THE
HAINAN
INCIDENT

THE
HAINAN
INCIDENT

A NOVEL

DM COFFMAN

Covenant Communications, Inc.

Dedicated to Gaoxing, Xiaofei, Guyung,
and the honorable judges of China

ACKNOWLEDGMENTS

This book has been years in the making. Based on personal experiences while living in China, I have woven truths with fiction to give it believability and interest—sometimes truth really is stranger than fiction! For this, I must acknowledge the beautiful Yalong Bay resort area of Hainan Island and the Li Culture Village. They do exist with all the positive aspects I have represented but without any of the negatives. Truly, they are a paradise and a vacation spot not to be missed.

The People's Republic of China does have a National Judges College in Beijing. My husband and I had the privilege of teaching some of China's young judges there. We were impressed with them, the facilities, and the staff. It is to those honorable judges—the dedicated men and women who uphold the laws of China—that this book is dedicated. May they continue to recognize the importance of the rule of law and their valuable role in their country's greatness.

We made many acquaintances in China who are now dear friends. I can't begin to name them all, but a few must be acknowledged in regards to this book: Hu Xiaofei (Frank), our wonderful friend and travel guide, resource for the history of Hainan and the Women's Army, and the person who kept us laughing with his charming humor; Du Guyung (Brian), whose spirituality inspired us when we couldn't see it in others; Wang LuoLuo (Hugh) and He Yi (Margaret), whose love and tenderness toward each other inspired the characters of Yi/Jason and Deckey/Sarah; Winnie Lao and members of the LDS Beijing Branch, who opened doors that otherwise would not have been opened; and Gesantunchop, my Tibetan student who introduced me to Tibetan ways and named the character Deckey—"his daughter."

Many people read the early drafts of this book. I am grateful for their insights and willingness to point out the weaknesses in my writing. Some of these people include Barbara Bamberger Scott (author), Bret Lott (author and novel-writing workshop instructor), the League of Utah Writers, Melissa Stricklan, Ben Bigelow, and Grant Wahlquist. And I am especially grateful to my husband, Gordon (Gaoxing), and my mother, Vivian Ralphs, for their untiring support, encouragement, and continual rereadings (there were a lot!), and to my editor and the people at Covenant Communications who saw the potential in this story.

CHAPTER 1

YALONG BAY RESORT, HAINAN ISLAND, SOUTH CHINA SEA
JANUARY 26–FEBRUARY 1, 2001

Yi slipped the electronic key card into the door of his luxury hotel suite and stepped inside. As usual, he left his flip-flops by the door. The marble floor felt cold under his bare feet. Setting his bag of swim gear down in the foyer, he moved toward the bedroom but then immediately stopped. The back of his neck tingled as a wave of adrenaline rushed into his system.

Someone had ransacked the bedroom.

His senses heightened. He listened for any sound indicating that the intruder might still be there. *Nothing*. His eyes darted across the plush sofas to the expanse of windows and tied-back draperies. The windows looked secure. With the exception of a few decorative pillows askew and a magazine opened on the coffee table, the sitting room was undisturbed.

Instinctively, Yi picked up the corkscrew from the silver platter on the wet bar and positioned the spiraled point between his second and third fingers. Moving toward the bedroom, he paused to open the door to the coat closet. *Empty*. He then checked the bathroom, bedroom closets, and balcony. *No one. And no sign of forced entry*.

His belongings from his suitcase, the dresser, and the closets were strewn onto the floor. The king-size bed sheets and comforter were partially pulled from the mattress. The nightstand drawers, although empty, had been removed. A chair was overturned.

Well, happy birthday.

As Yi surveyed the disarrayed room, anger began to replace the adrenaline pumping through his veins. He flung the corkscrew onto the now-empty dresser.

So much for five-star security! It was clear that whoever had done it had had a key.

Suddenly Yi's breath caught in his throat. He quickly grabbed the open suitcase off the floor and tossed it onto the bed. He felt for the hidden compartment. His heart raced as he pulled back the lining. The contents had not been disturbed. His American passport and US dollars were still there.

He closed his eyes. *Inhale. Exhale.* Years of martial arts training took over as he began to slow his heart rate through controlled breathing. Its calming effects helped him focus his concentration. He needed to assess what had happened.

The pounding in his chest subsided. He opened his eyes and began to analyze the room.

The money he had left on the table was still there. So was his airline ticket.

If not money, then what?

Taking a mental inventory, Yi realized what was missing.

The camera equipment.

His thoughts immediately went to the photographs he probably shouldn't have taken.

Had officials been monitoring already?

He had checked the hotel suite for surveillance devices when he arrived but hadn't found any. And he had registered under a Chinese passport. The local government wouldn't have suspected him as a foreigner unless . . . unless, somehow, he had jeopardized his cover. A queasy feeling crept into his stomach. He sat down on the edge of the bed.

Could he have given himself away before his assignment even started?

The nausea started to spread.

His mind raced to pinpoint when and how he might have made a mistake. He'd arrived in Guangzhou two weeks earlier. As planned, he immediately started immersing himself in the daily routines of life on the mainland. He watched the people, especially urban men in their thirties. He listened to expressions and nuances in their language. Word choices and tonal qualities identified a person's level of education and, often times, their hometown. He was fluent in Cantonese and Mandarin, but without the local mannerisms and up-to-date expressions, he would be pegged an "ABC"—American-born Chinese—which was the last thing he wanted.

He then thought about why he came to Hainan Island.

Should've stayed in Guangzhou.

No matter how hard he had tried to stay focused on familiarizing himself with Guangzhou customs, he couldn't let go of the fact that the Super Bowl was playing—on his thirtieth birthday—and his favorite team, the Baltimore Ravens, was in it. But Guangzhou television wasn't going to air the game.

The closest place to Guangzhou where the game was being televised was Hong Kong. Yi couldn't leave the mainland on his People's Republic of China passport unless he had a visa, which he didn't. Getting one would take too long, if he could get one at all. And using his American passport was definitely out of the question. Woodbury had made it very clear it was for emergency evacuation purposes only.

Simply put, Yi had wanted a diversion—something to take his mind off football.

Okay, more than football, he acknowledged.

As much as he hated to admit it, his assignment worried him. This wasn't his line of work. *Not even close.* But when Woodbury asked him, he felt a duty to help the countries of his birth and his heritage. It was the honorable thing to do.

Now he wasn't so sure.

As he picked up his belongings and put the bedroom back in order, Yi thought about the possibility of failing. He knew there were other young Chinese-American agents sent to China, like himself, to pose as judges in order to ferret out corrupt officials. Were they having as difficult a time getting started as Yi? He would probably never know. None of them knew who the others were or where they were located. All he knew was that he had to report to the Guangzhou Administrative Court one week from Monday.

Yi picked up the airplane ticket and read the itinerary: South China Airlines flight CS1322 to Guangzhou, February 1, 9:30 PM.

Maybe it should say "back to the US."

He dropped the ticket onto the table. Just because his ancestors were from the mainland and he had studied Chinese history and law in college didn't mean he could pull off undercover work. This was his first time to mainland China for goodness' sake! And, in the two weeks since he had arrived, he obviously hadn't fooled anyone. The beggars and street peddlers marked him as a foreigner his first day in Guangzhou, surrounding him and pulling on his clothes, insisting he buy their wares.

Now, having his camera equipment . . . *what, stolen? confiscated?* . . . could he be convincing enough to succeed in the assignment? He was an attorney after all, not an actor or a spy.

He walked to the balcony doors and stared out at the horizon, above the rhythmic waves breaking along the pristine beach. Was it the pictures he had taken? Or did someone know the real reason why he was in China? He shuddered at the thought.

Help me, Father. He offered a silent prayer then waited for any inspired guidance.

The military camp.

Yi glanced to the left at the group of tents in the distance. The soldiers in green fatigues were scurrying about as they had been when Yi had first seen them. He hadn't expected a military installation so close to a luxury beach resort. When he had arrived at the hotel and noticed the encampment, his curiosity had been piqued. What branch of China's military would conduct training at such an unusual location? As an expert on Chinese policy, Yi would be able to tell from their uniforms. Yet as he zoomed in with his camera, two surprising facts became clear: one, the uniform insignias were not any of those used by the People's Republic of China; and, two, there were non-Chinese soldiers among them. *That's unheard of,* he had thought. Then, without thinking, he had snapped some pictures to research when he returned to Guangzhou.

If the government had confiscated his camera, would they have trashed the room?

Probably not.

Yi ran his hand through his thick black hair, pushing back several strands that tended to fall onto his forehead.

Whoever did this wanted their presence known.

And unless they were blind in overlooking the airline ticket and cash left on the table, they wanted it known they were not there for money.

Another thought came to him, one he hadn't anticipated. *The Li-ren Culture Village.*

Yi had gone to the tourist area earlier that day.

He grimaced at how cavalier he had been in straying from the designated walking path. Absorbed in photographing some native children playing around the grass huts, he had followed them when they ran into the private area. What Yi had come upon was startling. Inside a makeshift plastic hut, clearly not part of the ancient village's planned tour demonstrating the Li tribe's simple life, was a sophisticated computer system—a state-of-the-art computer complete with high-graphics monitor and a communications station. The screen displayed a strange, metallic spiderweb-like symbol. He took several pictures of the whole setup and some close-ups of the logo to research later.

What did they expect? The modern juxtaposed with primitive was almost comical. Any tourist would see the irony and want pictures.

Except tourists weren't supposed to be in that area.

It was just so incongruent. Expensive equipment in a place without protection from the heat, rain, wind, and dirt—all elements detrimental to electronics. It didn't make sense. Certainly the village would keep their computer equipment and business records in a more stable environment, like a downtown office. The hotel concierge had said the village was a major tourist business on the island.

So why take the camera? Yi doubted the confiscation was simply the result of photographing a computer. There had to be more to it.

The logo.

It was different from the one on the village's entrance sign. Yi had hoped to check it out when he returned to Guangzhou.

That's got to be it. Whoever was linked to the symbol didn't want their presence in the village known. *Why?*

Yi took a deep breath.

Don't worry about that now. Focus on your mission.

He exhaled. Relief settled over him. Clearly the camera confiscation was not connected to his undercover assignment. He had simply made a silly tourist mistake.

Yi felt drained. He reclined on the bed and stretched out his lean, five-foot-ten-inch frame. The chandelier overhead sparkled in the setting sunlight.

That was close, Jason. You've got to be more careful!

***

Despite the camera confiscation and resulting paperwork, Yi spent the remainder of his vacation enjoying beautiful Yalong Bay. February 1 came all too soon. But a storm was rolling in, and Yi was eager to avoid it. He quickly loaded his gear and boarded the airport shuttle bus. He sat in an empty row away from the few other tourists already on board.

"Shame to leave such a paradise," a stylishly dressed Asian man in a silk shirt and linen pants commented. He and his female companion sat in the bus seats across the aisle from Yi. He spoke Cantonese, and Yi assumed he was from Hong Kong.

"I couldn't agree more," Yi answered back.

"So you speak Cantonese? I don't detect an accent. Where are you from?"

Yi was pleased his upbringing wasn't obvious. "Guangzhou."

"Oh, yes. Marvelous city. Excellent business opportunities. Heading there now, in fact. You a businessman?" the man asked as he reached in his shirt pocket and handed Yi his card.

"Administrative judge," Yi replied. He quickly located one of his own cards and, with both hands, extended it to the man in the customary manner.

"Even better," the man said with a smile. He pocketed the card without looking at it. "What flight are you on?"

"Thirteen twenty-two," Yi replied. Glancing at the man's card, he noticed his name was João Araújo. *Portuguese? Must be from Macau.*

He tucked the card into his notepad.

"Same flight then," the man continued. "It's a commuter express. Last one of the day. I imagine we'll all be on it." He looked at his watch. "Provided the bus leaves soon."

Yi couldn't help but notice the man's unusual wristwatch. The large, square black face was framed in rose gold, with a gold gear occupying the lower half and what looked like gold and red slot machine dials at the top. With the exception of the large numbers at the three and nine positions and the slender hour and minute hands, Yi wouldn't have know it was a watch.

"That's a curious timepiece," he commented. "I don't believe I've ever seen one like it."

"Probably not," the man said as he held out his arm. "This one is very rare. A vintage Jackpot Tourbillon."

"You mean the slot machine dials really work?" Yi asked, stunned.

"Oh, yes," the man replied, pulling on the small gold lever next to the watch stem.

Yi watched as the dials spun around. "Are you a gambler?" he asked, wondering why anyone would have such a watch.

The man laughed. "Let's just say I'm in the business."

Yi continued to stare in fascination.

"What's the purpose of the gear at the bottom?" he asked.

The man pulled his arm back and tapped on the watch's crystal. "The tourbillon gear—best in the world for accuracy. Somehow it prevents gravity on the mechanism."

"I'm not familiar with them."

The man nodded. "They are a bit pricey. On average about a hundred grand in US dollars. This one, substantially more," he added with pride in his voice.

Yi felt his jaw drop.

The man laughed. He seemed to enjoy the unsettling effect he was having on Yi. Of course a lowly Chinese judge would not have knowledge of such lavish things!

"Tourbillons have been around awhile. Napoleon owned one," he continued. He then added, as if an explanation were needed, "One of the many advantages of my doing business in Guangzhou." He smiled. "It was a gift."

Yi nodded cordially then turned to look out the window as a gust of strong wind blew through the palm trees. The now-constant rain was coming in an almost horizontal direction.

Thinking about the man's exorbitant watch, the gold gear at the six o'clock position suddenly seemed familiar to Yi.

The logo on the village computer.

There was a definite similarity. What looked like a metallic spiderweb could easily have been the cogs of an intricate watch gear. Yi thought about the symbol on the computer screen. There had been characters in the middle, like writing. They had not been Chinese or any other language Yi could read.

Probably Arabic, Yi thought, given the large population of Muslims on Hainan. When he arrived, he had been surprised by the strong religious influence on the local architecture. Gray clay walls with ogee-arched portals stood as gateways to clusters of shops and residential buildings.

Such plain features were a vivid contrast to the intricately carved and colorful wooden structures normally seen in Chinese cities.

A noise outside the bus drew Mr. Araújo's attention away from Yi.

Yi opened his notepad, wrote *tourbillon,* then briefly sketched as best he could the spiderweb/watch gear symbol. He would research the symbol and the military camp's uniforms when he got back to Guangzhou.

"Now, please come, please." The bus driver's flustered voice interrupted Yi's concentration.

Standing outside the bus in the rain, the driver was trying unsuccessfully to hurry along a group of what appeared to be American tourists struggling with oversized luggage and designer umbrellas. One teenage boy kept pestering a girl in line by pulling at her ear.

They've obviously been to the culture village, Yi thought with a smile, remembering the tribe's customary greeting of rubbing a guest's earlobe.

He watched the steady stream of colored umbrellas bob toward the bus from the hotel lobby. Several of them turned inside out from the gusting wind.

Expatriates, Yi thought. They often vacation in China before returning to the States during the Spring Festival holiday and winter school break.

***

The bus arrived at the airport on schedule. Had the driver called ahead, however, he would have learned there was no need to hurry. The flight was being delayed because of bad weather in Guangzhou. The plane, due to leave Hainan in little more than an hour, had not left Guangzhou yet. Given the severe thunderstorm raging there, it was unknown when the plane might leave.

"South China Airlines flight CS1322 to Guangzhou, scheduled to depart Hainan Island at 9:30 PM, has now been indefinitely postponed," the voice over the airport loudspeaker announced.

"Great," a tall American man with name-brand sunglasses on his head and an air of superiority about him complained. "We should have eaten at the hotel before we left."

"Let's find some empty chairs before they're all gone and wait it out," a lanky blonde woman, probably his wife, replied. "It's not like we have a choice, dear."

The hard-molded plastic chairs were small and attached together in rows positioned close to the ground. Sitting on them for any length of time would be uncomfortable for the average-sized American.

It could be at least two hours, possibly three, before the flight departed. With so many people stranded in such a small airport, Yi could see the impatience mounting in the Americans. And, feeling restless, he had to stifle his own urge to complain.

***

"Attention passengers, flight CS1322 to Guangzhou is now boarding," came the much-awaited announcement.

The clock on the wall showed 11:48 PM.

"It'll be at least 1:30 before we're back in Guangzhou and able to get these kids into comfortable beds," one of the exhausted parents with a child asleep in his arms said with a sigh.

Others slowly gathered their belongings and moved toward the boarding gate.

***

The pilot slid into the seat of the plane's cockpit and began the routine he had learned so well in flight school. His movements felt mechanical from the many months of training. He marveled at his ability to navigate the control panels with little or no thought.

For the short flight, there would be two pilots on board. Other than the requisite communications between airplane and airport tower and a minimal amount of pleasantries exchanged between them, the pilots avoided conversation with each other, focusing instead on their individual responsibilities. The plane took off without incident.

Twenty minutes into the flight, the airplane cleared the Hainan land mass, traveling over the South China Sea.

"This is your captain speaking," the pilot said into the microphone, trying to mask any nervousness in his voice. He ran his index finger around the inside of his collar. He cleared his throat before going on. "Welcome aboard South China Airlines flight . . ." He paused to verify the number. ". . . flight thirteen twenty-two for Guangzhou. We apologize for the delay."

His fist tightened as an almost imperceptible tremor crossed his wrist.

"I suggest doing a walk-through of the cabin area," he said to the copilot. "You know there are many foreigners on board. With the flight delayed, I am sure they are annoyed by the inconvenience. A walk-through would be a sign of goodwill."

The copilot nodded and exited the cockpit area. The pilot locked the door behind him. He then loosened his tie and unbuttoned the top button of his shirt. Usually wearing fatigues, he wasn't comfortable in the pilot's restrictive uniform.

A few moments later, the flight management systems were switched off, along with the autopilot, the transponder, and the radio communications systems. The pilot took over the manual controls of the now-silent airplane. An electrifying calmness settled over him. For two years he had waited for this moment. He forced himself to delay a while longer, to savor it, heightening even more the seductive feeling of power he now held. He took a deep breath. A half smile formed in the corner of his mouth.

His fingers tightened around the control yoke of the plane as he forced it forward, plunging the plane down. Yet he was careful to reduce power. Too much speed would cause structural damage to the plane. He wanted it to remain intact until the last possible moment before impact.

The smile spread fully across his lips as he heard screams from the cabin area behind him. Someone pounded frantically on the cockpit door. But he couldn't think about that now. He closed his eyes and began to dream of the paradise awaiting him as flight CS1322 crashed into the South China Sea.

CHAPTER 2

Meijuan didn't dare come during the day. Even at night she knew it was a risk. She pulled the collar of her thin coat up over her cheeks, clutching the lapels with her mitten-covered hands. Her breath created a frosty mist around her. She stood in the darkened alley across from the American embassy. The warm glow of white lights along the embassy's roofline, like the bright stars above Hainan, gave her courage. That was why she came at the Western holiday time of Christmas, when all the fancy decorations were up. Others walking along the street stopped and admired the twinkling lights. She could blend in.

Terrible layout, she thought as she studied the compound. Its location was isolated compared to other businesses along the street. Tall security gates and military guards stood in front. She knew she wouldn't be able to make contact with an American inside without going through the guards on the outside.

Chinese guards.

Her heart pounded. She had not anticipated them at the American embassy. Chinese officials despised her because she edited a subversive news magazine. She only printed the truth, but they hated her nonetheless. If she were caught trying to pass information to a foreign government, she would be locked away for a very long time—or worse. Her secret would not be told. She had to find a way to get the information she possessed into the hands of the American government without being seen by Chinese guards.

Standing in the alley, her coat collar pulled up around the faded facial markings of her tribal leadership, she thought about her recent visit home to Hainan Island. She had hoped to make peace with her son, Jiaoshi. But even after seven years, he had not welcomed her back. What she found instead was a hotbed of evil that, as she reflected upon it now, caused a shiver to run through her. For the first time in her life, she felt intense fear—not only for herself but also for the lives of many people. And it was all her son's fault. According to Chinese custom, that made it her responsibility too.

Must do this, she told herself as she crossed the street to the embassy gate. Four soldiers with rifles stood in a line in front.

As she drew closer, she could see that three of the guards were Chinese, but one was . . . *Caucasian? Yes!* She ran toward him.

"Halt!" the man shouted, arm raised, when she got within ten feet of him.

Meijuan froze.

He approached her slowly then asked in English, "What is it you want?"

"I . . . I . . ." she began in English, but no other words came to her.

"Ni wei shuo Zhongwen, ma?" She asked if he spoke Chinese.

Shaking his head, he turned and yelled for one of the Chinese guards.

Meijuan panicked. Unwilling to risk being recognized, she turned and ran.

"Hey!" the soldier yelled after her.

She never looked back.

***

Meijuan returned to her small room in the news magazine office. *Maybe the Internet will provide a solution*, she reasoned. She keyed in the words *United States White House* on the computer's search field.

After studying the list of possible websites, she finally logged on to what she thought was the official one. It listed telephone and fax numbers. Not feeling confident with her English-speaking skills, she felt it would be best and safest to write a letter. She would fax it to the White House. The magazine owned a small fax machine. She could easily send it when no one was around.

It took Meijuan five days to prepare the one-page letter carefully written in English. She breathed a sigh of relief as the fax machine scanned it in, signaling that contact had been made on the other end of the line. Now she would wait for the White House to send her an e-mail confirmation as she had requested in the fax. It was Monday morning, January 1. There would be New Year's celebrations going on in America. Possibly no one would see her fax for a day or two.

That's okay. She could be patient for a few days.

CHAPTER 3

The fax arrived at 10:03 PM on Sunday, December 31. It came in without any official cover sheet, so it was placed in the Routine Incoming basket for viewing whenever Ted Farley, internal communications specialist, got the chance. Policy stated that the fax had to be forwarded within forty-eight hours of the printout date on the fax header. With New Year's Eve celebrations going on, though, no one was in the mood to work. Consequently, by the time Farley saw the fax, it had already been sitting on his desk for more than a week.

"What the . . . ?" he mumbled as he read the fax's header date.

Farley had been written up before for taking too much time in forwarding incoming communiqués. It had cost him a point on his last annual review.

"Not again!" He tossed the paper onto his desk.

With twenty-three years of government employment behind him, Ted Farley was biding his time until retirement at the end of next year. Numbed by years of indifference, he sometimes felt that getting to work was the hardest part of his day. The last thing he needed was something disrupting his cushy routine: arrive at work around 8:45 AM, read *The Washington Post* until 10:00 AM, meet with some of the other communications guys to "chew the fat" and discuss the latest confidential communiqués that had crossed their desks, take an early lunch, maybe peruse his favorite entertainment website before the late lunch-goers came back, then play a few hands of solitaire on the computer, check out a few incoming communiqués, and call it a day.

Life was good—that is, until he came across the fax dated December 31.

Farley picked up the sheet again and quickly scanned the contents. The English was poor but clearly made reference to terrorist groups . . . in China. *That's a new one*, he thought as he scratched his balding head. Important information . . . *Oh, no!* The antiterrorism task force had given specific instructions that any incoming communiqués on the subject of terrorism, particularly from overseas, were to be sent immediately to the director of the task force committee.

Maybe the date will go unnoticed, Farley considered. Things had been chaotic during the transition to a new president.

He couldn't take the chance.

Probably a hoax anyway, he rationalized as he ran the fax through the document shredder.

CHAPTER 4

Frustration was setting in for Meijuan. Nine days had passed since she had sent the fax. She guessed that she was not going to receive any response from the White House.

She desperately needed to make contact with an American. *But where?* She couldn't approach the American embassy, and her fax to the White House had gone unanswered. Then she remembered an article she had written two years earlier entitled "The Silencing of Counterrevolutionary Attitudes of Students at Peking University." In her research she had learned that Peking University used foreign teachers. On the off chance that some of them might be American, she picked up the telephone and dialed the English Department at Peking University. A young woman answered.

"*Wei?*"

"*Wei, ni hao. Wo xuyao Meiguoren Yingyu laoshi.*" Meijuan explained she needed an American English teacher and that she was seeking assistance in writing an English news article.

"Yes," the secretary replied. "We have several young American students and an older American couple who teach English here. However, our semester is ending this week. Many of the teachers will travel during the Spring Festival break."

"May I have the information for contacting them?" Meijuan asked, hoping the woman wouldn't ask for her name or the name of the magazine.

"All of our foreign teachers stay in the Shao Yuan Hotel here on campus."

"And the name of the American couple?"

"Their name is Stillman."

"Xie xie ni. Xie xie ni." Meijuan quickly thanked the woman and hung up the phone before the woman could ask further questions.

It didn't take long to track down the telephone number and hotel room for the Americans. But, once again, her efforts proved unsuccessful. On the phone, the man didn't understand her, and she couldn't comprehend much of what he said. When she showed up at their door, they wanted to use a Chinese interpreter. She couldn't take that risk. It didn't matter. They were refusing to help her . . . something about not being one of their students. Even when Meijuan showed them the letter she had faxed to the White House, they wouldn't help her.

***

Frustration turned into discouragement and a sense of inevitability. Meijuan sat in her office reviewing news clips, trying to assuage her feelings of failure. If her English language skills had been better, she could have conveyed the vital information. There wasn't any more she could do.

Just then, in the *China Evening News,* two headlines caught her attention. The first one discussed the US president's upcoming inauguration celebration, and the second one announced:

> *The United Nations Council has enacted sanctions against Afghanistan's extremist movement . . . The United States and Russia are leading the drive to block travel by and supplies of arms to extremist members . . .*

Aiya! Not sanctions, she thought. *They will retaliate. Even more people will die.* This was much worse than she ever imagined.

She realized she had to keep trying. She had to find a way to communicate the information to the White House herself.

But not from Beijing. Too dangerous. An international call from Beijing would surely be monitored. Nevertheless, only the biggest cities in China had telephone lines of the high quality necessary for an international call. She decided on the city of Tianjin.

CHAPTER 5

TIANJIN, PEOPLE'S REPUBLIC OF CHINA
JANUARY 23, 2001 (CHINESE NEW YEAR)

The train from Beijing to Tianjin was unusually crowded. It seemed everyone was traveling to be with their families for the Spring Festival holiday—China's New Year. Meijuan had counted on it. Everyone would be busy with holiday plans. *Less chance for notice,* she had rationalized. The unfortunate part of such an important holiday, though, was that most shops and businesses were closed or fully booked for the celebration. Only by settling for a bed in a windowless room with no heat or plumbing was Meijuan able to find shelter for the night.

She waited until dark. Then, feeling it was safe to make the international call, she went looking for a public telephone in a vacant section of Tianjin. Many of the telephones (which were nothing more than a handset mounted to a pole with an orange, bubble-shaped overhang) were broken or missing. After three attempts she found one that worked. She dialed the long-distance number. Fearful of her surroundings, she cautiously glanced around. There were only a few people on the street. No officials. No parked cars.

A chill ran through her body as the strange-sounding language came across the line. She hesitated before trying to mouth the words she had so carefully practiced.

"Um . . . is this . . . American . . . White House?" she said as she twisted the phone's cord, her voice barely a whisper, wavering like a tiny bird's wings attempting first flight. It took her full focus and every ounce of courage she had to try to communicate with the American on the other side of the world.

Unfortunately, she didn't understand much of the reply.

"I have . . . important . . . information," she said, speaking as loudly as she felt she could, given the occasional passerby still on the street. Somehow, while struggling with English, she let down her guard. She was unaware of the stranger who had taken notice of her.

***

The Neighborhood Committee director prided herself on knowing everything that went on in her section of town. And this strange woman, who had rented a room alone during the Spring Festival holiday and who appeared very nervous, frequently looking over her shoulder, was obviously not from around there. As Neighborhood Committee director, she felt it was her duty to monitor this strange woman's activities. So she followed her. And when the woman stopped at the street phone, she watched.

The director moved in closer to hear what was being said. She had studied English enough in school to recognize the language, although she couldn't understand the words.

She placed a call on her cell phone.

***

Meijuan's conversation with the White House was not going well. She had so carefully written out the sentences, checked her grammar, and practiced the pronunciations, but her nerves kept getting in the way. She could only hope that the operator would put into the right hands the little bit of information she had been able to impart. There was more to say, but the sudden glare of headlights stopped Meijuan instantly. The unmarked car careened toward her. She knew she was in trouble. She dropped the phone and ran.

Finding a door slightly ajar, Meijuan stepped across the threshold of a darkened *hutong* alley. She glanced back at the telephone. The handset was still dangling from its cord. Two men in black suits got out of the car and walked to the phone. As one of the men put it to his ear, a middle-aged Chinese woman dressed in a dark blue Mao jacket and floral print pants came running up to them. She handed them a piece of paper then pointed in Meijuan's direction. The man hung up the phone. They moved toward the place where Meijuan was hiding.

Meijuan had seen the woman outside the room she had rented for the night, so the woman knew where Meijuan was staying. The address was probably on the piece of paper she had given the two men. There was no way Meijuan could return there. And it was too late to find another room or catch a train back to Beijing. She would have to spend the night on the streets of Tianjin.

Hunkering down into a dark corner of the abandoned *hutong*, she wedged herself between an old bicycle and a stack of crumbling bricks. The unsettled dust filled her nostrils. She stifled the urge to sneeze.

This is all Jiaoshi's fault!

Thoughts of her corrupt son brought painful memories to her mind. It had been seven years since he forced her to flee her beloved village on Hainan, where her ancestors had ruled for generations. She bore the Li facial tattoos to prove it, as did her mother and grandmother before her.

"You have interfered with my business affairs for the last time," he threatened his mother. "If you don't leave, you will be reported to authorities as a member of Falun Gong!"

Meijuan flinched at the mere mention of the government-despised religious group. She wasn't really a member, but an accusation was enough—especially for someone considered a leader in the community. The local officials would have made an example of her to convince others to avoid the consequences.

"You saw what happened to your friend," Jiaoshi had said to her. "The woman was arrested and taken away in shackles, disgraced in front of her family and neighbors, and then she was beaten."

"She was not Falun Gong!"

"No matter," Jiaoshi said with a wave of his hand, as if brushing her aside. "She did not do as she was told, so she was punished."

Before releasing her, the prison guards put out one of her eyes as a warning to others. Rather than go back to her home and endure the humiliation brought upon her family, the woman climbed up the rocky cliff of the nearby mountain and threw herself off. It was Meijuan who found her at the bottom of the cliff in a tangled heap.

"At least provide papers so I can register in Beijing," Meijuan had begged her son, realizing there was no other option.

"You don't think they will recognize your leadership ability by your facial tattoos?" he had mocked.

"Jiaoshi, you are a cruel man! You know these marks are known only on Hainan. They are our family's honor," she defended with tears welling up.

"It is a foolish tradition. Giving leadership to women—ha!"

"I see it threatens you," she responded as calmly as she could. She paused to let the words sink in. The almost imperceptible twitch of his nervousness told her she was right. But she also knew he would not back down.

"Please prepare my registration papers. I will leave Hainan," she had conceded.

But the papers never came.

Without *hukou* papers Meijuan had no value. She did not exist in the eyes of the government. Although she had been a leader in Hainan, anywhere else she was no more than a peasant. And life on the streets of Beijing could break the strongest of wills. What she hated most was the weather. Beijing winters were brutal. She would gather up scraps of cardboard or plastic sheeting—anything that would block the bitter wind—and seek shelter in hidden street corners. At least the freezing cold lessened the acrid smell of urine on the building walls.

When life became unbearable, Meijuan would dream of her childhood on Hainan Island. Remembering the soothing ocean sounds and warm, star-filled nights brought her peace. No matter what else she sacrificed, she would not compromise her heritage: the love of her village, her responsibilities as a leader, and the values her ancestors believed in. Those were her constant companions. She would not lose face to them.

She had eventually secured work with a small, counterrevolutionary magazine on the outskirts of Beijing. It didn't pay much, but it provided her shelter and a bed. She worked hard, learning all she could about news reporting. After a few years, she became the editor.

But her troubles didn't stop there.

"You absolutely must stop distributing negative statements about the government!" officials warned her many times. As editor of an underground publication, she had contact with similar organizations from which she learned many hidden facts—ones the government didn't want printed. On several occasions they shut the magazine down. Once, she was even arrested and beaten. Yet she had been determined to report the truth.

Despite the government's harassment, she enjoyed her work. But squatting in a dark, cold, and cramped *hutong* corner in Tianjin, alone on Spring Festival day, brought back the harsh realities from those earlier years in Beijing. In an unfamiliar city, fearful for her safety, Meijuan hoped she could secure passage on a train and be out of Tianjin before the authorities began looking for her in the morning.

CHAPTER 6

The telephone call came into the White House Telephone Center at 9:10 AM. It logged in as an overseas call, originating from Tianjin of the People's Republic of China. No line or caller identification coding was given. The call did not show up on the operator's computer list of known sources.

"White House, may I help you?" the operator gave her usual greeting, although the way her morning was going, she wasn't feeling at all helpful. Voluminous amounts of calls were still coming in after the president's inauguration only a few days earlier.

"Um . . . is this . . . American . . . White House?" a woman's faint voice said over the line.

"Yes, it is. May I help you?" the operator responded.

Silence on the line.

"Hello? May I help you?" the operator repeated.

"Um . . . I wish . . . speak to . . . um . . . American . . . president. Very . . . important."

"I'm sorry, I can't understand you. Would you speak louder please?" the operator said, starting to get a little annoyed.

More silence.

"Maybe this . . . not a good time. Too . . . dangerous," the woman said, sounding dejected.

Although unable to fully understand the faint voice on the other end of the line, the operator began to sense distress or at least some level of anxiety in the woman's voice.

"Honey, I can't help you if I can't hear what you're saying. You'll have to speak up."

Silence again on the line.

"I wish . . . to speak . . . with president. I have . . . important . . . information," the woman finally said, enunciating each word.

The operator stifled a chuckle as she said, "I'm sorry, but the president doesn't take calls on this line." *Is this a joke?* she thought. Who would try to reach the president of the United States over a public information line? "May I ask what this is regarding?" she asked, curious as to what this woman considered important information.

More silence.

"Wo bu dong, wo bu dong, ni hui shuo Zhongwen ma?" The woman, beginning to panic and obviously frustrated with trying to communicate in English, switched to Chinese.

"Excuse me? I'm sorry, I don't understand you. Please speak in English."

The operator was about to disconnect the line.

". . . *aiya* . . . please . . . I am editor . . . of news magazine in Beijing . . . I have . . . important . . . information about . . . Israeli-Palestinian war. I . . . I know . . . terrorist . . . groups . . . south in China . . . must warn *Meiguo* . . . umm . . . American . . . president. Please, you must . . . understand me. *Wo gaosu ni* . . . *aiya* . . . I tell you . . . very important!"

"I'm sorry, did you say terrorist groups? . . . In China? . . . Hello? . . . Hello?"

The line was dead.

Unsure whether the call had been legitimate or not, the White House operator filled out the follow-up call form with as much of the conversation as she had been able to understand. Since every incoming call to the White House was recorded, she knew the call could be reviewed for any parts she might have left out. She documented the call information registered by the computer, attached it to the taped cassette recording of the conversation, placed the form and the cassette in an interoffice memo folder, and addressed it to the director of the antiterrorism task force.

***

Nathan Greenwald, director of the anti-terrorism task force, studied the call printout as he listened to the cassette tape recording. The woman on the line sounded fearful and distraught, trying hard to communicate in English. *No command of the language.* He guessed also, from the background street noise on the tape, the call had been placed from a public telephone. *Not surprising.* The woman must have believed she was being monitored by the Chinese government and her own phone was bugged. The call definitely originated from China. *It could mean something . . . but maybe not.* His gut feeling told him it needed following up. He looked at his watch. 11:30 AM. *10:30 pm in Beijing—not too late to call.*

"Let's hope he's home," he mumbled as he dialed the international number.

"Hello, Stringer here," Colonel Jeffrey Stringer, military attaché assigned to the US embassy in Beijing, answered on the third ring.

"Jeff, ol' buddy, how ya doing? This is Nathan Greenwald calling from DC."

"Well, Nate, it has been awhile. I'm doing fine, thanks. How 'bout yourself?"

"Good, good. Say, I had an interesting message come across my desk this morning. The call was taken in the White House Telephone Center. The operator who took the call sent me the tape recording. A woman—sounds Chinese—called from what seems to be a street phone in Tianjin. The tape is difficult to understand, but she talked about terrorist groups. Here's the interesting thing, Jeff. She said they were in south China. Know anything about that?"

"Haven't heard anything specific. We've suspected some terrorist connection in China, particularly with the Uyghur minority group in the northwestern province of Xinjiang. But they're targeting China—seeking independence, that sort of thing. Nothing directed at Americans that we've been able to confirm and certainly nothing in the southern part of China."

"Could you follow up on it for me, Jeff? The caller said she was an editor for a news magazine in Beijing, reporting on the Israeli/Palestinian war. She said she had connections with these terrorist groups."

"An underground rag. There's a few of them around. Sure, I'll look into it, Nate," Jeff answered. "Can it wait a week though? I'm taking the family down to Hainan Island for a little vacation. Get away from this cold weather here. We fly back the evening of February 1, so I'll be back in the office on the second."

"I would appreciate it," Nathan said. "Let me know what you find out."

"Sure, no problem," Jeff replied.

"And enjoy Hainan. I hear it's nice there," Nathan said as he thought about how long it had been since he had taken his own family on vacation.

"Thanks. We're looking forward to it. I'll give you a call when I get back."

CHAPTER 7

Umar sat alone in the Hainan Net's operations center. His polished military boots were propped on the edge of his computer desk, a cup of hot tea in his hand. The hum of the fluorescent light overhead was the only sound besides the distant roar of the ocean's surf echoing within the cave. He relished these times of solitude. It gave him the chance to think about his family, whom he dearly missed.

The drought and war in his hometown of Kabul had caused much suffering. The death of his brother, Ulil, had been especially agonizing for him. He blamed himself. He was the older brother, so it was his responsibility to protect the younger one. Ulil had looked up to him, relied on him. They planned to leave Kabul and start their father's spice business in Islamabad. Their father had been a successful merchant, exporting to other countries. They often traveled with him on business to learn the skills of the trade. It was during those times that they experienced Westerners and their immoral ways. Foreign businessmen openly flaunted their wealth and power. They demonstrated no submission to a higher power. The boys' father tolerated these differences in the name of good business, but Umar and Ulil saw it for the evil it was.

When their father passed away, Umar and Ulil had turned to the influential leaders who spoke of ridding the world of such sin. They knew their father would not have allowed them to take up association with radical groups. But like many other youths, they wanted to believe the simple answers offered by the fundamentalist leaders. They yearned to wage war against the enemy. When they were with other young men who believed as they did, the excitement within them rose to a fevered pitch. Umar and Ulil joined the guerrilla fighters, dedicating themselves to the cause.

At first it was exhilarating. They fired M-16 automatic rifles and launched BM-12 antitank missiles, built car bombs using diesel fuel and chemical fertilizer, and practiced hand-to-hand combat. They ran obstacle courses and learned survival skills. They watched video tapes that showed the mutilated bodies of their enemies, the chant of "with blood, with blood, with blood" echoing in their ears. Their leaders encouraged them to bring honor to their families and themselves by becoming martyrs and thereby earning a glorious reward in the afterlife. Umar and Ulil envisioned themselves coming through the skirmishes unscathed to prove their invincibility and military prowess.

Instead of engaging in great battles, however, they spent their time sitting around watching their living conditions worsen. Supplies would run out. It would be weeks before replacements arrived. "Such hardships are a test of our faith," the leaders would say. But as Umar and Ulil heard and saw the constant contradictions, they became disillusioned. Things were not changing. After twenty-three years of civil war and its resulting poverty and disease, if anything had changed, it was that the situation was getting worse. Sickness and despair existed everywhere. Umar and Ulil decided to return to Kabul and prepare to leave for Islamabad, where they would set up their father's spice business again.

Then the bombing started. The guerrilla fighters were determined to take over Kabul from the tribal alliance. Umar and Ulil found themselves caught in the crossfire. As Umar and Ulil ran for shelter, bullets ricocheted around them. When Umar turned around to see where his brother was, an explosion hit Ulil from the back. The impact was so unexpected that, as Ulil lurched forward, a look of surprise-turned-to-reality spread over his face. He slumped into Umar's arms. Umar held his brother's shrapnel-riddled body as the life flowed out. Screams vibrated in Umar's ears. He wondered who else was suffering such torment. As he glanced around, he saw that he was alone. The screams were his own. As the warmth left Ulil's body, it also left Umar's, depositing in its place a cold hatred like Umar had never felt before.

***

Those images in Umar's memory were still vivid and painful. Cold beads of sweat began to form on his forehead as the heat grew inside him. Remembering how America had supplied weapons to the alliance— weapons that ultimately killed his brother—caused the hatred to again bubble up from his gut and bile to burn in his throat. But he was a patient man. He took off his green military cap and wiped his face with the back of his sleeve. Becoming a Hainan Net recruit two years ago gave him the opportunity he desired. They had funded his training as a pilot. One day soon he would taste the sweetness of revenge.

The beeps of the communications system starting up brought Umar back to reality and his job on Wild Boar Island. A coworker, Abikar, had come in and turned the consoles on. Umar swung his boots down off the desk and sat up in his chair. He clicked on the message icon on his computer screen, expecting a communication from Thailand. They were waiting for a transfer of funds to come in to pay for the next training session and to restock supplies. The inventory request arrived the day before for more detonation cord, high explosive charges, and firing devices. The order would ship out from Shantou next week.

"They are moving the testing farther out," Abikar said as he sat down in front of the communications console.

"Again?" Umar responded. "I thought after the crab incident, they had moved far enough."

Abikar laughed as he scratched his thick black beard. "That was amazing, wasn't it? Those thousands of crabs suddenly coming up on shore all at once like that. Unbelievable!"

"Except it almost gave away our position here," Umar said.

"Nobody linked the crabs to our explosives testing. Besides, some cash to the mayor would have put an end to any investigation. Everyone figured a change in water temperature or drop in the population of crab predators had caused them to come onshore. Anyway, no one cared why they did—they were happy to have so many crabs. People were scooping them up by the bucketfuls . . ."

"Hey, there's an e-mail from Kai," Umar interrupted.

He clicked on the message from Zou Kai, who worked in the American embassy in Beijing. The message was dated January 24 and read:

Americans on Hainan Island until Feb 1. Return flight to
Guangzhou is CS1322 leaving Sanya Airport at 9:30 pm.
All will be on board. Peace and blessings be upon you. Kai

"We should also be hearing from Wahid tomorrow," Abikar said, interrupting Umar's delight at the news in Kai's e-mail. "He'll be monitoring a large banking transaction, so watch for his e-mail. He is to let us know when the transaction is completed. You are then to move half of the money to the project's operating account."

The funds would be transferred from a Pakistani account to a Sanya bank correspondent account under the name of Li-ren Culture Village Enterprises. The transfer would be completed using the *hawala* banking system—*hawala* meaning "word of mouth" in Arabic. Pakistan was one of the few places where these kinds of transfers could take place. This was the best way for the Hainan Net's operations because the money changed accounts without actual funds crossing borders and without leaving a paper trail. Correspondent accounts allowed a bank to place deposits under its own name in another bank abroad without naming the original owner of the money. In other words, money mysteriously appeared in an account from an unknown source, and no one asked any questions.

***

That evening in a small fishing sampan moored next to the Sanya Bridge, amid the stench of decaying fish and floating pollutants, money exchanged hands—a large sum of money.

"A pleasure doing business with you," the Sanya official said to the soldier in green fatigues as he counted out the numerous bills of US currency. The mayor received handsome sums on a regular basis, although usually from his friend the Foreigner. But he didn't care who the money came from as long as it was a large amount and paid in American dollars. In exchange, he provided a favor. This time he simply had to arrange for a pilot not to show up for work.

CHAPTER 8

Wahid worked in the culture village on the main island of Hainan. Because he was Chinese and had grown up on Hainan Island, he was an excellent "front" man who could blend in with the look of the village. He dressed in the native Li costume and spoke the dialect. His conversations with potential recruits looked as harmless as a Li native discussing the local lifestyle with a tourist. When he had to leave the culture village on business, he dressed in Western clothing like a traveler. He could blend in almost anywhere.

He worked in the restricted area of the village in a tentlike hut, which was only big enough to hold two metal chairs and a table with a computer, monitor, printer, and network connection box. He had fashioned the hut from fiber-reinforced plastic to keep rainwater from leaking in. It wasn't the most ideal environment, but from there he could manage the Net's recruitment activities, away from the location of the operations center on Wild Boar Island.

Wahid had never been inside the operations center. On rare occasions Abikar, the center's senior communications specialist, stopped by the culture village to check on him. No personnel documents were to be transmitted to the center over communication lines. Wahid's primary contact was through routine e-mails and a courier, whom he knew only as Zhu. The courier carried official documents between the village and the center. Zhu kept him informed of all the center's plans. Dealing with Zhu, however, was a bit unnerving, and Wahid never had any warning of his arrival. The small-built man simply dropped down out of the trees, collected the documents, smiled, and often without a word disappeared back into the forest canopy. Apparently, the fastest way down the steep mountain was through the treetops. Dressed in black and with the dense foliage and loud noise of cicadas surrounding him, he moved undetected between the village and the shore.

Hidden away in the culture village yet close enough to provide a neutral contact point, Wahid could design and program the online advertisements promoting the Net, update the recruiting web page, conduct business, and meet with potential new members. This had proven the best way to recruit. And because there was no direct link back to Wild Boar Island, there was no possibility of exposing the Hainan Net. It was a perfect setup.

In addition to his web page work and recruiting activities, Wahid was supposed to monitor bank transactions. During those times he was not to leave the computer until the transaction completed and he could shut the machine down. But Wahid had become careless. Sometimes the transfers took hours, and it was hard to stay awake. Occasionally he would sneak off to a nearby grass hut and stretch out in a hammock for a quick nap. He had done it numerous times without a problem.

Today, however, as he turned back toward where he was supposed to be monitoring a money transfer, he noticed someone coming out of his hut. The person was putting a camera back into its case. Wahid's heart jumped. He watched as the man walked around to the other side of the grass huts, back to the main tourist area. He noted that the man was Chinese. By the looks of the expensive foreign camera and clothing, he was probably wealthy—possibly from Hong Kong or Taiwan. Wahid glanced at the computer and saw that the transaction had completed and the screen had reverted back to the network's web page. On the display was the insignia of the Hainan Net and some Arabic characters welcoming new recruits to take up the cause. This was worse than if the man had seen the banking transaction in process. At least that might have appeared to be a legitimate transaction for the culture village. But this—this was much worse.

Wahid quickly shut down the computer, threw on a western shirt, and rushed to catch up to the man with the camera. Thank goodness he was still in the village! Wahid followed from a safe distance. The man seemed to be just a tourist. But Wahid couldn't take any chances. At the very least he would have to confiscate the camera. Beyond that, he didn't know. He had never killed anyone before.

He followed the man with the camera back to his hotel. Wahid's eyes widened in astonishment at the opulence of the resort's accommodations. He had to force himself not to stare. Trying to look as if he belonged, he casually stepped into the elevator after the man with the camera. A smile passed between them. Wahid looked down at his shoes and hoped the rapid beat of his heart was not audible. When the elevator stopped, he waited.

"After you," the man said politely.

Wahid realized he hadn't pushed a button for another floor.

Startled and not knowing where to go, Wahid stepped outside the elevator. He grinned sheepishly then shoved his hand in his pocket as if searching for his key. He was sure the man with the camera could see him shaking.

"Have a nice day," the man said as he passed and headed down the hallway. Wahid watched until he turned a corner, then he followed. He needed to see which room the man entered. Afterward, Wahid would wait in the lobby downstairs until he left again. Hopefully it wouldn't be too long of a wait, although the luxury of the five-star hotel was appealing. For this, Wahid felt guilty and would pray for forgiveness.

Not more than half an hour later the man appeared in the lobby dressed in a swimsuit and tank shirt. A tote bag with a towel sticking out hung on his shoulder. He walked over to the resort activity counter. It looked like he was signing up for something.

Ah, very good! Wahid hoped the man didn't have his camera with him.

He watched him walk out to the beach then stood and nonchalantly made his way to the elevator. Upon arriving at the right floor, he began looking for a housekeeper.

"Thank goodness I found you," he said to the floor maid restocking her cart. "I have forgotten my key, and I am in a big hurry to an important meeting. I must get back into my room, 404. Could you please help me?"

He handed the housekeeper one hundred yuan. She accepted and opened the door without further question. Wahid quickly slipped inside and closed the door.

Again amazed by the lavish furnishings, he ran his hand over the upholstery of an armchair as he moved into the sitting area. Warm beams of light shining through the floor-to-ceiling glass windows cast flecks of colored rainbows across the room. The soft cushions beckoned to him. How different it would be to rest here instead of in a hammock! He was tempted to stay awhile. But as he flipped through the pages of a magazine on the glass table, the modern images repulsed him. He needed to locate the camera and get out of there.

He moved quickly toward the bedroom. As he passed the spacious marble bathroom, the big white bowl extending up from the floor caught his attention. He had never seen a Western-style toilet. He had heard about them—very unsanitary compared to squatting over a hole. He hesitated only a moment before going in for a closer look. He lifted the lid. Water. *So wasteful!* And mounted on the wall above were a small television box and a telephone. *Such extravagance!* It reinforced in Wahid's mind the importance of the work he and his comrades were doing.

In the bedroom, he scanned the contents for the camera bag. *There!* It was sitting on the floor next to a small table with a suitcase. He felt the urge to grab the bag and run. On second thought, he decided the room must look like a robbery had taken place, like someone was after more than just a camera. He scattered the contents of the suitcase and the closets around on the floor, pulled out dresser drawers, stripped off some of the bedding, and overturned a chair.

That should do it.

As he reached for the camera bag, he noticed some cash and an airplane ticket on the table where the suitcase had been. For religious reasons, he couldn't bring himself to take the cash. It was bad enough he had to take the camera. He picked up the ticket and read the name and itinerary: Yi Jichun. Flight CS1322 departing Sanya Airport on February 1, 2001, at 9:30 PM. A smile creased his cheek and a surge of relief rose up inside him.

Setting the ticket back down on the table, he took the camera bag and quietly exited the room.

CHAPTER 9

Loud screams and persistent crying emanated from the airport waiting area. For Yi, the noise was unbearable. He knew a long wait under these circumstances would leave him with a bad impression of a place that, except for his camera equipment being taken, was the closest thing to paradise he had ever experienced.

When the delay of the Guangzhou flight was first announced, a flurry of people rushed to the ticket counter seeking other possible flights. Yi didn't even try to approach the counter. He hated crowds. And in China he learned that many people didn't bother with lines; they simply pushed in front of anyone between them and the counter or tried to cut in from the side. If you pointed out to them that there was a line in which they should queue up, they would look at you as if they had no idea what you were talking about and thank you very much for pointing it out. Yi loved his heritage and was proud of his ancestors from China, but this was one characteristic he had no tolerance for.

He had guessed right. With the exception of a few American expatriates, almost everyone else on the flight pushed in around the ticket counter, cutting in front of each other, ignoring any sort of queue, hoping to get to the ticket counter first. From the looks on the faces of those who made it to the front, they were obviously being told there were no other flights to Guangzhou. Dismayed, they returned to their seats to wait for the announcement of when the Guangzhou flight might be rescheduled. The Americans who had queued up cast looks of disgust and voiced their annoyance when they received the news that no other Guangzhou flights were available. They would simply have to wait, which was something Americans didn't do well—Yi included. At the first opportunity, he sought out an airline representative.

"Are there any other flights heading out soon to a place even remotely close to Guangzhou?" he asked the representative. Hopefully he had thought of the idea before others came up with it. After all, he only needed to get to someplace in the southern part of the mainland. From there he could take a train or bus into Guangzhou.

"There is one flight at 10:30 PM to Shenzhen," she replied. Shenzhen was only a forty-five-minute train ride from Guangzhou. The Hong Kong express trains passed through Shenzhen every two hours on their way to Guangzhou. He estimated he could still be home by half past midnight.

With his warmest voice and most charming smile, Yi asked the inevitable question, "Any chance you could get me a seat on that plane? It's really important that I arrive home tonight."

His handsome smile had been successful on other such occasions, and he hoped it would work now. The attractive young woman lowered her eyes and smiled back.

"I'll try," she said and started keying into her computer.

Yi looked around him. The airline had not posted boarding signs for the Shenzhen flight yet. As soon as they did, there would be another mad dash to the ticket counter as others realized the possibility of an earlier flight off Hainan Island. Yi was glad he had thought of it first.

"Yes, I can change your ticket to the Shenzhen flight leaving at 10:30 PM. Would you like window or aisle?"

"Aisle would be great." He handed her his ticket and passport.

"You are lucky," she added. "There are only a few seats left on the Shenzhen flight."

She lowered her eyes again and smiled as she handed Yi his boarding pass and passport.

"Thank you, pretty lady," he said, covering her hand with his as he took the ticket from her. A splash of pink color came to her cheeks.

Yi picked up his carry-on bag and moved to the other gate. As anticipated, when the boarding sign for Shenzhen was displayed, everyone—particularly the American expats—made a dash for the ticket counter. Yi noticed the man and woman from Macau, with whom he had chatted on the bus at the hotel—*João Araújo, was it?*—had also exchanged their tickets for the Shenzhen flight. Everyone else was told that the plane was full. And there were no other flights to the mainland before Guangzhou flight CS1322.

***

Yi arrived back in his Guangzhou apartment at 12:40 AM. He set his luggage down and headed for the bathroom. It had been a long day, and he wanted nothing but sleep. Unpacking could wait until morning.

He awoke to a beautiful sunny day, a drastic change from the weather of the night before. After making himself a cup of herbal tea, he turned on the television to catch the morning news. The anchorman's voice came on:

"Once again, there has been a tragic airplane crash off the southern coast of China. At approximately half past midnight last night, South China Airlines flight CS1322 from Hainan Island to Guangzhou crashed into the South China Sea. Rescue teams have been searching the area, but there appear to be no survivors. Many of the 207 passengers were American, including several high-level officials and their families from the American embassy in Beijing. An investigation is underway to determine the cause of the crash. As of now, it is believed the crash was due to severe weather in the area. We will report more on this breaking development as we learn of it . . ."

The cup of tea slipped from Yi's grasp as he realized the flight that had crashed into the ocean was the one he should have been on.

CHAPTER 10

"I believe I have a place that will interest you," Jiaoshi said to the dark-complexioned man as he picked up his stack of chips from the casino table. Jiaoshi spent much time at the Macau casinos and in Hong Kong, where interacting with international businessmen increased his access to power. These connections gave Jiaoshi opportunities that mainland local officials did not have, along with exposure to information he wouldn't receive through proper government channels.

"Really?" the Foreigner responded with indifference, focusing instead on his glass of Glen Garioch whisky.

"I'm sure you know the owner here—Mr. João Araújo?"

The Foreigner nodded then casually glanced around the room.

"He has informed me that you are seeking a private location near the South China Sea for the purpose of conducting some . . . training?" Jiaoshi said, trying to sound discreet yet eager to seize a new opportunity. "As mayor of the capital of Hainan, I am in a position to offer you the use of a private island."

The Foreigner turned his head toward Jiaoshi and looked at him for the first time. He studied Jiaoshi's face and attire. The quality of his suit and tie indicated he had income other than the mere salary of a government official. And the fact that he was in Macau indicated the man had connections as well as access to falsified government documents.

"The Communist Party is known for its strict policies in dealing with outsiders," the Foreigner said. "I am not interested in copious amounts of paperwork and monitoring."

Jiaoshi laughed, trying to hide his nervousness. "Hainan is a remote area, my friend. Beijing officials seldom venture that far south."

"It's not a chance I'm willing to take," the Foreigner replied. He took another sip of his drink.

Afraid the opportunity was slipping away, Jiaoshi blurted out, "I assure you I am in complete control of that area, my friend. You will not be bothered by government officials."

Jiaoshi thought about the other provincial officials and how much money he would have to pay them to cooperate. *No problem.* Even if he had to pay them large sums of money, he speculated that this venture would make him a very wealthy man.

"Leave me your business card. I will come next week to see this island," the Foreigner said. He stood to leave. He would verify the man's credentials through his friend, João Araújo.

Jiaoshi proudly presented his card.

***

The next week the Foreigner arrived on Hainan Island. Jiaoshi took him to see Yalong Bay and Wild Boar Island.

"This area of Yalong Bay was previously used for China's military training," Jiaoshi reassured the Foreigner. "It would not be unusual to see a military camp here once again. And as you can see, Wild Boar Island has the privacy you are looking for," Jiaoshi beamed, proud that he was the only one in Hainan who knew of the island's hidden cave.

The Foreigner nodded as he surveyed the area.

Uncomfortable with the Foreigner's silence and concerned that it might be an indication of disinterest, Jiaoshi rambled on about the location's many features.

"And just as importantly, my friend, our growing tourism means there will be many large money-making ventures here. The government will not question large sums of money passing through our local banks." Jiaoshi paused, smiling anxiously.

The Foreigner had to admit the conditions seemed ideal. And given the added privacy of a hidden cave, the area was even more promising than João had indicated. The Foreigner was pleased.

"Construction will have to be done inside the cave in order to make it suitable to our specific uses," the Foreigner commented.

"Whatever you need; I will arrange everything for you," Jiaoshi quickly responded. "I am sure I can get you the best construction prices." He was having difficulty containing his exuberance.

"Under the circumstances, Mr. Bao," the Foreigner began as he scanned the expanding resort across the bay, "I think it would be best if my organization handled the construction ourselves and used our own workers. We must avoid drawing attention to our activities and our location. For that reason, it is best if local workers are not involved." He smiled. "I'm sure you understand."

"Of course! Secrecy is one of the many services I provide," Jiaoshi responded sheepishly, not wanting to say anything that might cause the Foreigner to change his mind. "I guarantee you'll have secrecy. Total secrecy."

"How much money would you require to fully secure this deal?" the Foreigner asked.

That was the question Jiaoshi had been anxiously mulling over in his mind. Now that he was faced with giving an answer, his anxiety became overwhelming. He didn't want to appear too greedy or lacking in the knowledge and experience of such transactions, but he would be a fool if he didn't get as much as he could in this once-in-a-lifetime opportunity. He pulled at his lower lip and stared at the ground, as if hoping a price would magically appear in the sand.

The Foreigner waited patiently. As tiny beads of perspiration began to form on his brow from the heat trapped inside his Italian wool suit and starched shirt, he dabbed lightly at his forehead with his folded linen handkerchief. The fine white silk threads of the single monogram—a cursive letter *X*—turned a pale gray from the salty liquid.

"Uh, I do not wish to sound greedy, but, of course, this is a premium resort area, as you know. Um, so for your use of the old military training area on Yalong Bay and full rights of use to Wild Boar Island and its cave, and, of course, the many benefits to you for my valuable services and high-level connections, I would have to say, um . . ." He hesitated a moment, his heart racing. "I would have to ask a fee of one million per year, in US dollars, deposited into a Swiss bank account."

There. He had said it. The number was now out there, real and tangible. He fully expected the Foreigner to counter with a smaller amount, which was okay—he had figured it into his calculations. He was prepared to accept substantially less. He would still end up quite wealthy.

He held his breath as he waited for the Foreigner's response. The seconds passing seemed like an eternity.

"Fine," the Foreigner said without any emotion.

CHAPTER 11

"Ah, it is so good to see you again, my son," the white-haired man said to the Foreigner as they shook hands and kissed each other's cheeks. "You are well?"

"Yes, sir, I am well. A little tired maybe but well."

"It is to be expected, given all you are doing—the traveling and organizing. So many details to arrange," the white-haired man said as he patted the Foreigner on the back. "Come, you must say hello to everyone. They are eager to see you, and, of course, we are all looking forward to your report."

In a private corporate boardroom in Belgium, eight men in expensive suits sat around a mahogany conference table. The Foreigner took a seat to the left of the white-haired gentleman and looked at his Breguet Tourbillon watch. It was 5:00 AM.

"Let us begin," the white-haired man said. The room became silent, and all eyes turned in his direction.

"The first item on our agenda is the status report by our guest," he said, gesturing to the Foreigner. "We can assume plans are going as scheduled, yes?"

"As scheduled," the Foreigner replied, nodding.

"Then please apprise us of your activities since we last met," the white-haired man stated with interest.

"Thank you," the Foreigner began. "Gentlemen, as you directed, I have acquired property in the southern Asia region . . ."

***

Six months later, in the private corporate boardroom in Belgium, the eight men again took their seats around the mahogany conference table. It was 5:00 AM.

The Foreigner arrived at 5:02 AM and was greeted warmly by the white-haired gentleman who hugged him and kissed each cheek in the traditional European fashion.

"Welcome, my son," he said to the Foreigner as he entered the room and closed the door. "It is good to see you once again."

"It is good to see you, sir," the Foreigner replied. "You are looking well."

"Yes," the white-haired man nodded. "Now come, help yourself to some fresh hot coffee and a pastry. We provide only the best."

The Foreigner walked to the sideboard and poured himself his usual cup of Grand Earl Grey tea, squeezed in a wedge of fresh lemon, and stirred in one teaspoon of raw sugar.

"I think we are ready to begin," the white-haired man said. He nodded to one of the directors, who went to the side credenza and placed a call on the telephone.

At 5:05 AM, four men in gray polyester suits strained by the size of their steroid-swollen bodies arrived outside the boardroom and took their posts. They were armed—trained to kill and emotionless about the number of times they had done so. They stood guard. They knew their jobs, which they had performed every first Sunday of every quarter for the past five years. Their orders were given by telephone from a man they had never seen, but tidy sums appeared in each of their bank accounts right on schedule. And it was a generous sum for two hours' work on Sunday mornings four times each year. Additional amounts could be earned by carrying out special assignments, such as coercion or elimination. Those jobs were paid separately but still by direct deposit into their bank accounts. Overall, they could count on a six-figure annual income.

Today, as with all the Sunday meetings, their orders were to guard the boardroom area and eliminate any problems. They had never seen anyone enter or leave the boardroom, nor could they hear anything being said inside the soundproof room. The only indication that a meeting was going on was a call from the private line located on the other side of the doors. The guards would then wait at their posts until a second call came approximately two hours later, relieving them of their duties.

Inside the boardroom there would be no written report, documents, or recordings of the meeting.

The Foreigner removed from his pocket an unmarked computer disk. He inserted it into the boardroom's projection system computer.

"Gentlemen, since our last meeting, much has been accomplished in setting up Hainan Net operations," the Foreigner began with confidence. "I think you will be pleased at the progress."

He proceeded to the front wall of the boardroom and flipped a switch, lowering a projection screen. He clicked the remote in his hand. A map of Southern Asia and the South China Sea came up on the screen.

The directors nodded and smiled.

Using a laser light source, the Foreigner pointed to the southern coast of Hainan Island.

"First, the cave on Wild Boar Island has been fully constructed into an operations center with a communications hub and biological weapons laboratory."

"You are absolutely sure it is well hidden and secure?" one of the directors interrupted.

"One hundred percent sure. The island had been privately owned by a family who did not make the existence of the cave known. I acquired the island from the only surviving family member, who assured me there was only one entry. Of course, we destroyed it after installing our own fully secured entrance."

"What reliance do we have that this man's knowledge of the cave won't cause us problems in the future?" another director asked.

"We pay him handsomely for his cooperation and silence," the Foreigner responded.

"Why pay him at all?" one of the directors remarked. "Why not just eliminate him? My experience has been in these situations that these people become never-ending drains on cash."

"You are correct. But in this case, the man is also the mayor of Sanya— the capital of Hainan. And as such, he serves a useful purpose in securing government favors and in seeing to it that our presence on the island goes unnoticed by other officials. He also ensures that our banking activities with foreign entities go unimpeded—something China usually disallows or monitors closely, which we do not want." The Foreigner paused before going on. "To put your mind at ease, sir," he said with a smile, "when his useful purpose ceases to exist, so will he."

The director who had posed the question nodded, as if satisfied with the Foreigner's response.

"Now, as for the center's security," the Foreigner continued, "state-of-the-art surveillance equipment has been set up around the perimeter of the island, and radar equipment has been installed to monitor air traffic. No one can get near the operations center without setting off silent alarms, which are monitored around the clock. In addition, a gas recovery system has been installed to make detection of biological fermentation processes virtually impossible. The elaborate communications systems have the capability of sending and receiving encrypted satellite transmissions between our other points of operations, including Bangkok, Hong Kong, Pakistan, Afghanistan, the Philippines, and Columbia. In addition, a private area network has been set up with remote sites located inside a tourist area on Hainan, where recruiting is being conducted, and in a local bank, where wire transfers are handled from our Pakistani bank."

"What about training facilities?" a director asked.

"In addition to our military training camps in Afghanistan and the Philippines, we have set up training on Hainan—near the shore, just across from Wild Boar Island. As a matter of fact, it's one of China's old military training facilities."

"So nothing appears out of the ordinary, then?" a director commented.

"That's correct. To locals and tourists, it looks to be simply a continuation of China's national military training," the Foreigner stated as he moved to the sideboard and poured himself another cup of tea.

He took a sip before continuing his report.

"Demolition testing and training are being conducted at several points in the South China Sea," he said as he pointed to the map. "There is a storage area for smaller demolitions within the cave on Wild Boar Island. These are used for underwater testing and training near that area. Larger-sized demolitions are stored in our facility in Bangkok for use on cargo and cruise ships. Those are being tested farther out at sea."

"How well received are the recruiting and training efforts?" someone asked.

"I would say very well received. Our recruiting numbers are higher than projected. We have recruited and trained more than seventy new soldiers in the past six months. Their dedication is most impressive, I must say," the Foreigner stated proudly.

CHAPTER 12

"I think I may have someone for your program," Senator Boyle said as he took a seat in Trenton Woodbury's office. "He's a young Chinese-American male, late twenties, who works in my office. Name's Jason Yi. Works under Dave O'Reilly, my China specialist. This kid's sharp—a Georgetown Law School grad, fluent in Mandarin and Cantonese."

Woodbury, head of the WTO Legislative Committee, picked up the phone and punched in some numbers. "Bill, this is Trent. I need a thorough background check, and I mean thorough. Name's Jason Yi. Boyle will give you the details. I want to know if this kid so much as crossed the street the wrong way . . . Yep . . . As soon as you can."

***

Three weeks later the report arrived. Woodbury immediately opened it and removed the file. The cover sheet outlined the information contained in the report, which included Jason's background from childhood and the backgrounds of his parents and grandparents—where each had been born and where they had lived; physical characteristics, general health and medical records; overview of the San Francisco neighborhood where Jason grew up; interviews of neighbors' perspectives about Jason, his parents, and grandparents; what schools Jason attended, his grades, comments from teachers; sports activities; driving record; criminal record; friends' names and interviews; job history and employer interviews; marital status and sexual orientation, including background information on any persons to whom he had been romantically linked; political affiliations; time spent out of the country, where he went and why; and any specialized skills.

Woodbury turned to the summary sheet, which stated:

Yi Jichun (nickname Jason), born in San Francisco, California, on January 28, 1971, the only child of Yi Ming and Fu Yu Xuan, both of whose parents emigrated from Canton to California in the 1940s. Grandfather Yi Meung Su (deceased) was an herbal doctor; father is an accountant schooled at Columbia University . . . Jason Yi graduated high school at the age of sixteen. He received his bachelor of arts degree in Chinese languages from the University of California at Berkeley, then attended Georgetown Law School in Washington DC, specializing in international law. Admitted to the bar in Washington DC, and California . . . Described by associates as honest, intelligent, possessing tremendous fortitude, athletic, chivalrous, charitable, somewhat quick tempered but avoids quarreling . . . Skills include advanced Jie Quan Dao (martial arts) and SCUBA (to 200 feet). . . . Religious affiliation: LDS (served a two-year mission in Taiwan from 1990 to 1992 for The Church of Jesus Christ of Latter-day Saints).

Hmm, Woodbury thought. . . . *Mormon . . . Not surprising. The CIA likes to see LDS agents fill their ranks. Very reliable and trustworthy.*

"Good," he spoke out loud then continued reading the report.

Yi's driving record showed two speeding violations and one minor accident, which occurred in his first year of driving.

No warrants or arrests.

The medical report showed male, Asian, height 5 feet 10 inches, weight 163 pounds, excellent health, appendectomy at age eleven, no known allergies, eyesight normal but recommended reading glasses.

Unmarried, with no children.

Woodbury closed the folder and picked up the phone.

"Boyle," the voice responded after several rings.

"The report on Jason Yi looks good. Why don't you bring him in. Let's see what he's willing to do."

***

Jason worked on Capitol Hill. He had interned there each summer between semesters while attending law school. In 1997, after graduating from George-town Law School, he was employed by Senator Randolph Boyle's office, working under Dave O'Reilly, specialist in China affairs and WTO review legislation.

Senator Boyle served on the Senate Appropriations Committee and was concerned about a proposal for the funding of a United States–sponsored World Trade Organization training program for judges in China. The program would prepare China's judicial system for rule of law requirements under permanent normal WTO trade status—the level China was expected to be granted when the WTO voted in November. Boyle saw the proposed training program as a waste of money.

***

Meeting Jason for the first time, Woodbury was pleased with what he saw. Jason was exactly the image needed for the assignment. He had an aura of professionalism and confidence about him but not arrogance. Above average in height for a Chinese man, his shoulders were broad and straight, his arms muscular but not massive. His torso narrowed at the hips, and he was slightly bowlegged, as were most natural athletes. He had a round yet masculine face with a hint of tan to his golden complexion, probably indicative of an enjoyment for the outdoors when he could find the time. His thick black hair fell back from his high forehead and curved slightly where the ends touched the top of his shirt collar. He was direct in his eye contact yet not threatening, and his smile was broad and charming. He looked to be from a healthy lifestyle.

After shaking hands, Woodbury gestured for Jason to sit in one of the two tufted leather armchairs positioned in front of his massive mahogany, leather-top desk. Senator Boyle sat down on the burgundy sofa along the wood-paneled side wall.

"As you may know, Jason," Woodbury began, "one serious problem in trade relations between the United States and China is the large quantities of counterfeit products manufactured there. Foreign businesses are hesitant to invest in joint trade ventures with China because of the counterfeiting."

He waited for Jason's response.

Jason merely nodded—he was very much aware of China's problem with counterfeiting. He had written several reports on the subject for Senator Boyle.

Woodbury continued. "The committee has agreed to appropriate funds for a judicial training program in China if—and that's a big *if*, son—the US is allowed to assist in uncovering counterfeiting rings by sending in specially trained Chinese-American agents to serve for a short time as local officials in China's provincial governments."

Jason tried to stifle a chuckle as he replied, "I don't mean to be rude, sir, but the Communist Party would never open up enough to allow Americans into official areas where they could have access to classified government information, even for a short period of time."

Woodbury cleared his throat before responding. "I appreciate your candor, Jason, but I think you'd be surprised at what the Chinese government is willing to do under the circumstances—especially in seeking permanent normal trade status in the WTO and with their bid for the 2008 Olympics on the line. The United States and China are working together to crack down on counterfeiting and local corruption. This is important to the United States because many American companies already established in China are losing large sums of money to counterfeit products. Other businesses are hesitant to sink money into opening up mainland markets because they know it's a sure bet they'll end up competing against knockoffs of their own products. Besides American investment losses, China is losing out on billions of foreign capital. And, as I said before, they know if they don't get this counterfeiting mess under control, it could seriously jeopardize their trade status and their bid for the Olympics. Truth be told, they're having a devil of a time cleaning up this mess on their own."

"The counterfeiters are paying large sums of money to local Chinese officials to look the other way, making it difficult if not impossible to catch them," Boyle added.

Woodbury continued. "Given permanent normal trade status, China's judges will have to familiarize themselves with and adhere to the rule of law. You're probably aware of this, Jason, but judges are a relatively new concept in the Chinese legal system. Prior to 1979 there were only a handful of them throughout China. After the Cultural Revolution, there was such a shortage of judges that local officials were appointed whether they had any legal training or not. This resulted in inconsistencies in the interpretation of the laws and gave too much power to local officials. It became a breeding ground for corruption. Of course, now there are several thousand judges throughout China, and they must have an education and pass a national judicial exam. Nevertheless, the problem still exists."

"I'm aware of China's history, sir," Jason replied with a smile, wondering where the conversation was going. He'd assumed he had been called into the meeting in Trenton Woodbury's office to discuss some research he had done recently on China's trade relations.

"Yes, of course. And, as I'm sure you're aware, Chinese culture and politics can heavily influence the outcome of a legal matter. Very little—not even the law—is as important as family and one's political connections."

"Family members take care of one another," Jason offered in his culture's defense. "Favors are paid back through other favors. It's called *guanxi*, and it's an important part of Chinese culture."

"But they've got to learn to abide by the rule of law," Boyle interjected sharply.

"Yes, sir," Jason agreed. "But there are some things the United States could learn from China."

"The law must be supreme, Jason," Boyle went on. "That's the rule of law. You know it, the World Trade Organization requires it, and China will have to abide by it if they want to succeed in international trade relations. The way things are right now, if someone is accused of a crime—even if he's guilty—his family, friends, and business associates would say or do anything to get him off. And the judges are nearly as bad, lining their own pockets. The United States and other foreign businesses are just not willing to go in and invest billions of dollars in a country where the judicial system doesn't hold to the law."

Jason knew this was a sore subject with Boyle. As far as he was concerned, the United States would be throwing good money after bad in funding a judicial training program for China's judges.

Sensitive to the fact that the meeting might seem confrontational to Jason, Woodbury stood and moved to the front of his desk. He sat on the edge nearest to Jason. The faint scent of aftershave reached Jason's nose. *Old Spice.*

In a warm, fatherly tone, Woodbury continued. "Jason, China knows their judicial system has problems. They want to succeed in the WTO, and they are willing to embrace the concept of the rule of law. That's a big change for them, and they know it's going to take time and effort on everyone's part. That's why we're willing to help. And believe me, China wants our help. This WTO judicial training program, although primarily funded by the United States, is sanctioned by China's Supreme People's Court and the Ministry of Education."

"They've already agreed to let us send in Chinese-American agents to pose as local Chinese officials," Boyle said.

"Only China's president and a few of the highest officials will know about the project," Woodbury added.

"Sir, I'm sure you recognize the danger in that. If a foreign agent were to be caught, it's likely he or she would be executed before word could reach those high-level officials," Jason said, concerned for the safety of the agents who would be risking their lives.

"Your concern is valid, Jason. I assure you, we are aware of the dangers," Woodbury responded.

"Well, that's at least a first step," Jason replied and paused before going on. "Sir, I appreciate the opportunity to discuss this with you and the senator here, but exactly how is it you would like me to help in this project?"

The room fell silent.

"I would be happy to put together a report on what WTO information the agents would need to know," Jason added. "Details on Chinese law . . ." He paused, surprised that neither Woodbury nor Boyle seemed to be forthcoming with a response. The two of them exchanged looks as if expecting the other one to answer.

Woodbury cleared his throat again. "Jason," he responded, "we would like to send you as one of those agents."

Again the room fell silent.

"Well, you certainly are straightforward," Jason laughed, hoping to hide his sudden uneasiness. This was not at all what he had expected, which annoyed him because he prided himself on recognizing hidden agendas. He had completely miscalculated the purpose of the meeting. He glanced over at Boyle as if to say, *Why wasn't I given a heads-up on this?* but Boyle was now engrossed in a folder he had open in his lap. He took off his reading glasses and looked up as Jason began to speak.

"Why me?" Jason said with total seriousness.

Woodbury deliberately didn't tell Jason about the detailed investigation that had been done on him. He knew that telling Jason he had been investigated without his knowledge or authorization would make him angry and defensive.

"For the very reasons you mentioned. You know WTO procedures, and you're familiar with Chinese law and international trade." Woodbury then laughed. "And I guess it doesn't hurt that you're of Chinese ancestry and fluent in the language."

"I see. I look and sound the part," Jason responded with a hint of sarcasm. "That's not a lot to go on when your life is on the line in a Communist country."

Jason let a few moments pass and then shook his head. "I'm honored, sir, but I'm not trained in undercover work." He glanced over at Boyle who was still looking down, this time twisting his wedding band.

Silence again.

"I understand, Jason. And, truth be told, that's probably an advantage," he added with a slight chuckle. With complete seriousness, he continued. "I'd personally see to it that you were well trained and well compensated." He stressed the word *well* both times.

Boyle looked up. He knew the money angle Woodbury had presented wouldn't be enough to get Jason to accept the assignment. "Jason, you would be doing a great service for America, the WTO, and more importantly, China."

Jason thought for a moment before responding. "If I were to do this . . . and that's a big *if*, sir—" Jason smiled, enjoying the use of Woodbury's own words to show he now controlled the outcome of the discussion, "—we can work out the numbers later. Right now I want to know what I would have to do over there and what protection the United States would provide for me."

Woodbury nodded. "Fair enough. In short, we would send you someplace in China where you would pose as an administrative judge. The exact province would be determined by the amount of suspected corruption among local officials—possibly Guangzhou in Guangdong Province. A lot of counterfeiting factories are set up there because of the close proximity to shipping ports. Furthermore, you would attend the WTO judicial training program in Beijing for approximately three months. In your capacity as a judge, we want you to interact with other judges, learn from them, and scope out fraudulent activities they may be involved in or know about. In other words, blend in and absorb information. There would be about forty judges total, coming from all over China. As you know, Jason, most of China's judges are young like yourself, so you should have no trouble blending in and making friends."

"And the protection?" Jason asked again.

"For your own sake, son, the less you have the better."

"You mean non-official cover? That would mean no diplomatic protection." Jason could feel little beads of sweat beginning to form under his shirt collar. "The last thing I need is to be caught spying in an Asian Communist country and have the United States turn their back on me."

"Don't get caught." Boyle tried to interject some humor, thinking a little levity would lessen the tension now developing in the room. Woodbury's steely glance let Boyle know his humor was not appropriate or appreciated.

"Jason, if we sent you under official cover, we would have to assign you a position through the US embassy. That puts you too far removed from local Chinese officials and totally defeats the purpose of the program. Non-official cover is the only way to go here."

"So you're going to hang me out there without any protection whatsoever?" Jason couldn't believe what they were asking of him.

"Definitely not," Woodbury replied. "You'll have the expertise of the Central Intelligence Agency behind you in establishing your identity there and in creating the necessary background documentation for your cover. You'll be given new identification documents under your Chinese name, with People's Republic of China papers, including a Chinese passport, residence card, bank account, a law degree from a top Chinese university, and national exam results for your judicial certification. The paper trail will be thorough, I assure you."

Jason was still unsure about whether he wanted to get involved.

"What about other agents? Will there be others I can contact over there?" he asked.

"You'll be the first of five NOC operatives, maybe more—we don't know at this point. But to answer your question, no, you'll have no knowledge of or contact with any of the other agents. You won't even know where they're located. For your safety, son, it is best that way." Woodbury tried to sound reassuring.

Boyle wanted to redeem himself from his earlier humorless remark, so he mustered up all the sincerity he could. "Jason, whether I like it or not, Congress is going to appropriate the funds for this program. It's pretty much a done deal. So if we're going to spend the money, we need to do it right. I recommended you because I knew you were trustworthy and would see that the job got done. We need this to be a success, Jason. Nipping this counterfeiting problem in the bud is a major step in the right direction for China . . . and the United States."

Jason considered Boyle's words.

"How long would I have to stay over there?" he asked.

Woodbury shrugged his shoulders. "Can't say for sure. Possibly a year. These organized corruption networks run along cultural, linguistic, and in some cases strong family lines. They will be difficult to penetrate even for a native speaker."

Jason thought about the improbability of penetrating such an organization as well as the strong possibility that if he were caught he would be killed.

Boyle broke the silence. "Another thing, Jason. I know how important your religion is to you, but you must be aware that it is not recognized by the government of China. It would jeopardize your cover if you were to have any contact with your church or its members or to conduct any religious practices there."

"I realize that," Jason responded, a hint of uncertainty beginning to show in his voice.

"But, rest assured, Jason," Boyle continued, "there are many US agents serving undercover throughout the world that are of the Mormon faith. Because of their convictions and dedication, they are highly successful at it, as I'm sure you would be."

Jason nodded. "Tell me about the training," he asked.

Boyle answered. "The training's excellent, and it is very thorough, Jason. First of all, you'll spend six months in special Foreign Service training learning how to operate under a false identity and how to blend in with your surroundings. They'll teach you what to do if your cover is compromised—like what signs to look for and what to do if you're being followed, or if your rooms are monitored, what to listen and watch for, et cetera, et cetera. And driving skills—how to throw off a tail, ram another car to disable it if necessary, that sort of thing. Of course, self-defense, which I understand you are already skilled in."

Jason had to admit he was intrigued. And the more he thought about spending time in the country of his roots, despite the danger, the more he felt it was what he needed to do.

"Is that everything?" Jason asked.

"Son, that's only the beginning," Woodbury said with a smile.

***

Six months later, Jason completed the specialized training and signed the Foreign Service documents. They gave him new identification papers, including a Chinese passport using his real name, Yi Jichun, with instructions that he was to tell no one, not even his family, about the assignment.

But he did tell someone—not all of the details but enough to discuss how undercover work would affect his membership in the Church. He told his bishop.

"Jason, the Lord knows what's in your heart," his bishop counseled. "If after much prayer and contemplation you feel this assignment is the right choice, then I believe the Lord takes into consideration the fact that you will be unable to attend Church meetings or have scriptural material with you. These things are not yet sanctioned by the Chinese government. So, I imagine, having such items in your possession would mark you as an outsider."

"There's one other thing." Jason hesitated before going on. "I'll be sharing a dormitory room, and I'm told there are no private bath areas. Wearing different clothing from the others could jeopardize my cover. If I'm unable to wear my garments, am I still protected?"

The bishop thought for a moment. "There are some instances when garments shouldn't be worn. I believe that during those times, as long as you stay close to the Lord in your prayers and thoughts, you are protected. Remember, Jason, you always have the Holy Ghost with you. Listen to His promptings."

Jason nodded. He knew what the bishop said was true.

They both sat in silence for a moment as Jason contemplated a year without the things he cherished most.

As though the bishop knew Jason's thoughts, he added more words of comfort. "Many fine Latter-day Saints serve in these capacities, Jason. Just follow the guidance of the Spirit, and keep within the boundaries of your undercover training."

Jason recalled the warning from the Foreign Service director: "Being undercover is a lie, and you have to live it. It is your only protection. From here on, use the name Yi Jichun as a constant reminder of your cover. Never let your guard down, not for a moment. Doing so could cost you your life. And don't overlook your surveillance detection procedures. If you are being watched and you compromise your cover, you may not get out alive. With Communist Chinese identification papers on you, Mr. Yi Jichun, the United States could have a heck of a time getting you back!"

CHAPTER 13

Ürümqi, Xinjiang Uyghur Autonomous Region, People's Republic of China
January 22, 2001

"Are you sure these documents will pass inspection?" the Foreigner asked in Chinese with a European accent. He scanned through the production certificate and shipping documents, looking for any differences in the papers from previous shipments.

"*Dwei, dwei, dwei*, yes!" the manufacturer said to the Foreigner with a big grin, showing several rotted and missing teeth. He wore a soiled lab coat over his threadbare suit, two sizes too big, with trouser cuffs frayed in the back from being walked on. He continued proudly. "The Xinjiang Drug Administration official now assigned to Golden Camel Herbs and Medicines manufacturing plant is my uncle. It is no problem! You get best deal because he is family. He takes less money than the other official to say heroin is *Lingzhi* herbal medicine," he said, pointing his gnarled finger at the certified contents statement. "It is very good for you, very good."

The Foreigner knew drug authorities at provincial levels had the same power as China's State Drug Administration to examine and authenticate the production quality of drug manufacturers. The benefit of this practice was that it allowed for "trust" productions—manufacturing without the administration's actual examination. Licenses could be granted without proof that the stated drug was actually manufactured. Producers were finding ways to maximize their profits by creating low-quality drugs, counterfeiting name brands, or manufacturing illegal drugs, such as heroin.

High-grade heroin from the Xinjiang Uyghur Autonomous Region of China was some of the purest found anywhere in the world. But it was extremely dangerous to move, and getting caught by the government of the People's Republic of China for manufacturing or smuggling illegal drugs meant swift execution. Consequently, anyone involved in the handling of a shipment expected upfront, large cash payments under the table. Selling usually took place in the coastal area of Guangdong Province—not only because it was easier to move large quantities out of the country quickly from that area but also because it was important to keep the government out of the already volatile area of Xinjiang. Located on China's northwestern border, the Xinjiang Uyghur Autonomous Region was heavily populated with minorities who had, for some time, been active in seeking independence from the Communist People's Republic of China.

"But you are using the same truck driver to drive it to Guangzhou, right?" the Foreigner asked, handing the production certificates and shipping documents back to the manufacturer. Noticing ink smudges on his fingers from handling the documents, he carefully pulled his handkerchief from the breast pocket of his Italian wool suit and wiped his hands.

"*Dwei*, same driver. Very reliable," the manufacturer answered as he took a drag on his cigarette, coughed, and then hacked up a wad of phlegm that he proceeded to spit onto the floor. "His truck is being loaded now."

"Let's have a look, shall we?" the Foreigner said.

"Yes, yes, of course," the manufacturer replied, taking one last puff from his cigarette and then dropping it on the floor as he headed toward the loading dock.

The Foreigner crushed the smoldering cigarette with his shoe before following the manufacturer out. He had invested a lot here. He didn't want to see it go up in flames.

The boxes were being loaded into the back of a blue panel truck. Two scrawny workers hand carried them, disappeared into the darkness, and then returned empty handed. The corrugated boxes were stamped on the side with the Golden Camel Herbs and Medicines logo and the product name, "*Lingzhi*, Ganoderma Lucidium." The Foreigner walked over, picked up a box, and after removing something from his pants pocket, sliced into the side of the box as if it were butter. Pulling out a foil packet, he tore the corner with his teeth and then touched some of the white dust with his tongue. A smile came to his lips. He handed the box to the manufacturer.

"Where's the driver?" the Foreigner asked.

The manufacturer scurried to the cab of the truck and pounded his fist on the window. The driver must have been asleep inside. He jumped out of the truck, rubbing his eyes.

The Foreigner looked at his Breguet Tourbillon watch, eager to get back to the airport where a private jet waited for his return flight.

"Count it and then sign for it," the Foreigner said as he took an envelope out of his jacket pocket and handed it to the driver.

The driver took the cash out of the envelope, folded the stack in half around the index finger of his left hand, and began flipping through the twenty-dollar bills, counting. He loved the feel of American money. He had been especially pleased when the manufacturer told him payments would be in US currency. With the instability of the Chinese banking system, US dollars were preferred. He had collected quite a tidy sum for himself already. He only needed to make a couple more shipments like this and then he would be off to Singapore. His cousin was arranging his passport.

As he finished counting, the manufacturer handed him a clipboard, which he signed. He then tore off a piece of paper and handed it to the Foreigner.

The Foreigner nodded at a black Mercedes parked nearby. Its lights came on immediately as it pulled toward the dock.

"You know who to contact if there are any problems," he said to the manufacturer as he got into the back seat of the sedan. "Your wire transfer will take place after the shipment clears Guangzhou."

"No problems, no problems," the manufacturer said nervously as he stepped out of the Mercedes' path.

He hacked and spit again. No, he did not anticipate any problems. Other than the unexpected visit by the Foreigner, things had proceeded as they had in the past. The production run had been flawless—some of the best heroin they had ever produced—and it had been packed in the foil pouches, like the *Lingzhi* powder. His uncle had done a good job on the production certification documents, so no problems there. And they had manufactured just enough *Lingzhi,* an expensive mushroom spore extract used as a nutritional supplement to enhance well-being and boost the immune system, to fill the top row of boxes inside each case. Shipping inspectors throughout China knew the high price of the *Lingzhi* powder—about two hundred US dollars per box in China for a five-day supply, six hundred and fifty dollars in the United States—and how manufacturers would complain about their losses if the inspectors damaged any of it during inspection. So the inspectors were often reluctant to open the cases. If they did, it was usually only one box from the top row. He knew a little cash could be provided if an inspector thought to look elsewhere.

He also knew the truck driver would be successful in delivering the full shipment to Guangzhou. This driver had seen firsthand what happened to the last driver who tried to steal some of the heroin for his own profit. If the full shipment wasn't delivered on schedule exactly as planned, the driver knew the Foreigner would kill him.

CHAPTER 14

"Right on schedule," Wang Yan said with a smile as he waved the truck through the security gate of Guangzhou's port authority.

The other officials were already waiting on the dock when the heroin shipment arrived from Ürümqi. Each one knew what authorizations he would provide on the documents declaring the contents of the shipment as "herbal supplements" and stamping the export certificates as inspected and duty paid. It was one of the benefits of shipping out of the port of Guangzhou. As one of the three economic zones in China, Guangzhou was allowed greater freedoms for international trade than other regions of the mainland. Beijing officials tended to look the other way when it came to activities in an economic zone.

"You know the routine," Wang Yan stated indifferently.

The others nodded and set about the work they had done numerous times before. For their efforts, they knew they would be paid handsomely in US currency. They also knew the penalty that would be inflicted upon them if procedures were not followed exactly as directed. What they didn't know, however, was who else was involved in the other phases of the operation and what the heroin was being used for.

"What do you think this shipment's worth?" whispered Gong Yu Tian, the official responsible for collecting the export taxes and fees.

"I would say . . . at 720 kilos . . . the street value in Hong Kong would be in excess of about three hundred million dollars," Xin Wen, the official in charge of inspection, replied.

Gong Yu Tian whistled through his teeth. "Wouldn't you like to get your hands on that kind of money!"

Xin Wen shook his head. "You know the penalties, so don't even think it, Yu Tian. This shipment leaves first thing in the morning. Personally, I'll be glad when it's out of here."

The heroin shipment would leave Guangzhou by cargo ship, moving down the delta to Hong Kong then out into the South China Sea. From there it would cross the Pacific Ocean and eventually end up in the Republic of Colombia, South America. Upon its arrival there, a large sum of money would be transferred to a bank account somewhere in Pakistan.

But those details weren't the Guangzhou officials' concern. Their responsibility was to get the shipment safely out of China. In order to do that, the paperwork had to be properly prepared, some amount of fees collected, and any problems paid off or dealt with accordingly. The Guangzhou officials could not let down their guard until the shipment was loaded on the international cargo ship and it had left the port.

***

Gong Yu Tian knew he was in trouble. He had gotten greedy. He had been skimming off tax money on the heroin shipments for some time, charging more than the typical fees assessed and pocketing the difference. He had amassed a fortune and hoped to retire soon to the northern coast where he had purchased a large home overlooking the sea.

Unfortunately, this time the Foreigner was following the shipment through every step. The manufacturer had notified the Guangzhou officials that he had unexpectedly shown up at the manufacturing plant in Ürümqi, and it was likely he would show up in Guangzhou. The manufacturer also told them the Foreigner had carefully reviewed the production and shipping documents. Gong Yu Tian knew if the Foreigner reviewed the Guangzhou documents, he would see that money had been taken.

If Gong Yu Tian left town immediately, the Foreigner would surmise he was the one who had stolen the money and would track him down. No matter where he went, he was sure the Foreigner would find him. And he had no doubt about what would happen to him then. He had to find a way to get the Foreigner off his trail. Gong Yu Tian could think of only one way—turn the shipment in to the drug authorities.

Gong Yu Tian knew about the increased monitoring by the Chinese State Drug Administration and other government agencies and the increased number of drug busts carried out by the new drug force. Last month the drug force was tipped off to an illegal shipment of fake medicines manufactured in Guangzhou that was being shipped to Japan. The medicines were nothing more than dirty commercial-grade talcum powder mixed with a binding agent. Most likely tipped off by a drug manufacturing competitor, the drug force confiscated the shipment and arrested the manufacturer. His trial, as with all drug-related trials, was a speedy one, and he was executed a month later. Gong Yu Tian reasoned that if he could have the Foreigner arrested and executed, he would be able to get away with the money he had skimmed from the Foreigner's shipments. Nevertheless, he would have to act fast since he had no idea when the Foreigner might show up.

After returning to his office, Gong Yu Tian quickly altered the latest shipping documents to the correct taxes and fees and left the file on his desk. He then told his colleagues he wasn't feeling well and left for home. If he packed quickly, he could place the call to the drug force authorities and be on a train by early evening. He planned his strategy as he raced down the street, his heart pounding. First, he would stop by the bank on his way home and withdraw the money he had skimmed from the heroin shipments. Second, he would pack up some personal things from home, including the last payment in US currency, which he had legitimately earned. If his neighbors asked where he was going, he would tell them he was going to visit his family in Xi'an. Then he would leave for the train station where he would purchase a ticket to Qingdao—the location of his home overlooking the sea. And, finally, he would call the drug force's office from the train station, just before the train was to leave, and tell them of the heroin shipment waiting at the dock.

After leaving the bank, breathing a sigh of relief that his large cash withdrawal had gone without incident, he headed for home unaware of the telephone call being made from the bank.

***

The cell phone vibrated, and the Foreigner answered.

"The withdrawal has been made," the bank representative stated.

"The full amount?" the Foreigner asked.

"Yes, sir. The full amount. Mr. Gong seemed to be in quite a hurry."

"Thank you."

***

The Foreigner took out his Black Talon knife and cleaned his manicured fingernails as he sat in the darkened apartment of Gong Yu Tian. The bag of US currency, which Mr. Gong had hidden under his bed, was now at the Foreigner's feet. He had planned this trip to China to deal specifically with this latest little problem. But since he was making the trip anyway, he was instructed to stop in at the manufacturing plant and check on things there as well. As repulsed as he was by the Ürümqi drug manufacturer, he had at least proven to be reliable. The Guangzhou official, however, had been skimming funds from the operation for some time. The bank account was the final proof. The deposits to the account exactly matched the inflated amounts from each of the heroin shipment's export tax documents. *The benefits of working for an organization with access to any bank account in the world,* the Foreigner thought smugly. There was no hiding money from him. He was capable of tracking any sum, anywhere.

The Guangzhou shipping officials apparently needed a reminder of how serious it was to not carry out their responsibilities exactly as instructed. The Foreigner didn't really enjoy killing—it was so messy. But it left a profound, and therefore invaluable, impression on others who might have similar thoughts about betraying the organization.

***

Gong Yu Tian stopped for a brief chat and cup of tea with his neighbor before going upstairs to his apartment to pack. He was excited, even giddy, about this new change in his life.

"I never told you I had a wealthy uncle in Xi'an?" He feigned surprise to the neighbor. "Well, I don't like to boast. I am a humble man who doesn't deserve such good luck."

"What will you do with your uncle's money?" the neighbor asked in envy.

"Oh, I haven't thought much about it," he responded, eager to get upstairs and be on his way. "Probably give to charities. I have such simple needs for myself, you know."

As he left the neighbor's apartment, he thought about the new life he would now lead. This neighborhood was beneath him. If he hadn't been so greedy, he could have left a long time ago. He was glad his working days were finally over. He would live out the rest of his life in the style he always felt he deserved. He smiled as he turned the key in the lock of his door.

Stepping inside the doorway of his tiny apartment, the curved tip of a knife caught him in his belly.

"*Ni Hao*, Mr. Gong," the Foreigner said with a further thrust of the knife.

Gong Yu Tian collapsed to the floor. The wound, while serious, would not kill him immediately. A hazy film began to form over his eyes and a warm lightheadedness clouded his mind. Shadowy impressions formed of the Foreigner placing the money Gong Yu Tian had withdrawn from the bank into the bag where he kept his payments of US currency. The Foreigner turned and smiled down at him.

"That was quite a nice sum of our money you collected, Mr. Gong. It is a shame you won't need it any longer."

Gong Yu Tian reached for the bag.

"You know, my friend, in my country we have a most effective punishment for those who steal."

He grabbed Gong Yu Tian's right hand and cleanly cut through the wrist—a technique mastered through years of experience.

"Greed is a sin, Mr. Gong," the Foreigner said as he carefully wiped the blood from his knife with his handkerchief. He then picked up the bag of money and left the apartment.

CHAPTER 15

The words repeated over and over in Yi's mind: "You must live the lie at all times. It is your cover, your only protection." But Yi no longer cared. Stunned by the morning's news of the crashed plane he was supposed to have been on, he broke a key rule of his assignment. He knelt down and prayed.

If my room is being monitored, let them think I like hard floors, he rationalized.

After finishing his prayer, he stayed on his knees a while longer. A warm sense of peace came over him, and he felt reassured that he was accomplishing a service the Lord wanted him to do. The feeling was invigorating. He needed to get out of his tiny apartment.

Yi wasn't due to report to work until Monday, but he decided to visit his new office anyway. Since it was Friday, he hoped the Guangdong Province Office of Administration would be operating at a slower pace. He could chat with some people, make some connections, and get his bearings.

Because the office complex was located only a few miles from his apartment, he had acquired a bicycle to ride to work. The exercise would do him good, and it would give him a chance to observe his surroundings. Yi loved adventure. In the course of his thirty years, he had sought it with enthusiasm. And if risk played a part, the thrill was that much better. But now, being undercover in Guangzhou, even with renewed spiritual confirmation, Yi was having occasional doubts about his abilities. He wished his grandfather were around to talk to. His thoughts drifted back to a conversation he'd had with his grandfather years ago.

"What is on your mind, *suner*?" his grandfather's voice whispered in his ear, calling him by a term of endearment meaning "son of my son."

"*Yeye*, tell me about a time when you were afraid," six-year-old Yi asked.

"Oh, *suner*, there have been many times," his grandfather replied. "But once, when I was just your age, I felt most afraid. It was one night while I was watching Grandfather as he fished on the great Hongshui River. I loved to watch him with his *luzi* fishing birds. He would put a collar around each bird's neck, large enough not to harm the animal but small enough so the bird couldn't swallow any fish. Then he would go out on his flat bamboo raft, leaning against his wooden pole to push off to the center of the river. The birds would stand at the raft's edge, waiting for his signal, eager to catch fish. A lantern at the top of a pole on the raft lit the area so I could see them from the shore. Once the signal was given, the birds would dive into the water like bolts of lightning, streaming down in search of fish. When they returned to the raft Grandfather would take the fish from their mouths and toss them into a large basket at the front of the raft. Those eager birds would then dive back into the water to catch more fish. They seemed so happy—they had big smiles on their faces, and they were having such fun. I wanted to be with those happy birds, so one night I begged Grandfather to let me go out on the raft with him. He told me I could go only if I held on tight to the lantern pole because the bamboo raft was very narrow and had no sides, so it would be easy to fall into the river. But I wanted to touch one of those happy birds, so I let go of the lantern pole. And you know, *suner*, I tumbled into the river. Down, down, down I went like a heavy stone to the bottom."

"Couldn't you swim?" young Yi asked, spellbound.

"No, and neither could Grandfather. I was sure I would die at the bottom of that river and the gods would punish me forever for having disobeyed Grandfather."

"But, *yeye*, you didn't die."

"No. At the point when I thought I would surely die, a voice whispered to me, 'Open your eyes, *suner*; just open your eyes.' So I did."

"And what did you see, *yeye*?" Yi asked eagerly.

"I saw one of Grandfather's happy birds darting back toward the raft, and I reached out to it. The next thing I knew I was holding on to Grandfather's bamboo pole, and he was pulling me onto the raft."

"And did he scold you for letting go of the lantern pole?"

"No, when I told him what had happened, tears came to his eyes, and he told me about a time when he was most frightened as a small boy. He said his grandfather had told him, 'Open your eyes, *suner*, just open your eyes.'"

Many times Yi's grandfather had used that expression to encourage him to look beyond the obvious. It was one of the reasons why Yi had been open to hearing the missionary discussions and joining the Church. Now in Guangzhou, in the land of his heritage, Yi felt the advice from his grandfather was more important than ever. Being spiritually in tune and alert to his surroundings would be the keys of success in this assignment.

Feeling a need to familiarize himself with the streets and neighborhoods of Guangzhou, Yi took a slight detour into a park before continuing on to the office. The activities there brought back more memories for Yi when, as a child, he bicycled with his grandfather to the Portsmouth Square Park in San Francisco. His grandfather played elephant chess with other men from the neighborhood. Yi couldn't help but smile at the similarities from long ago. Men sat hunched over their plastic elephant-chess playing cloths with their round wooden chess pieces, intently discussing their best strategies and betting they could win against any stranger. Other folks from the neighborhood came to the park for their morning tea and chat. Old men brought bamboo birdcages covered in blue cloths, and after carefully hanging them in the trees and removing the covers, the air filled with soothing chirps and flutters as the birds basked in the fresh air and warm sunlight. In the open grass areas of the park, larger groups gathered to do their morning *tai chi'quan* exercises, moving in slow motion as if they were under water—some thrusting plastic swords, others waving silk scarves.

As Yi took in the sights, his mind wandered back to his outings with his grandfather. Occasionally, young Yi and his grandfather would take a dragon kite with a long, rainbow-colored tail. San Francisco breezes were great for kite flying. Yi could count on the kite being carried so far he could scarcely see it. His grandfather once told him the kite was like their relationship. At some point he wouldn't see his grandfather anymore; but like the tight pull on that kite string, assuring them the kite was still there, Yi would know his grandfather was always with him.

His grandfather died suddenly from a heart attack when Yi was only twelve years old. Angry at first, Yi immersed himself in sports at school. One of his team members played in a Church basketball league and invited him to join. He started attending the Church's meetings and later took the missionary discussions. It was then that he began to understand fully the eternal nature of the family. His grandfather's analogy of the kite string took on new meaning for him. He felt the connection especially strong when, after fulfilling a Church mission to Taiwan, Yi was able to perform his family's temple work in the Oakland Temple.

Over time, however, thoughts of his grandfather began to fade. His studies at UC Berkeley and then Georgetown Law School had been exhausting. And the pace he had to keep while working for Senator Boyle in Washington DC had not allowed him much time for anything other than work.

Having precious memories brought back of his grandfather also stirred the raw feelings of his loss. More than ever, Yi longed for the guidance of his grandfather's wisdom. And since coming to mainland China, he felt an even stronger pull on that invisible string connecting the two of them.

***

"I'll need to see your residence papers and job identification documents," the security guard at the entrance to the Office of Administration building said.

"Yes, of course," Yi responded as he took the papers out of his briefcase. Drops of sweat started to form around his neck as he anticipated the guard's reaction to his fake identification.

Please, Lord, let them pass.

The guard read through the papers carefully, looking up at Yi several times as if scrutinizing him. He scanned Yi's residence card into a machine and punched some keys on a computer. Yi could feel a lump beginning to form in his throat. He swallowed to clear it and then smiled.

"We didn't expect you until Monday, Mr. Yi," the guard stated then folded the papers and handed them back.

"Yes, I was hoping to have a look at my office. And if Mr. Jia is in, I would like to meet with him today," Yi stated in an authoritative voice, trying to sound like a judge. Mr. Jia was the senior official over Guangdong's Administrative Court and the person to whom Yi would report.

"Oh, yes, of course, Mr. Yi. I will notify his secretary that you are here," the guard replied. He then picked up the handset of a large, red rotary-dial telephone and gestured for Yi to take a seat in the waiting area. Observing his surroundings, Yi noted the austere decor of the concrete-block Communist government building and its drastic distinction from the colorful wood and tile structure of the Sun Yat-sun Memorial across the street. A large bronze statue of Dr. Sun Yat-sun faced the government building as if he were overseeing the important activities taking place there.

A short time later, an attractive middle-aged woman came to the waiting area. Yi stood and extended his hand.

"Mr. Yi," she said, bowing slightly instead of shaking Yi's outstretched hand. Yi discreetly returned his right hand to his black suit pants pocket. The official uniform of a judge in China was a black suit, thin black tie, white long-sleeved shirt, and a red Communist pin worn on the left lapel. The pin had been provided to him with his fake identification papers, and Yi had had his suit made by a Guangzhou tailor just days after he arrived. Although it was not a workday for Yi, he knew that coming to the office required him to be in uniform.

"There are some papers I will need you to fill out," the woman said, her eyes lowered. "And I'm afraid Mr. Jia is unable to see you right now. He is in an important meeting with a member of the Supreme People's Court."

"I understand," Yi replied. "It was foolish of me to come in before my scheduled starting date. Mr. Jia is such an important man." Knowing the culture, Yi knew if he appeared embarrassed for his thoughtlessness, the woman would be sympathetic to him not losing face.

"I am sure when he finishes his meeting, he will want to meet with you today," she said.

Yi realized what she said was a lie. There were protocols to be followed on the starting day of new hires, and a man of Mr. Jia's position would not make such formal introductions without the proper ceremony and other essential dignitaries around him. Yi's official start date wasn't until Monday, and he had made a mistake coming in before that time.

"I think, if it is okay with you, I will complete these papers and meet with Mr. Jia as scheduled on Monday," he said as he handed back the forms.

"Yes, of course," she answered with a big smile, this time looking him in the eyes.

"But first, before I go," he returned her smile, "would you be so kind as to point me in the direction of a men's room?"

A puzzled look briefly crossed her face before she lowered her eyes again. "A water closet? Certainly. Come with me, please."

He followed her up a flight of stairs and down an empty corridor. Many of the office doors were closed and the rooms darkened. He noticed the names and titles of the occupants as he walked by, noting that the offices were not for judges but for county administration officials. One door read "Shipping Inspections" and another "Export Tax Collection."

They stopped in front of the men's water closet entrance.

"I'll only be a moment," Yi said to the woman.

"If you wouldn't mind seeing yourself out, Mr. Yi, I am needed back in Mr. Jia's office."

"Of course," Yi replied. "Thank you for being so kind. I look forward to seeing you again on Monday."

They exchanged smiles, and the woman left.

Given the empty corridor and darkened offices, Yi did not expect anyone else to be in the bathroom. So he was surprised to hear conversation as he entered the room. No one was immediately visible. The sounds came from two adjacent stalls, the doors of which extended from the ceiling all the way down to the raised floor of the squat toilets. Not even the shoes of the occupants could be seen. Yi entered a stall farther down and quietly latched the door.

". . . Yu Tian was a foolish man! He should have known he would be caught," one voice said in a harsh whisper. "It's not worth being murdered and disgracing one's family."

Murdered? Yi's attention was piqued. Who did he say had been murdered? Someone named Yu Tian. That was interesting. One of the darkened offices they passed on the way to the bathroom belonged to a Gong Yu Tian, Export Tax Collection. Were they talking about him?

"Better to take a chance and become wealthy yourself rather than let the money go to someone else. If we don't do it, they'll find others who will," the second voice whispered back.

"Well, I'm not taking any more chances," the first voice said.

"What do you mean? You can't stop now," the second stated. "It's your job to complete the inspection documents. If you stop, you'll end up like Yu Tian. You know it!"

A flushing sound covered the first voice's response, followed by the sound of stall doors opening and banging shut. They had obviously not heard Yi come into the bathroom. Yi waited.

"We'll not speak any further of this. We're at risk speaking of it now. We continue as is. Now we had better hurry down to the dock . . ." The voices trailed off as Yi finished and quietly exited the stall, making sure the door didn't bang closed behind him. He quickly rinsed his hands and shook the water off, seeing no paper towels.

This could be an important link to Guangzhou's corruption, Yi thought. It warranted further investigation.

Yi headed back down the empty corridor to Gong Yu Tian's office. He knocked lightly on the opaque glass window. No response. The office was dark, so Yi turned the doorknob. It was locked. His heart sank. Then he remembered the training he had received back in the States. Never really expecting to use them, he did possess the tools to unlock the door.

No. He shook his head as adrenaline poured in. *This is going too far.*

But the information here is important to your mission. The impression surprised him, and he wasn't going to ignore it.

He slipped the slender metal pick out of its case and inserted it into the lock. Within seconds the door was open. He glanced down the corridor before stepping inside the office and closing the door behind him. He waited a moment as if in anticipation of someone bursting in to catch him in the act.

The lights from the corridor provided sufficient illumination through the door's glass for Yi to see without turning on more lights. He moved around to the desk and sat down.

Well, Mr. Export Tax Collector, what were you doing that cost you your life?

Yi scanned the files still on Yu Tian's desk. *Probably taking payoffs from the sound of it.* He thought back to the conversation in the men's room. *But why did they kill you? And who are "they"?*

Yi picked up the top file and began to look through the contents. As he scanned what looked to be standard shipping documents, something caught his eye. The name on the shipping documents was Li-ren Culture Village Enterprises, Hainan. The documents listed them as the owner of a shipment of herbal supplements manufactured in Xinjiang Province destined for the Republic of Colombia in South America. The bank representative shown on the documents was a Pakistani bank in Islamabad.

For a local tourism business, you sure are internationally connected. Yi remembered his visit to the quaint village on Hainan, the pictures he had taken of the computer system there, and the resulting camera confiscation. A foreboding feeling swept over him.

Besides the strange logo and military uniforms, research Li-ren Culture Village Enterprises.

Putting everything back in its proper place, Yi quietly left the export tax collector's office and hurried to exit the building. He tried to look casual as he walked past the guard at the entrance, but his heart was still pounding.

Mixed emotions tore at his soul. Had the answer to his prayer only hours earlier included this? He had felt so confident in his apartment. Yet since the meeting in Trenton Woodbury's office less than a year ago when he accepted the assignment, he'd had to lie, sacrifice his religious practices, sever ties with the Church, and now commit a crime.

Can this be right?

***

A quiet weekend in his apartment studying *Ensign* articles online and doing laundry helped restore Yi's confidence in himself and his work. Monday morning came without event, and Yi was actually looking forward to the week ahead filled with boring paperwork and orientation meetings before reporting to the judicial training program in Beijing.

CHAPTER 16

A polished black sedan with blackened windows sat parked inside the west gate of Peking University. Frank and Sylvia Stillman noticed it as soon as they left their campus apartment. They hesitated, not knowing if it was the right car or not. All they had been told was that a driver would pick them up at the west gate at 4:00 PM. It was now 3:52 PM. The car looked as if it had been there a while. They set their luggage down, looked around, and waited. A few minutes later the driver of the black sedan stepped out of the car. Without saying a word, he opened the back door and gestured for Frank and Sylvia to get in. He then loaded their luggage into the trunk.

Since there were other foreign teachers at Peking University, Frank and Sylvia assumed the driver had been given a physical description of them: a tall Caucasian male in his mid-sixties, with thick, silver-gray hair and a Van Dyke beard, and a female in her late fifties, a little on the heavy side ("grandmotherly round," she would say), with dyed auburn hair. They both wore glasses.

Frank asked the driver if he spoke English. He smiled and said he did not. Frank looked at Sylvia, guessing she was probably thinking the same thing he was thinking: the driver was not what they had expected. He certainly wasn't at all like Beijing taxi drivers. This man seemed refined and well educated. His countenance gave off a level of worldly confidence, like someone who had studied or traveled abroad. He was meticulously dressed—not in a uniform but in stylish Western blue jeans, ironed with a crease down the front, and a striped, knit polo shirt tight enough to show off the definition of his well-formed biceps. A leather cell phone case hung from a finely braided leather belt, and his shoes were polished leather loafers. He could have stepped right out of an issue of *Gentlemen's Quarterly* magazine. On the front seat next to him was a military weapons catalog.

His driving was aggressive. He wove in and out of traffic like a professional. And just before arriving at each tollbooth, he placed a six-by-eight-inch card with large red Chinese characters in the left corner of the windshield. He did not stop or pay any toll money. He barely slowed down.

After a fifty-minute drive across town, the Stillmans were delivered to the National Judges College. Located on the outskirts of Beijing, the surrounding areas looked more rural than big city. The guard at the college gate saluted the black sedan as it pulled through the gated entrance. Frank and Sylvia scanned the facilities: a small, modern campus with white-tiled buildings, simple in design—quite different from the traditional buildings at Peking University.

A young woman dressed in a brown suit stood at the curb of what looked like an administration building. She appeared to be awaiting their arrival.

"Welcome, Mr. and Mrs. Stillman. I am Ms. Lu, the administrator of the National Judges College." She extended her business card with both hands, each end held between a thumb and index finger.

"The driver will take your luggage to your room." She smiled. "You need not worry. Please come this way."

The Stillmans followed the woman into a large reception room elegantly decorated with traditional Chinese furniture. One large oriental carpet, thick with sculpted floral designs, covered the highly polished wood floor. Embroidered tapestries and water-colored scrolls of majestic mountain scenes hung on the walls around the room. Along the wall to the right were black lacquered screens with floral carvings and inlaid mother-of-pearl. Across the room to the left, facing the entrance doorway, were two ornately carved wooden chairs with a carved table in between and two small, round tables at each end that were topped with colorful and intricately patterned porcelain vases. Each side wall bore the same style of wooden chairs and tables, grouped in twos facing the center of the room. There were a total of six chairs on each side. Each chair contained a square seat cushion made of bright red silk with gold emblems—flying bats forming a circle with a Chinese character in the middle.

A Caucasian man crossed the room toward them, his right hand extended and a smile on his face.

"Frank, Sylvia, it's great to meet you," Samuel Giles, director of the WTO judicial training program from New York University, said. "Your university speaks very highly of you." He shook hands with both of them.

"It's a pleasure to meet you too," Frank responded.

"I take it your stay in China has been a pleasant one?"

"Delightful," Sylvia stated enthusiastically.

"May I introduce Mr. Gao, our vice president," the administrator said.

The vice president extended his business card to Frank, also using both hands as the administrator had done. An interpreter stood by his side.

"Welcome to the National Judges College," the vice president said in excellent English, a warm smile on his face.

"It is an honor to meet you, Mr. Gao, and to have the opportunity to teach here," Frank replied with a slight bow.

"Please, let's be seated," the vice president said as he led Frank toward the center chairs. He gestured for Frank, as the senior law instructor of the American teachers, to sit in the left center chair. The vice president sat in the right center chair. Sylvia watched, pleased to see her husband recognized in such high regard.

The administrator gestured for Sylvia and the WTO director to sit on the left side of the room. She and the interpreter sat on the right. A young woman wearing an ankle-length red *chi pao* dress began to serve jasmine tea in delicate bone china teacups with saucers and lids.

"Is this herbal tea?" Sylvia asked hesitantly, concerned that it be acceptable to their religious beliefs yet not wanting to offend.

The young hostess nodded.

The vice president stood and began to speak, slowly but in English. "The National Judges College is a small school compared to the campuses of Peking University and Tsinghua University, but we have an important purpose in training the legal officials of China. We train China's law clerks, court administrators, attorneys, and judges. Our students serve throughout China in the local People's Courts and in the Supreme People's Court here in Beijing. We are a new school, yet we have trained hundreds of important officials here. And now our judges need training for work in the World Trade Organization. This program is important to China and is sanctioned by our Supreme People's Court. It is our honor to have such fine American teachers here to teach in the Sino-US WTO judicial training cooperation. We welcome you."

The guests applauded, and the vice president sat down.

The WTO director then spoke. "This training program, in cooperation with both governments, is being sponsored by three US universities. Temple University is providing the master of law portion, New York University will focus specifically on the WTO rules and regulations, and Brigham Young University, with its world-renowned language training programs, has been asked to conduct this three-month session in English language assessment and introduction to American rule of law. The other foreign teachers will arrive in the morning. Among the five of you, the forty judges will be taught Monday through Friday from 8:30 AM until 9:00 PM. Friday afternoons will be their free time, and those with families may choose to return home on the weekends. Because of administrative meetings scheduled for Monday, March 19, there will be no classes held that day. And we will observe the national Labor Day holiday on May 1. Other than those dates, this program is all they will do for the next three months. These judges have come from all over China, leaving their families and jobs, to concentrate solely on their studies here. It will be an intensive program. However, while the training is going on, this college will continue to function in its capacity as an educational facility. Therefore, we must confine our training activities to the classrooms and areas we have been assigned. Furthermore, we must be mindful of the other teachers and students here. Now, it is my understanding that the first two days will consist of oral and written testing for English language level assessment of the judges. The judges will then be placed in three groups based on their language proficiency."

The administrator continued the briefing. "After the judges have been assigned to their groups, we will have an official welcoming ceremony. Come, I will show you to your office. And if you need anything at all, please call me."

The reception ended. After shaking hands with everyone, the Stillmans followed Ms. Lu out of the administration building.

***

Yi's week of orientation at the Guangzhou court proved to be nothing more than sitting in an empty office reviewing court documents and procedures. He was eager to start interacting with other judges in the judicial training program. He arrived in Beijing on February 11 and arranged for a taxi to take him from the airport to the National Judges College. Surprised at how much smaller and older the taxis were in Beijing than in Guangzhou, he was reminded of the little red taxi he had ridden in on Hainan Island. The Beijing taxi was the same cheap *Xiali* brand, not much more than a tin can on wheels. He almost laughed out loud when he noticed two tiny microphones on each side of the Beijing taxi's front windshield.

"What are those devices on the sides of the windshield?" he asked the taxi driver in Mandarin. Of course, Yi knew they were microphones, but he wanted to see how the taxi driver explained them being there. Yi guessed the driver had been instructed to record conversations of foreign or suspicious-looking passengers.

"Oh, those are for security, in case the taxi is stolen," the driver immediately replied.

"I would imagine that not too many of these old taxis get stolen," Yi teased. "You know, I just came from Guangzhou, and their big, new taxis don't have security devices in them." Yi couldn't resist goading the Beijing taxi driver. The driver didn't respond.

It took the taxi driver ninety minutes to locate the National Judges College. He had taken back roads from the airport instead of staying on the ring roads or expressway. Yi didn't care. He was fascinated by the scenery. The poor living conditions were surprising to him given the near proximity to the country's capital. Rows of stacked bricks with an open doorway every fifteen or twenty feet and tin or plastic sheeting for a roof provided the housing for many. Yi noticed a woman throw a large bowlful of water out a doorway. He was sure they didn't have plumbing. A river of gray liquid with floating debris accumulated nearby.

Despite years of hardship, Yi thought, *the Chinese people are truly blessed. How special they must be to Heavenly Father, that He would send*

*one out of every six of His spirit children to a Chinese home on earth—
more than any other nationality.*

The taxi arrived at the National Judges College at 2:15 PM. A uniformed guard stood at attention on a raised platform. Yi read the characters on the front wall to be sure he was in the right place. The college did not look as Yi had imagined. The campus was small, about the size of a city block, with buildings no taller than four or five stories and no traditional architectural features of sloping rooflines, animal carvings, and colorfully painted eaves. These buildings were of a simple square design with small, plain white and yellow tiles covering them. Yi noticed that one of the buildings, located toward the back of the campus, was topped with several high-powered antennae and expensive satellite dishes.

Yi paid the taxi and carried his suitcase to the security gatehouse. He showed the guard his identification papers.

"Leave your suitcase," the guard directed as he handed Yi his papers and an orientation packet. At the push of a button, the metal accordion-style security gate retracted.

The packet included a map of the campus, his dormitory room number, and a schedule of activities starting with registration, an opening ceremony with dinner, and two days of language testing by American teachers. Yi walked inside, studying the map to determine which direction he should go.

He dreaded the idea of two days testing with Americans. He had hoped to avoid them as much as possible until he assessed the other judges. His English proficiency level needed to fall within the other judges' range. If not, his identity could come into question. He headed for the dormitory.

The building was a concrete square, four stories high with no elevator. Yi's room was on the third floor at the end of the long central hallway. Several judges stood outside their rooms, smoking and chatting nervously about the impending language tests. The cigarette smoke hung thick in the air.

Four judges were assigned to each room, which contained two sets of small metal bunk beds not much bigger than cots. The bedding consisted of two inches of batting on a wooden board and a thin blanket folded neatly at the foot. A table and four chairs took up the space in the middle of the room. The floor and walls were bare concrete.

"Welcome!" someone shouted in English as Yi came through the door. "You must be Yi Jichun, the last of our little group," the man said in Mandarin. "Welcome!"

The boisterous roommate threw his arm around Yi and led him to the bunks where the rest of the men were sitting. Yi detected alcohol on the man's breath. "Welcome! Welcome!" he said again, laughing and patting Yi's back several times. Yi wondered if he knew any other words of English.

"Hello . . . my name is . . . Yi Jichun," Yi replied in halting English. "My English name is . . . Ja-son . . . but you can call me Yi." The roommates laughed and applauded at his efforts in speaking English.

"Oh, you speak very good English, very good!" the inebriated one said in a loud voice. "Very good English!" he repeated again. It seemed what he lacked in English skills he made up for in volume.

Introductions were made in Mandarin as they exchanged business cards. Those who had decided to use English names during the program told how they had chosen them. Some had been given an English name by a foreign teacher when they were in middle school or college. The outspoken one with alcohol on his breath had given himself "Henry" as his English name. "Like the king," he said. He seemed quite confident in his English, except he had the annoying habit of repeating himself. He introduced the others.

"This is my good friend Lincoln. Good friend. Yes, my good friend Lincoln. He is from Dalian. He is a . . . is a . . . a maritime judge. That's it, a maritime judge. He gave himself the English name of Lincoln, like the president. Yes, the president of the United States, Abraham Lincoln."

"I chose the name Lincoln, like the American president, because he was a very honest man. I want to be like him—very honest," Lincoln said and patted his chest.

"It's nice to meet you, Lincoln," Yi replied in English. He then told him in Mandarin that he was from Guangzhou and interested in maritime law, that he looked forward to talking with him more about it, and that he too was an honest man. Lincoln returned his warm smile.

"I was given the English name of Jerry by my English teacher," the other roommate spoke up in excellent English. "I'm not sure if I'll use the name though. It's a cartoon name—for a mouse, I think."

"Oh, yes, I think you are right," Yi chuckled. "But I still like the name Jerry. It has a happy sound to it." Yi could tell that although their living conditions were meager, he was going to enjoy spending the next three months getting to know these fine gentlemen.

"Come, we must go for our . . . for our register before the open ceremony," Henry said to the others, like a parent directing his children.

***

The forty judges promptly assembled for the official opening ceremony. Most of them were dressed in black suits, ties, and white shirts. Even the female judges wore black pantsuits and ties. They were seated in a modern wood-paneled auditorium. A banner hung over the long dais where the honored guests were seated. It read "The First Sino-US WTO Judicial Training Cooperation."

The WTO director spoke. "Welcome to the first Sino-US WTO judicial training cooperation. Let us first recognize our honored guest, the vice president of the National Judges College, Mr. Gao Xiang."

Everyone applauded as Mr. Gao stood and bowed.

The WTO director continued. "Over the course of the next three months, you will have the opportunity to receive intensive training in American law and legal English to prepare you for the World Trade Organization training you will receive in the United States. Now let me introduce our distinguished faculty."

As the director read each guest's name, he or she stood, and the judges applauded.

"Mr. Frank Stillman, our distinguished attorney from Washington DC, will teach you the fundamentals of American law. His wife, Sylvia, a legal administrator and business executive, will assist him and teach legal concepts and terminology. Dr. Bender, a professor of linguistics from Brigham Young University, will work with you on your oral English skills and proper pronunciation. Ms. Harris, a professor of English as a second language— also from Brigham Young University—will work with you to improve your English writing skills and teach you how to write legal documents. And Mr. Papworth, an expert in computer-aided learning, will teach you online legal research and computer-aided intensive English reading."

The director then outlined the rest of the program. "At the end of these three months, the top two students will receive scholarships to the United States for a fifteen-month master of law program at Temple University. The eight judges with the next highest scores will receive scholarships to attend a Temple University master of law program taught here in China by American law professors at the prestigious Tsinghua University. Then at the end of twelve months, those eight judges will go to the United States for an additional three months of study at Temple University to finish their degree. The remaining judges, at the end of these next few months—provided you complete this intensive program—will travel to the United States for one month of World Trade Organization training at New York University. This is a vital first step in preparing China for permanent normal trade status in the WTO, and you are the first judges to carry this program forward. So, once again, welcome to the WTO judicial training cooperation. Now I would like to introduce attorney Frank Stillman."

The judges applauded again.

As he stood and looked out at the friendly faces before him, Frank couldn't help but notice how young the judges appeared. He guessed their average age was in the midthirties. *Boy, not in the US! It takes years to become a judge.* He thought about his own legal career. He wouldn't admit it to anyone but his wife, but he disliked practicing law—hated the confrontations. He much preferred teaching.

"Your honorable judges, may it please the court," Frank said. "That is how an attorney in America addresses a judge. I am honored to stand before forty of China's distinguished judges."

The judges smiled proudly.

He continued his speech. "Two years ago my wife and I retired from hectic jobs. I am a retired Washington DC lawyer specializing in administrative law. Sylvia is a business manager and legal administrator. After graduating from George Washington Law School, I spent thirty years in private practice and government work. On occasion, I also taught international law courses at a university near our home in Virginia. Mrs. Stillman managed a law firm in Washington DC, which she loved. But, for me, the government work was beginning to wear me out. I felt I needed a change. And Sylvia wasn't about to let me become a couch potato in retirement! So China became our new experience together through Brigham Young University's China Teachers Program. We spent our first year in Guangzhou, where I had the opportunity to teach American law.

Mrs. Stillman taught business and English. We were then transferred to Peking University, where we've taught for the past six months. We have loved working with the wonderful students and faculty at both schools. And now Mrs. Stillman and I are eager to get to know each of you."

The judges applauded more loudly than ever.

***

"I do not believe you are from the Guangzhou Administrative Court," one of the judges said to Yi in Cantonese at the judges' welcoming party—an evening of karaoke and drinking. "I have never seen you there." He handed Yi his business card stating his high-level position in the Guangzhou courts.

Yi could feel his face start to flush. He was grateful the room was dark. The last thing he wanted was a confrontation about his identity.

Yi guessed the man was about forty years old. He wore a finely tailored suit and silk tie. His shirt was European cut with French cuffs adorned with gold cuff links. He was holding an imported beer in his hand, and Yi noticed a large gold ring on one of his fingers.

"Yes, I was transferred there only recently," Yi replied in perfect Cantonese. "My name is Yi Jichun. I am happy to make your acquaintance . . . Tan Yang," he said, looking at the printed name. Yi then presented his own card.

The man studied it before putting it in his shirt pocket.

"I don't know why you would be transferred there," Tan Yang remarked. "We manage well with the staff we have. Guangzhou has a unique way of doing business. We don't need anyone coming in who doesn't know our ways of operation. We certainly don't need foreigners and the WTO telling us how to operate."

Yi assumed the man's agitation was exaggerated by alcohol.

"I am most appreciative of the opportunity to learn how things are done in Guangzhou, Mr. Tan, especially from people such as yourself," Yi fawned. "You obviously are doing well. I too wish to make money and provide for my family."

The man relaxed and smiled. "Then I think you will succeed in our administrative court. We have many such opportunities. You will learn soon enough. Come, let's have a beer together."

Yi smiled and looked at his watch. He had rehearsed this scenario many times. "I would love to, Tan Yang, but I have to make a personal call." Taking out his cell phone, he quickly left the room.

CHAPTER 17

"Who will win the scholarships?" was the question on everyone's mind. The competition was fierce for the opportunity to attend Temple University's Master of Law program in the United States. With the exception of only a few of the senior judges (and Yi), all of them wanted to study in America. The two slots, reserved for the students with the highest training program scores, were highly coveted. But what the judges had only recently learned was that the five judges with the lowest scores would be sent home without any additional WTO training. This put a cloud of gloom over everyone's spirits and made the competition more intense. To alleviate some of the pressure, the administrator arranged a day trip to the Great Wall.

Within minutes of everyone getting on the bus, the whole atmosphere changed. There was excitement in the air. Thoughts of the scholarships were put aside. The underlying current of pressure and competition suddenly vanished. People laughed and joked with each other as if they were best friends.

Yi sat next to Lincoln. Jerry sat across the aisle from Yi.

Finally, a chance to loosen up, Yi thought with relief. *After six weeks in China, all I've got is a murdered official linked to an international herbal shipment registered to a primitive island village that has a high-tech computer system with a spiderweb logo. But I haven't a clue as to how they're connected or why!* He ran his hand through his hair. *Jason, you've got to come up with a lot more than this to keep Boyle from thinking you're wasting US taxpayers' money!*

Yi watched out the bus window as the landscape changed from city freeway to winding mountain lanes. In the distance he could see the gray stone wall running along the top of the rolling mountains. These were not gently sloping hills. Yet the Great Wall followed the terrain up and down like the back of a long twisting dragon, with stone parapets as its rocky spine.

Suddenly, the bus began to slow down. It moved to the far right-hand lane then pulled onto the shoulder of the highway. Everyone looked to the front of the bus to see what was happening.

The bus driver quickly exited the bus. He hacked and spit as he went around to the back to open the engine compartment door. Black smoke billowed out. A sudden silence came over the interior of the bus. Several judges stood to get a better view and to stretch their legs.

A few minutes passed before the driver came back to the front of the bus. He was holding a cell phone to his ear. He glanced at his watch and then put away the cell phone.

"The bus company is sending another bus. This one cannot make the climb up the mountain," the driver said apologetically.

"How long before the other bus comes?" the administrator asked the driver.

"Soon, soon," the driver responded as he reached for the keys still in the ignition. He lit up a cigarette and stood looking down the side of the mountain. Several judges got off the bus and lit up cigarettes as well. As the temperature was quite cold outside, however, most of them finished and hurried to get back on the bus.

Tan Yang stepped back on the bus and flicked the butt of his cigarette out onto the ground. He scanned the seats as if looking for someone in particular. Walking down the aisle, as he came to the row of seats where Yi was sitting, Tan Yang broke the silence. He spoke in a voice loud enough for everyone to hear. "Yi, why don't you tell us about the bomb incident at Tsinghua University. The judges' directory says you were there in 1992."

The bus fell silent again. All eyes were on Yi. He could feel his body heat increase as his face began to flush.

"I remember reading about that in the newspaper—it was all over China," a judge spoke up, breaking the silence and diverting the attention away from Yi.

"Yes, I read about it too," someone else said. "What was it like at Tsinghua when the bomb went off, Yi?"

Yi's mind raced to recall the incident. Had he read something about it in any of his research? No. Nothing came to mind. In fact, he had no idea what Tan Yang was talking about. Not only had he not read about the incident, but the Foreign Service failed to brief him on any incident at Tsinghua University in 1992. He would have to bluff his way through Tan Yang's interrogation. *Help, Lord!*

"Well?" Tan Yang said impatiently. "We're waiting for you to tell us about it."

Yi chuckled nervously. "I haven't thought about that incident in quite some time, Tan Yang. Thanks for bringing it up." He paused as he quickly thought of what he could say. Then he smiled. "Believe it or not, I was not on campus when it happened. If I remember correctly, it occurred while my grandmother was quite sick. I had returned home to be with my family." Yi hoped his answer was believable.

Tan Yang wasn't satisfied.

"But everyone must have been talking about it on campus when you returned. What did they say?" Tan Yang persisted.

Yi could feel his heart pounding. *Breathe.*

"They said basically what was printed in the newspapers, Tan Yang. So you probably know as much as I do—unless you don't read the papers." Yi began to laugh. "Who can fill Tan Yang in on what the newspapers had to say about it?"

Everyone around them began to laugh at Tan Yang.

"The bomb went off in the teachers' cafeteria, Tan Yang," someone shouted from the back of the bus.

"And the man who did it was from Guangzhou. Maybe Tan Yang knew him!" someone else howled.

"Or maybe he was family," another added, and everyone laughed even harder.

"Forget it!" Tan Yang waved his hand away and then took a seat a few rows back from Yi.

"At least no one was injured in the bombing," Jerry leaned over and told Yi, who nodded in agreement. "The guy told the Beijing police the reason he had done it was to get some attention," Jerry added. "He must have been crazy!"

"Then maybe he is a relative of Tan Yang's," Yi added in jest, laughing with relief that the scrutiny was over.

But Jerry didn't laugh. A confused look crossed his face. Yi knew immediately he had made a mistake.

"You mean *was*," Jerry said, carefully studying Yi's face. "He was executed shortly after the appeal."

Yi looked embarrassed. "Of course. *Is. Was*—sometimes my English is not very good. Sorry."

Jerry rolled his eyes and smiled. Yi leaned back and closed his eyes to help his head stop spinning. *That was close!*

Before any more could be said, a new tour bus pulled up. Everyone began to cheer. This one was new and modern, and it had heat. Within forty minutes, they arrived at the Badaling section of the Great Wall. The administrator got off the bus to purchase tickets, while the driver parked. Everyone headed toward the entrance area. Both sides of the street were filled with small tourist shops and coat rentals. The high elevation and winter season helped profits soar for businesses renting to the tourists who underestimated the cold—which was pretty much everyone.

The judges crowded around the rental booths. Several began trying on coats and hats. They laughed at each other for how ridiculous they looked. The coats were old, green military greatcoats, thickly padded and full-length, with brown wool collars and bright gold buttons. The round fleece hats with tied up ear flaps looked like Russian *ushanka* hats. A red Communist star marked the front.

If only the people back in the senator's office could see me in these! Yi thought. No matter how silly he felt, the coat and hat were very warm, and that was most important.

The temperature on the mountain was bitter cold. The biting wind whipped through the red and yellow flags positioned along the ramparts of the Great Wall. Yi, Lincoln, and Jerry began to climb the steep and uneven steps of the Badaling section. Yi thought about the wall's history—once a mighty fortress against invading Huns. With each steep step, he pondered the number of bodies buried beneath him because the builders of the Great Wall didn't stop to remove any dead or dying workers; they simply built over them.

The three judges resolved to reach the highest peak. They climbed until the restored section ended and there was nothing left of the original wall except piles of broken stone.

"How about we take a break," Yi suggested. The others nodded.

They located some large rocks and sat down to eat the snacks they had carried in their backpacks.

Yi took a swig from his water bottle. "So, Lincoln, how do you like practicing maritime law?"

Lincoln hesitated. "To be perfectly honest, I used to love it," he said finally, a hint of sadness in his voice.

"What do you mean *used to?*" Yi responded. "You're great at what you do. From the way you've talked about your work in class, I was sure you loved practicing maritime law."

Lincoln shrugged. "There's not much to it as long as we do what we're told—if you know what I mean."

Yi looked at Jerry to see if he knew what Lincoln was talking about. Jerry shrugged his shoulders.

"I take it there's some questionable activity going on," Yi commented. "Well, hey, most courts have some level of dishonest dealings. It can't be that bad, can it?"

Yi must have struck a nerve in Lincoln because he poured out his feelings as if a floodgate had opened.

"Don't make light of it, Yi!" Lincoln retorted. "It's gotten so bad we're losing out in establishing China as a major international shipping force. I personally know of numerous cases of corruption that have discouraged foreigners from investing here in transport services—opportunities China needs. It makes me sick that we're robbing ourselves of greater international prominence. China is ready, but our own people are holding her back."

"I understand how you feel, Lincoln," Yi said. "I read somewhere that China's economic losses from corruption have exceeded ten billion *yuan* over the past five years."

"It's not just economic losses," Lincoln continued. "Corruption harms the image of our country. If we lose face to the world, the damage is far greater than economic."

"True. But what can be done?" Jerry interjected.

"Well . . . we need to enforce the rule of law." Lincoln's hesitation made it sound as if he didn't believe his own words.

"How can we apply legal reasoning and enforce laws when we're most often told what our decision will be?" Jerry asked. "We can't apply the law as we've studied it; we must apply whatever ruling is given to us by our superiors—whether or not it holds with the laws of our constitution and the Supreme People's Court." As an afterthought he added, "Our law degrees were a waste of time."

"I agree," Lincoln said. "In our courts, judicial decisions are often made with a telephone call from someone higher up. Whatever you're told the ruling will be, that's what you rule whether you like it or not."

Remembering what Boyle had said in Trenton Woodbury's office, Yi added, "I know of senior judges who decide cases based on who offers the largest amount of money over dinner."

"Yes, that happens," Jerry nodded.

The three of them sat in silence, contemplating what had been said.

Lincoln spoke first. "The shadow of our government system is becoming more and more crooked. Soon the stick will not be able to stand."

"I don't get your meaning," Yi said.

Lincoln passed it off with a wave of his hand. "My father used to say it. He often quoted the old saying, 'A crooked stick casts a crooked shadow.' Well, I'm seeing a lot of crooked shadows."

Yi nodded. "If only people could see the damage corruption brings. They may think it benefits them, but in the end it hurts everyone."

The conversation waned as they shared their snacks.

Between bites, Jerry commented, "In my province a common practice for accumulating wealth is to skim funds off foreign joint ventures. Many high-rise construction projects end up in bankruptcy before the buildings are completed. You see it all the time. Overseas investors pay money into a bank account here, then the local partners pad their expenses and skim funds until the venture is insolvent. When the foreigners bring legal action, we as judges are expected to rule in favor of our fellow Chinese. It makes a mockery of our constitution and judicial system."

Once again they ate in silence.

This time it was Yi who spoke. "Just because it happens doesn't make it right. We shouldn't give in to corruption just because everyone else is doing it." He paused before going on. "I believe in the rule of law. And I think we can each make a difference."

"We'd lose our jobs," Jerry replied sullenly.

"Well, it would take some time," Yi defended. "But it has to start somewhere." He remembered the words of the ancient prophet Alma concerning the planting of a good seed. "Like a tree, if we are diligent in our labors, it will grow. And with patience and long-suffering in nourishing it, the tree will bear fruit most precious and pure above all that is pure."

"That's very poetic," Lincoln said as he and Jerry stared at Yi.

"Oh, it's something I read somewhere," Yi answered a little sheepishly, knowing he had bent the rules of his cover by paraphrasing scripture. He then added with conviction, "But I believe it is true."

"I agree," Lincoln concurred.

"I'm willing to try," Jerry added.

An idea came to Yi. "This is going to sound crazy, but I'd like to put together a list of names or perhaps titles—yes, I think titles would be best—of officials, by province, who are known to be involved in corrupt activities." He paused before going on. "What do you think?"

Jerry and Lincoln stared at him as if he had two heads.

Lincoln cautioned him. "You know, Yi, we discuss things in private that cannot be shared in public."

"It won't be made public."

"Why would you want to make a list?" Jerry asked.

Yi had to be careful how he worded his response.

"I'm curious to see if there are any similarities or connections between activities and provinces. There probably aren't any—at least I hope there aren't—but I think it would be an interesting analysis."

Lincoln couldn't help but laugh out loud. "I think there will be a lot of connections! And then what will you do?" he added with a serious tone in his voice.

Yi thought for a moment. "As Professor Stillman would say, 'I'll cross that bridge when I come to it.'"

They all laughed at Yi's use of a common American idiom.

"By the way, Yi, why do you think Tan Yang was questioning you about the bombing at Tsinghua?" Jerry asked, suddenly serious again.

Yi shook his head. "I have no clue. I can't imagine why he was making such a big deal about it. I mean, I obviously wasn't paying much attention to what people were saying at the time. It's been nine years since it happened and with everything going on with my family, I guess I blocked it out." Yi really hated lying.

"I'd be careful. I think Tan Yang has a grudge against you—for whatever reason," Lincoln warned.

"Unfortunately, I think you may be right," Yi replied.

***

The bus traveled back to the college in silence. Most of the judges slept from exhaustion. One section of the Badaling area had been so steep that people had to crawl on their hands and knees. All would agree, however, that it had been well worth it.

Yi sat quietly pondering conversations he'd had with judges since coming to the judicial college. By and large, he felt they were hard-working, honest, and honorable people. With the exception of a few like Tan Yang, Yi's impression was that these judges were not willing participants if they were engaged in unethical practices. Some were involved because there was nothing they could do. If they went against the dictates of their superiors, they could lose their jobs, their income, and their status in their communities. Yi now had a better understanding of why the Chinese judges admired the separation of powers within the American system of government and the protection it afforded American judges to rule based upon the law. He also realized his endeavors might not be as productive as Senator Boyle had hoped. Very few of these judges, Yi believed, were responsible for corrupt activities.

Surprisingly, that realization brought a sense of relief to Yi, not only because he now held many of these judges in the highest regard and would not want them brought down by charges of corruption but also because, somehow, their honor and integrity were interconnected with his own. Their actions reflected upon his name. He realized that what he felt toward the people of mainland China went far beyond a general love of mankind or even his affection for his grandfather's homeland. Yi felt the bond of blood shared by their common ancestry.

***

By the time the bus arrived back in Beijing, the sun was setting behind the western mountains. It wasn't a vibrant sunset, however, that caught everyone's attention. What was suddenly so peculiar about Beijing was the color of its air. A dust storm had blown in from the Gobi Desert and turned Beijing a vivid orange. As if on Mars, everything had an eerie rust tint. The orange fog was so thick the buildings on either side of the street could not be seen. Pedestrians and bicyclists held handkerchiefs up to their noses and mouths. Some women tied scarves over their whole head, even their faces. There was no wind. No visible particles of sand hung in the air. It was as if a bright orange mist had settled over the entire city.

The students moved quickly to gather up their belongings, exit the bus, and get to their dormitories before breathing in too much of the polluted air. Yi found himself left behind because he'd misplaced his cell phone and didn't find it in time. Stepping off the bus, he noticed Tan Yang waiting for him. Yi tried to avoid eye contact. He turned toward the dormitory.

Tan Yang grabbed him by the arm.

"I don't know what you're up to, Yi Jichun, but I don't believe you were ever at Tsinghua University! In fact, I don't believe you're who you say you are. And when I can prove it, you'll regret having gotten involved with the Guangzhou court!"

CHAPTER 18

"I've admired you for some time," the Foreigner said in Russian to Dr. Sonja Koreshky.

They sat in the back corner of an empty restaurant nestled in the heart of Almaty, once Kazakhstan's capital and central Asian hub on Marco Polo's Silk Route.

Dr. Koreshky turned her eyes from the picturesque mountain view through the windows on the other side of the dimly lit room and studied the handsome man sitting across from her. She was attracted to him. Men of such refinement were rare in Russia. Economic upheavals since the fall of the Soviet Union had left most people—including men of power and status—feeling destitute and pathetic, in most cases using alcohol to numb the pain. Emotional frailty mixed with the stench of liquor and poor hygiene repulsed her. She had left her own husband, who once was head of the state's division of finance. Now he was a filthy, mean drunk who resented her career and her self-control. He had called her "Ice Queen" and had taken every opportunity to ridicule her in front of friends and peers. She had finally left him when he had become physically abusive. Her method for coping was to focus on her job as chief virologist with the Spectrum Research Institute for Viral Preparations in Koltsovo, Russia.

"I am pleased someone of your caliber would take notice," she replied with a warm smile and lifted her glass of merlot to her lips, pausing before taking a sip. *Yes, I am extremely happy you have taken notice,* she thought and began to imagine this handsome foreigner taking even more of an interest in her.

He watched as she sipped her wine. The faint light from the table's candle reflected a yellow glow in her wine glass, giving the burgundy liquid the appearance of blood. The Foreigner smiled as he thought about the evening's finale.

"I am intrigued by the fact that you speak Russian flawlessly, yet you speak with a European accent, one I am unable to pinpoint exactly," she remarked.

He smiled. "It seems my speech has been influenced by my extensive travels. I am afraid I have picked up some nasty habits."

"What you call 'nasty habits,' I find positively charming," she flirted.

"Madame Koreshky." He began to shift the conversation to the purpose of their meeting.

"Please, call me Sonja. I want us to be close friends."

"Sonja." He paused as if savoring the name. "It is an added personal pleasure for me to meet you. Your expertise is of great importance to my company, but I also hold you in the highest regard. I must confess that I have a weakness for attractive and intelligent Russian women."

He took a small sip of his wine. This heightened Sonja's desire for him as she watched him savor what was still his first glass. Many Russian men probably would have gulped it down and continued to pour one glassful after another. She herself was on her third. He had barely touched his wine through dinner.

"It pleases me that you find me attractive," she replied.

"And I have to say," he added with a beguiling smile, "I find your testing methods to be refreshingly direct and thorough. Quite like my own, I might add."

She reached across the table and moved her fingertip lightly over the back of his hand, which still held the stem of his wine glass. He brushed against her finger with his own.

"Then we are kindred spirits, darling," she said as she placed her hand on his, feeling the warmth from the wine and her emotions spreading through her body.

"I especially admire the thoroughness with which you tested your smallpox strain in Aralsk," he said, not pulling his hand away but rather placing his other hand on hers so she couldn't pull away.

He watched for her reaction to the knowledge that he knew the secret of her open-air testing, relishing the power such confidential information provided him yet maintaining the amorous game they now played.

Only for a brief moment, her eyebrows lifted slightly. She gave no other indication of surprise.

"There were two virulent strains, my dear," she responded clinically. "We released both into public areas in Aralsk and then monitored the outcomes to determine their effectiveness."

He studied her for a moment. "Many innocent people died, Sonja. Was that not a concern of yours?"

"Not really," she said coldly and without hesitation. "Many people did die, but the gains were well worth the loss. One of the strains proved to be substantially more deadly than the other and resistant to vaccine." She added proudly, "The results were exactly what we had hoped for."

He lightly stroked the top of her hand. "And the only way to know for certain was to test the strains on a large, unsuspecting population."

"Yes, of course," she said as she reveled in his intense, almost-black eyes.

"And the flulike virus—it has been thoroughly tested as well?" he asked.

"With a sixty percent death rate. The subjects manifested severe acute respiratory distress and other flulike symptoms within three days of exposure, followed by pneumonia-like characteristics of difficulty breathing and high fever. Rapid dehydration brought on death within ten days in the elderly, the very young, and those with weakened immune systems," she stated with clinical precision.

"How did the Kazakhstan government react to such an epidemic?" he asked.

"Oh," she chortled, "we could not test it here. Not after the smallpox test. No, we tested this virus in a rural part of Southern China. We needed a concentrated population in a less-developed area, one that couldn't respond quickly enough to stop the full effects of the virus. And, of course, we needed a government that would cover it up."

He studied her a moment longer.

"I think one of the things I find most attractive about you, Sonja, is that we do think alike." He half smiled, causing a slight crease in his cheek that emphasized his perpetual five o'clock shadow.

She leaned closer and spoke softly. "I hope we find that we are alike in many more ways."

He slowly pulled his hands away from hers and dabbed the corners of his mouth with his napkin. He was becoming tired of the seduction. Although she obviously worked hard at keeping herself trim and attractive for her fifty-eight years of age, he still found her repugnant and wished the ordeal to be over. He casually glanced at his Breguet Tourbillon watch.

"I assume you have the virulent strains with you that my company wishes to purchase?" he asked.

"Russian smallpox, ebola, and our recently developed deadly flulike virus. Yes, my dear, I have them carefully packed for you in a secure, temperature-controlled travel case." She set a small black box on the table. "And you have my cash payment?" she queried.

"A small price to pay, it would seem," he said as he picked up the briefcase beside his chair and laid it on the table. "In US dollars, as you requested." He paused before questioning further. "And as stipulated in our agreement, Sonja, there is no record of this transaction?"

"Of course not. You are dealing only with me," she assured him.

Hmm, just like when you dealt with the Iraqis in 1990, he thought, *which we wouldn't have known if you hadn't deposited the money into your bank account.* He chose to keep that little secret to himself.

"Excellent," he responded.

"Well then?" she said as she folded her napkin and placed it on the table.

He hesitated just a moment before asking, "Might I ask where you are staying this evening?"

Normally, she would not give out personal information during this type of business transaction—for security reasons as well as a preference for keeping her personal life private. But this man excited her, and it had been far too long since she last enjoyed a handsome man's company.

"I have a room at the Hyatt Regency, just a short walk from here. And like this restaurant, it has a spectacular view of the Alatau Mountains and the city lights."

"Ah, the Regency," he mused aloud. "A lovely hotel and convenient to the airport. An excellent choice, Sonja. May I accompany you back to your room?"

"I would like that very much. I do hope, however, that your interest in seeing me back to my room includes more than just the mountain view," she said coyly.

"My dear Sonja," he said softly, "you must be reading my mind."

She took another sip of her wine, finishing off her third glass.

She smiled. "We do think alike."

The Foreigner gestured to the waiter across the room and paid cash for their dinner.

"Shall we?" he said as he stood then helped Sonja with her chair and coat.

"Of course," she replied and carefully lifted the small black box from the table.

He pulled on his black leather gloves and picked up the briefcase. Deciding not to wear his overcoat, he draped it over his arm and the briefcase. He then placed his other arm around the small of Sonja's back as they walked to the door. On the street, he extended her his arm.

Such a gentleman, she thought as she tucked her hand around his muscular bicep.

***

The elevator was empty as they rode to the tenth floor of the Hyatt Regency. No one passed them in the hall as they walked arm in arm to room 1043. Sonja noticed her hand tremble slightly as she placed the key in the lock.

Inside the room, the Foreigner laid his briefcase and coat on a chair near the door, took the black box from Sonja's hands, and carefully set it on the lamp table. He then helped her out of her coat and tossed it on the bed. Standing behind her, he kissed her lightly on the back of her neck.

She purred, tipping her head to the side and closing her eyes.

Sliding one hand slowly around her waist, he reached into his pocket with the other and took out the Black Talon knife. Silently, he released the blade. With one swift motion of the razor-sharp talon, he slit her throat. By the time she opened her eyes, her life had ended.

The Foreigner went into the bathroom to wash off the knife and his gloves. He noticed blood splatters on the sleeve of his Italian wool suit.

"Pity," he muttered.

He put on his overcoat, picked up the black box and the briefcase, and left the hotel room. His departure from the hotel went as unnoticed as their arrival. After turning the corner of Zhambly Koshesi Street at Saint Nicholaus Cathedral, he hailed a cab to the Almaty Airport, where his private jet awaited takeoff. The filed flight plan listed the destination as Sanya International Airport on Hainan Island.

CHAPTER 19

Three weeks into the program many of the judges were still struggling with basic English, relying on simple questions they had probably learned in middle school.

"Do you like Chinese food?" a shy female judge asked who had not yet spoken out in class. The Stillmans often joined the judges for lunch in the faculty cafeteria, encouraging them to practice their English.

"Yes, very much," Sylvia answered. "We eat Chinese food in America all the time. You know, it is one of the three most popular styles of food in America."

"What do you think of China?" another judge asked.

"We admire the Chinese people . . . for their long history, their pride in their motherland . . . and for their desire to make things better. This is an exciting time of growth and international relations, and we are happy to be a part of it," Frank expounded.

"How did you . . . come to teach in China?" Yi asked, pretending to struggle a little with his English.

Frank explained, "After noticing an advertisement that Brigham Young University was looking for people to teach in their China Teachers Program, I jokingly said to Sylvia, 'Sylvia, what would you say if I suggested we go to China to teach for a year or so?' She didn't laugh as I had expected. As a matter of fact, she said she thought it was a great idea."

"Truth be told, I thought he was kidding," Sylvia interjected with a laugh.

"But as we thought more about it, we liked the idea. As Sylvia pointed out, I needed to retire. I wasn't enjoying my work as much anymore.

And we weren't tied to the Washington DC area. Our children were grown and starting their own families. Financially, it was a good time. We submitted our applications, interviewed with the administrators of BYU's program, and, before we knew it, we were on our way to China."

"Why did you leave Peking University? That is China's oldest and best university . . . like Harvard," one of the judges stated proudly.

"Yes, we loved teaching there," Frank answered. "The students were very dedicated to their studies. But BYU also needed us to teach in this program, and we were eager to have the opportunity to teach American law again and meet some of China's fine judges."

"Oh, we loved Peking University," Sylvia interjected. "The campus is beautiful, and the people are wonderful—the students, faculty, and the hotel staff and security people there. They were all so kind and helpful. We would have done just about anything for them." As an afterthought she said, "That's why it was so hard to turn that strange woman away." Turning to Frank she added, "Remember her, Frank?"

"What strange woman?" the judges asked in unison.

"How could I forget her?" Frank responded, wishing Sylvia hadn't brought up the incident. "I wasn't sure but what we'd be forced to leave China after her visit!"

The judges gasped.

Frank waved his hand. "Just kidding." He loved to startle them.

"So what happened?" a judge asked. They were all eager to hear another one of Frank's adventure stories.

"Well, it was late on a school night. We were tired and had settled in for the evening."

"No, Frank," Sylvia interrupted. "I was still packing in the other room when you answered the door, remember?"

"Oh, yes, that's right. We were planning to travel over the Spring Festival holiday before coming here to the Judges College. Anyway, we were staying in the Peking University campus hotel for foreign experts. Thank goodness they provided security. Otherwise, I don't think we would have gotten any rest! We loved having students over for visits, but since our classes came early, we asked that they not visit us after 9:00 PM."

Sylvia laughed. "That didn't stop them, though. We occasionally got calls much later than that."

"So when a knock came on our door at a quarter to ten on a school night, we just assumed it was one of our students. I didn't hesitate to open the door. Standing there, however, wasn't a student at all, but an older woman—probably in her midsixties."

"With the Chinese, it's so hard to tell. You all have such youthful looks," Sylvia said with a grin. Her face then became pensive. "Except for this woman. Her face was dark and leathery and seemed to have marks of some kind. Almost in a pattern."

"Like dots?" Yi asked, remembering the pattern of tattoo marks on the faces of the female Li tribe leaders on Hainan.

Sylvia nodded.

Frank continued. "Anyway, I knew the minute I opened the door that it was the same strange woman who had telephoned us a few days earlier. And I got the same feeling of agitation and anxiety from her in person as I had sensed over the telephone. Call it a gut feeling, but the woman was just plain weird. There's no other word to describe her. Now here she was, standing in our doorway, uninvited."

"She called you the week before? How did she know your telephone number?" a judge asked.

"That's a good question, along with how did she get our name and address and how did she get past the security guard in our apartment building so late at night? Well, it wasn't much of a conversation because I could barely understand her. The woman insisted on talking to us, but she didn't really speak English, and the little she did know, I was having a difficult time understanding," Frank explained.

"We still have no idea how she got our name and telephone number. That's part of the mystery . . ." Sylvia continued the conversation with the judges as Frank's mind wandered back to the phone call.

"Stioman," she had said over the phone. *"I wish you to help me with English. It is very important."*

"Are you one of our students?" Frank asked politely.

"No, not student. Editor of magazine. My English no good. I need you to help me . . ."

"I'm very sorry," Frank interrupted, "but we cannot work with anyone other than our students. Our contract specifically states we are not to take on other work assignments."

"Please, Stioman. I pay you."

"I'm sorry. We can't violate our contract. Besides, our semester ends this Friday. We will be traveling over the Spring Festival holiday, and then we will be moving to another college. I'm really sorry."

"But this very important, very important," she pleaded.

"I'm afraid the answer is no." Frank then hung up the phone. He felt it was the only thing he could do. She would have gone on for hours, he was sure of it.

Frank's attention was momentarily drawn back to the lunchroom conversation as one of the female judges commented, "That is unusual for a Chinese woman to visit without an invitation—especially late at night. It is not our custom to . . ." And as the conversation continued, Frank thought more about the strange woman's visit.

Standing face to face with her, he could see his instincts had been right. She was not going to take no for an answer. He had made himself clear over the phone that they could not help her. Nevertheless, here she stood in their doorway.

She did not look like a Peking University professor or any of the hotel staff. There was an overall unhealthy look about her—a kind of dullness to her appearance. And she looked very distraught. Frank wondered who she was, where she had come from, and more importantly, why she was contacting them.

She was tall for a Chinese woman, about five-foot-seven, and considerably thinner than most—practically emaciated. Her black hair hung in thin strands about her shoulders. Her skin had a brown, leathery quality to it, as if she had spent much time in the sun. Most Chinese women avoided sunlight, even carried umbrellas in sunny weather to keep their skin as white as possible. In addition, her cheeks had small dark spots, maybe pockmark scars, in a kind of circular pattern. Basically, although she carried herself with a hint of gracefulness, she appeared more peasant than professional.

She stepped into the room before being invited. She didn't even take off her shoes. Opening a piece of folded paper, she began immediately. "This true? This true? I must know if true!" She continued talking in what sounded like Chinese as she tried to push the piece of paper into Frank's hands.

Relying on the few phrases of Chinese he had learned, Frank conveyed to the woman that he didn't understand or speak Chinese.

"You no speak Chinese?" She now looked completely dejected. "My English no so good. I wish you speak Chinese. This terrible, this terrible," she said as she shook her head, dull strands of hair crossing her shoulders.

"*Is there something we can help you with?*" *Sylvia asked when she came into the main room, leaving her packing duties. She wondered who had come to visit so late at night.*

"*Please, sit down,*" *she said to the woman.*

The woman wore a lightweight, dark brown polyester overcoat tightly cinched at her waist. It was nothing more than a thin raincoat—far less than what was needed in Beijing's winter weather. She didn't attempt to take the coat off. Everything about her spoke of distrust and fear, yet she seemed determined to say what she had come to say. She carried a large tote purse, open at the top, with folded papers tucked inside. Next to the papers was a small, portable tape recorder. It looked of high quality—a contrast to the rest of her image. Frank and Sylvia looked at the tape recorder, then at each other. Were they being recorded?

"*This true?*" *the woman asked again, holding out the creased and somewhat wrinkled piece of paper. It looked like a printout of an Internet web page. It contained the seal of the United States White House, a quote from the newly elected president asking for assistance in fighting terrorism, and a reference to available ambassador positions.*

Frank took the piece of paper from the woman and skimmed it, noting the URL address at the bottom. It certainly looked like the real thing.

"*Yes, I would say this is true,*" *he said and handed the paper back to her.*

"*Are you interested in a job at the White House?*" *Sylvia asked, perplexed. "The jobs referred to are embassy jobs—they are only for high-level American citizens. Are you an American citizen?*"

"*No, no . . . I try to contact White House. My English so bad. I try to write letter . . . I write carefully, very carefully, a letter . . . and, how you say . . . fax it here,*" *she said as she pointed to the White House fax number listed on the web page printout. "But the White House no respond. I no receive any response. But this very important, very important!*"

"*How about if we call our friend upstairs to come and translate for us?*" *Sylvia said. "She's married to an American, but she is Chinese and . . .*"

"*No! I no speak to Chinese. Can no be trusted. Too dangerous. Why you no speak Chinese? My English very poor.*" *She shook her head. "Please, you call White House. You tell them very important information.*"

"*You want us to call the White House?*" *Frank said. He couldn't help but laugh. His mind began to race, trying to think of some way out of this awkward situation. "From here?" he said, pointing to the hotel's phone in their room. "This is not an international phone; this is a hotel phone. We can't call. Besides, we don't have any connections with the White House. We're only teachers here."*

"If you have important information, you should take it to the US embassy here in Beijing," Sylvia added.

"Yes, that's an excellent idea," Frank stated. "I'm sure they can help you."

"I try. No good. Too many Chinese people. Chinese guards at gate. I can no let them see me. They try to stop me. I no talk to Chinese guards. Too dangerous."

As the woman became more upset, it became more difficult to understand her.

"This letter I fax to White House. You read. You understand," she said as she handed Frank another folded piece of paper. It had a round symbol on the bottom of the paper—maybe a logo or something. The letter was typed in English.

Yi interrupted Frank's thoughts with a question. "Professor Stillman, what did the woman want that she would seek you out and then come to your home so late at night? It must have been something important."

Frank frowned. "Oh, she wanted help with a letter she was trying to write in English. Unfortunately, our contract with Peking University stated that we were not to work with anyone except the students. I had to tell her we couldn't help her."

Sylvia sadly shook her head. "We felt bad that we were unable to help, but we didn't want to violate our contract with the school. We didn't know who she was."

"So what did you do?" a female judge named Sarah asked.

"Well, Sylvia had an idea," Frank replied. "She suggested we contact a Chinese American friend here in Beijing."

"Oh, yes. Libby." Sylvia giggled. "Now there's an amazing woman! We met her while attending our church's branch in Guangzhou. She was visiting from Beijing, and when she found out that we were going to be moving to Beijing, she introduced herself to us. She told us that although she was Chinese and her English wasn't the greatest, she was an American citizen living in Beijing. Well, we exchanged business cards and contacted her when we arrived here. We've become close friends, and she's helped us on more than one occasion."

"As we have helped her," Frank pointed out.

Sylvia giggled again. "Yes, we have. Being with Libby is like being in a whirlwind. You get drawn into the middle of things before realizing what's happened."

The judges seemed to enjoy Frank's and Sylvia's storytelling—at least what they could understand. Listening to English conversation was good practice for them.

As Frank told another story of their experiences with Libby, Sylvia thought back to the phone call she made to Libby the night the strange woman showed up at their door.

"Wei?" Libby answered the phone.

"Libby, this is Sylvia Stillman. I'm so glad you're home. I apologize for the late call."

"It no matter. I'm here talking with my good friend, Doris, visiting from San Francisco. Here, you talk to her. Oh, I tell her all about you, my good professor friends."

Libby put her friend Doris on the phone.

Sylvia heard an awkward chuckle on the line. "Hi, Sylvia, this is Doris."

"Welcome to Beijing. How long are you here for?" Sylvia asked, trying to make polite conversation but wanting to keep it short.

"Only a few days on business," Doris replied.

"Well, enjoy Beijing." Sylvia hoped being blunt wouldn't offend the woman. "Doris, would you mind terribly if I asked Libby for some help on a rather urgent matter right now?"

"No, not at all. I'll put her back on. It was nice talking to you."

"Thanks. Same to you."

Libby came back on the line. "Doris and I been shopping today . . ."

"Look, Libby, I need your help," Sylvia interrupted. "A woman showed up at our door this evening. We don't know who she is, but she's quite distraught. She doesn't speak much English, and we can't understand her. Would you talk to her and then tell us what she wants?"

"Sure, sure, no problem," Libby replied.

Sylvia motioned for the strange woman to come to the phone.

She began to speak in rapid Chinese. Not two minutes later, however, she handed the phone back to Sylvia. Sylvia couldn't believe it. Libby was so amazing! In two minutes, she had accomplished what they had been unsuccessful at for more than forty-five minutes.

Sylvia got back on the line. "Thanks, Libby. That sure was quick. What does the woman want?"

"No matter," Libby said, serious for the first time. "Just get her out of your house!"

Recalling Libby's words and the tone in her voice triggered again the feelings of unease from that night. Sylvia had never heard Libby so serious. It felt as if she and Frank had done something terribly wrong by letting the woman into their hotel room. Now Sylvia was sorry she had brought it up in front of the judges.

As Frank ended his story about Libby, Yi guided the conversation back to the strange, late-night visitor. "So was your friend able to help her?" he asked.

"No, not really," Frank replied, shaking his head.

"I know you said you were just joking, but why would you think you might have to leave China as a result of the strange woman's visit?" Yi inquired. "I don't understand."

Frank smiled and looked down at the table. He had hoped the judges would tire of this interrogation. But since China's judicial system is based on an inquisitional system, he suspected that would not be the case. As their teacher, he needed to maintain their trust. He felt it best to be direct.

"We just didn't know what to do," Frank said, looking around at the judges. "We didn't want to offend anyone. The woman seemed determined to stay, and we didn't know how to ask her to leave."

Sylvia jumped in. "It was as if she had nowhere else to go. Anyway, I gestured toward the door and told her that Mr. Stillman would walk her out. I then whispered to Frank to please go with her to make sure she left the building. While he was downstairs, I noticed she had gone off without her letter. There it was, still sitting on the lamp table," Sylvia said, shaking her head. "Of course, we had no way of returning it to her."

Frank flinched. He had not wanted to discuss the letter in any detail.

"What did it say?" Yi asked.

"Oh, I don't remember the details," Frank lied. "It didn't make a lot of sense."

Sylvia went on. "But the interesting thing was the spiderweb symbol at the bottom of the page, like an insignia of some kind."

"What do you think it meant?" Sarah asked at the same time Yi asked, "What did it look like?"

"I don't know. I have no idea," Frank replied with a shrug, wishing Sylvia had been less talkative about the letter.

"But what did it look like?" Yi asked again.

Sylvia responded before Frank had a chance. "Well, it looked like an intricate spiderweb, but metallic-like, with some Middle-Eastern characters in the middle. Arabic or maybe Hebrew. You know, bent nails kind of thing."

Yi felt the color drain from his face. The description sounded exactly like the symbol he had seen on the computer in the culture village on Hainan.

"Are any of you familiar with such a symbol?" Frank asked the judges.

Most of them shook their heads. No one seemed to know anything about it. Yi thought it best not to pursue a conversation about it in front of the other judges. He needed to talk to the Stillmans alone. And he needed to see that piece of paper.

CHAPTER 20

"Thank you, sirs, for your willingness to meet earlier than scheduled," the Foreigner stated after the eight men had taken their usual seats around the conference table. "As the Hainan Net's setup is now complete and fully operational, I felt it was important for me to provide you with the latest report."

"You have indeed made great progress," the white-haired man said. "Now if you would please tell us about the status of our other resources. How are our ship captains and sailing vessels progressing? Are they, too, ready for live operations?"

"Yes. For the past two years, we have maintained trained crews routinely sailing cruise and cargo ships between Hong Kong and Bangkok and from Guangzhou and Shantou in Southern China to various Asian ports as well as to Colombia, South America. Now that the operations center in Hainan has been completed, we have better, more direct and secure communications with these units. And as you know, we now have several trained recruits with airline piloting and navigation skills."

"May I ask," a director, who had been silent to this point, said, "what has come of the virulent strains we have heard so much about. Isn't your operations center equipped to handle bioweapons? If so, were you able to obtain them?"

The Foreigner smiled before answering as he remembered his encounter with Dr. Koreshky. "Yes, I had the pleasure of doing business with a most charming and accommodating Russian virologist."

"But the project is still underbudget," the director said, a puzzled look on his face. "We estimated that with the purchase of the strains you would be over budget by three million dollars."

"Let's just say she was dying to satisfy our needs," the Foreigner replied with a smirk.

Several of the directors snickered at the Foreigner's pun to avoid discussing the unpleasantries of his work.

"And the strains have been quality tested?"

"Yes," the Foreigner said. "According to our lab experts, the strains are 100 percent active and of the highest potency. In fact, the mutated strain of smallpox I was able to acquire is considered to be the most resilient known throughout the world."

"Excellent! Then we are ready to proceed with plans," the white-haired man said as he stood up from the conference table. He then walked to the front of the room and took the remote control from the Foreigner. He pressed a button, and a map of the United States and Central America displayed on the screen.

The Foreigner returned to his seat.

The white-haired man spoke. "For several years now, we have watched as the United States has interfered with political activities in the Middle East. The distrust and hatred toward Americans that have built up there now make it feasible to set our plans into motion. In order to proceed, however, we must create a diversion for the United States. Gentlemen," he paused before continuing in a more lighthearted voice, "we must convince the United States that their full attention and services are needed elsewhere."

The directors joined him in a buoyant laugh.

In a serious tone he continued. "We must create a situation significant enough to divert America's attention away from our interests in the Middle East. Rogue terrorist attacks would not be enough. And if anything, they could heighten America's scrutiny of and sanctions toward the Middle East. No, this must be big enough to engage their military as well as civilian resources. I therefore propose, gentlemen, that an attack be carried out upon the Panama Canal."

"The Panama Canal?" one of the directors questioned, and from the puzzled looks from the other directors, it was obvious the same question was on their minds.

"Why not hit the United States directly?" one of the directors asked.

The room was silent as other directors nodded in agreement.

"That, my friends, would not only increase America's scrutiny of certain key Middle Eastern areas because they would assume the attack came from an Islamic terrorist group," the Foreigner stated, "but would also probably result in a US–sponsored military overthrow." He now had the directors' full attention.

He paused to let the devastating scenario play out in their minds.

"It would be years before you could get the United States and their allies out of your little playground," he said. "And I don't believe that is the outcome you desire."

The room was again silent.

"Okay," one director broke the silence. "But why Panama? They don't even have a military."

"Precisely," the white-haired man declared. "Without their own military, the United States would have to come to their aid. The US is not going to allow the Panama Canal to be jeopardized in any way. By attacking the canal, the United States would be forced to resume control of operations at least until repairs could be made."

"That's right," reflected one of the directors. "Although the United States turned over all the canal's operations to Panama two years ago, the stipulation was that if the canal were ever in jeopardy, the US would take back operations. Panama has no military, and 99 percent of the canal's operations have been privatized by the Panamanian government."

The directors pondered the proposal.

"Since we can assume you are talking about an attack using one of our ships, what's the possibility that the ship's identity can be traced back to our operations?" a director inquired.

"An excellent question," the white-haired man responded. Looking at the Foreigner, he said, "Would you please explain to the directors how we acquire and register our ships?"

"Certainly. Gentlemen, as you may or may not know, the international maritime trade is largely unregulated. As a result, the industry loses track of many ships—not only ours but others as well—because they are frequently given new, fictitious names and then reregistered with fake corporations as the owners. Tracing a ship back to its real owner can be an impossible task, if you want it to be."

"Thank you." The white-haired man turned to face the map again and pointed with the laser pointer to the Pacific entrance to the Panama Canal. He continued. "After being positioned into the second of the Miraflores locks on the Pacific side, one of our reregistered cruise ships loaded with explosive cargo will be detonated, taking out the locks, the harbor crew, and a substantial portion of the canal, rendering it impassable."

"The canal's sophisticated scanning equipment would pick up explosive cargo long before our ship could get anywhere near the canal entrance, let alone positioned into a lock," one director said, shaking his head, skeptical of the plan's viability.

"And why a cruise ship?" another interjected. "Wouldn't a less expensive cargo vessel be more practical?"

"We can handle the scanning issue through financial arrangements. We have several Panamanian employees who are willing—for a large sum of money, of course—to arrange for the scanning to appear clear," the white-haired man replied with confidence. "As for the use of a cruise ship, they are faster than other vessels, and because of their size and nature, they are less likely to come under scrutiny. And as I'll point out in a moment, the passengers may be quite useful."

"You're not suggesting we blow up a ship full of people, are you? You know I'm opposed to such action," one of the directors commented.

"Certainly not," the white-haired man replied. "The ship would be emptied of its passengers at that point."

"Sir, would destroying one lock result in a large enough diversion?" the Foreigner asked. "It seems to me the United States could rebuild any damaged sections of the canal within a matter of months, if not sooner. And while the canal is impassible, land transportation systems could be used to move shipments across to the other side. You wouldn't be preventing shipments, merely delaying them. If I'm not mistaken, the railroad that runs along the canal has been modernized and can reach speeds of up to seventy miles per hour. Although its use is primarily passenger transportation and tourism, it could easily be converted for cargo, especially since it's one of the few operations still managed by the United States. If I remember correctly," the Foreigner paused for a moment, "I believe the canal's railroad is operated by Kansas City Railroad."

"Your knowledge of Panama is quite impressive, young man. And you are probably right that hitting one of the locks along the canal would not be a large enough disaster on its own," the white-haired man remarked. "That is why there would also be attacks on the railroad; the Chagros River, which supplies the water to operate the locks; both the Centennial Bridge and the Bridge of the Americas; the military refueling stations on both sides of the canal; and on seaports along the western United States."

"There is no way we could get a ship loaded with explosives into a US seaport," a director exclaimed. "Not with the use of Vehicle and Cargo Inspection Systems technology for port security. There's no way we could succeed. Why, it's ridiculous to even consider it!"

Another director chimed in. "And VACIS technology is becoming obsolete. I understand the United States government now has the capability of creating a three-dimensional image of cargo carriers using something like a . . . a nuclear beam or something."

"A neutron beam scanner," the Foreigner corrected. "It's called Pulse Fast Neutron Analysis. It reveals dangerous substances by detecting the cargo's chemical makeup."

"See? Their technology for port access is too advanced," came the retort.

"Point of fact, sir, no," the Foreigner replied, shaking his head. "Use of PFNA technology is still quite limited. In reality, most US seaports only inspect about 2 percent of all incoming cargo. The rest rely on a filed manifest—a written list of the cargo's supposed contents—sent twenty-four hours before setting course for the United States. So although somewhat risky, US seaport attacks are quite possible."

"Gentlemen! Please, we are getting away from the point. I can see now that if we were to attack US seaports, the United States as well as international shipping communities would be on guard, which would render an attack on the Panama Canal pointless. So please, hear me out."

The white-haired man paused while the directors quieted down. "In addition to an explosive attack on the Panama Canal, I propose the use of our newly acquired flu virus as part of the diversion. The virus would be released on the cruise ship prior to the passengers disembarking. Their symptoms would not be significantly apparent until after they had traveled to their respective homes in other parts of the country—

exposing numerous others along the way. By the time the emptied cruise ship reaches the Panama Canal, the United States will be in such a state of chaos trying to isolate the virus and determine its origin that the addition of the canal explosion would together occupy the United States' full attention. There's no doubt about it."

Smiles came to the directors' faces as they realized the plan was a good one.

"I second the proposal," a director eagerly said.

The white-haired man breathed a sigh. "I thought you might see things my way. Now," looking at the Foreigner, he said, "how long will it take to prepare for such an operation?"

The Foreigner thought for a moment. "We need to do some testing with the flu virus to determine the best method of exposure and the exact time frame to outbreak, and so forth." He paused as he thought a moment more. "And I would also like to research and test the amounts and types of explosives needed to completely destroy a canal lock the size of the Miraflores."

"I agree," the white-haired man said. "Careful calculating and planning are needed to ensure a successful outcome." As an afterthought he added, "And how are you set for finances?"

"The heroin shipments out of Ürümqi continue to provide more than adequate funds," the Foreigner replied with a smile.

"Then can we schedule completion, let's say, in six months?"

"We can," the Foreigner answered, nodding. "Six months would put the attack during the canal's busiest season, which runs from September to December. The most effective time would be early in October."

"Well then, you have more than ample time. We'll schedule execution of this plan for October. In the meantime, you will provide us with monthly progress reports."

The board's secretary then put the plan to a vote.

"All those in favor say aye."

The vote was unanimous.

CHAPTER 21

Yi had been unable to speak to the Stillmans privately. It seemed every time he approached them or stopped by their apartment, other judges were already occupying their time. They wanted every possible chance to practice their English skills and receive insights into the legal training—anything to get an edge in the competition.

But Yi's curiosity about the letter, which he believed was linked to Hainan Island, was becoming a nagging obsession. He had researched the logo on the Internet but hadn't come up with anything. When he keyed in *tourbillon gear,* he found several pictures that bore a strong resemblance to the symbol. Information about the gear stated it was superior in precision because it operated independently from the rest of the mechanism. But how did that relate to an ancient culture village? What would they be independent from? *Isolated by their primitive environment?* Maybe. Yi needed answers.

He thought about the judge in the training program who was listed in the directory as being from Hainan. Maybe a conversation with her could provide some clues about the culture village and its link to the strange symbol. It would also give him a chance to get better acquainted with her, which was something he had been planning to do anyway. They had worked together on some assignments in class, and Yi was impressed with her legal reasoning and language skills. All he knew about her was what he had read in the directory: "Deckey (English name Sarah Decker) is a junior judge with the Sanya Civil Court of Hainan Province. She was born December 7, 1969, in Damxung near the capital city of Lhasa, in Xizang Zuzhiqu Province, Tibet Autonomous Region. She studied law at Fudan University in Shanghai then trained at the Shanghai courts for nine years. Her interests include art, classical music, foreign cultures and history, and the welfare of the Tibetan antelope."

***

Yi found Sarah studying alone in one of the small rooms the college had set up as a law library. Unlike American law libraries with labyrinths of shelves loaded with thick books, this library had only a few shelves along the walls with a couple of rows of tables and chairs set up in the middle of the room. Yi sat down in the chair across from Sarah. She glanced up, smiled, and then continued her reading.

Yi began talking anyway. "You know, we haven't had a chance to talk about anything other than the American judicial system. We've worked together in class, but I feel I hardly know you . . . which is a distinct disadvantage," he said with his most charming smile.

Sarah blushed, and a slight frown creased the corners of her mouth. "I know many of the judges are taking time to socialize here, but this program is very important to me. The competition for the master of law scholarship is so intense." She shook her head. "It's not likely to happen, but I would like to be one of the judges chosen to study in America. It has always been my dream. So, you see, I must study."

Yi could see the concern in her face. "But you speak English so well. I think your ability is the best of all of us here in the training program. And you have one of the sharpest legal minds I've ever known. Your intuition is uncanny!" He reached across the table and placed his hand over hers and gave a gentle squeeze. "How can you not be chosen?"

Embarrassed by Yi's outward display of affection, yet delighted by his warm touch, she looked him in the eyes and smiled. "Thank you for the compliment, Yi. I can only hope you are right."

Yi had to admit he was attracted to Sarah. Not only was she brilliant in the law, but she was charming and beautiful as well. About five-feet-five-inches tall, she had a slender yet shapely figure and silky black hair that cascaded down to the middle of her back. Her mannerisms were gentle and delicate, yet she was straightforward and uninhibited in her legal challenges in class. Somehow she seemed to make the judicial training program more enjoyable for Yi and lessened the monotonous review of American law basics. As an attorney, his knowledge went far beyond what was covered in the program, and it was difficult for him to feign not knowing the answers. Yet he had to appear to be studying and struggling as much as everyone else. If he didn't, he risked being exposed as a fraud—especially with the Guangzhou judge, Tan Yang, keeping a close eye on him.

So Yi wasn't surprised when Tan Yang walked in to the library.

Sarah quickly pulled her hand from Yi's and sat up straight in her chair, hoping the Guangzhou judge had not noticed them touching. Public displays of affection were frowned upon in the Chinese culture, especially between male and female acquaintances. She began reading her book again. Tan Yang sat at a nearby table and only briefly glanced at Yi before opening his briefcase and taking out a book.

"So where did you learn to speak English so well?" Yi was determined to continue the conversation with Sarah despite the intrusion by Tan Yang. "I assume you studied abroad."

"Oh, I wish that were true," she leaned in and whispered so as not to disturb the other judge's reading.

Leaning closer to her, Yi could see that her skin was like fine porcelain, and her large, wide-set black eyes had long upper lashes—an uncommon characteristic in Asian women.

"It's because of my schooling and work in Shanghai," she continued. "I had the opportunity to study English courses taught by American teachers at Fudan University and to work with foreign businessmen in international law. In fact, the American teachers at Fudan were from Brigham Young University."

"Really?" Yi asked. "Do the Stillmans know them?"

"I haven't asked," Sarah replied. "But I wouldn't be surprised because the BYU teachers are very close—they all belong to the same religion and meet together every week. They are very devout people."

"How do you know that?"

"The teachers at Fudan told me a lot about Mormons. That's what they are called because of a special book of scripture they have. I asked if they would let me read it, but they said they couldn't give me a copy because of their church's agreement with the government. I've done a lot of research on the Internet, though. They are a generous and hardworking people. Their beliefs are quite honorable. I have to say I agree with many of their teachings."

Yi suddenly felt uneasy and exposed.

Come on, Jason, it's not stamped on your forehead—she can't tell you're Mormon.

"But it's not a sanctioned religion here in China," Yi pointed out.

"I know. But I found it fascinating."

Time to change the subject, Yi thought.

"Sarah, I noticed in the judges' directory that you were born in Tibet. I've never been there. What was it like growing up?"

"Well, it has been quite a while since I was in my hometown," she responded. "After finishing middle school, I came to Shanghai—for school and then my job in the court system. I've lived and worked in Shanghai for the past nine years. But to answer your question," she beamed, "growing up in Tibet was wonderful." She again glanced over at the judge at the other table, worried that their talking, even quietly, might disturb him.

Yi didn't care if Tan Yang was disturbed or not. He wanted to learn more about Sarah and what she might know about Hainan. He suspected Tan Yang was more interested in their conversation than in his reading anyway.

He tried to remember something about Tibetan culture that he could mention to Sarah. "Can you tell me about those long Tibetan horns—what are they called?"

"You know of the Tibetan trumpets?"

"Not by name, obviously, but I've seen pictures. I'm curious as to how they're played. Some are so big it looks like they would be too heavy to lift."

"They are. That's why they rest on stands to hold them up." She smiled and again set aside her book. Yi could see that if he wanted to keep a conversation going with her, he needed to keep her talking about her hometown.

"They're used during the Tibetan *Xodoin* Festival—one of my favorite holidays as a child," she went on. "The festival is also called the Opera Festival because of the numerous opera and folk concerts. But the word *Xodoin* means 'yogurt banquet' in the Tibetan language. The festival is held on the first day of the seventh month of the Tibetan calendar, usually early August, and lasts for about two weeks. It starts with an opening ceremony in our capital city, Lhasa. When I was young, my whole family would make a special trip there for the beginning of the festival. I loved going, especially to hear the folk music. Anyway, the trumpets are blown as part of the opening ceremony. Tens of thousands of Tibetans gather in the square in front of the Potala Palace. Then when the opening ceremony ends, everyone returns to their hometown to continue the celebration." Sarah blushed, realizing she had been rambling. "Oh, I've gone on and on about my homeland. I'm sorry. But, you see, I love it so much."

Yi was intrigued by the way her face lit up when she talked about her home. The animated inflections in her voice gave her a perpetually cheery nature and caused her round cheeks to draw up until her eyes became fringed slits. He was especially mesmerized by the tiny dimple that formed every time she smiled. Yi realized he could spend hours watching and listening to her.

"Sarah, please go on. I'm intrigued by your hometown and culture."

"Okay. What would you like to know?"

"Well, is yogurt the only food served during this festival?" Trying to be funny so she would smile again, he tried another joke. "Or does it also include roasted yak?"

Sarah didn't laugh.

Bristling somewhat but wanting to be polite, she paused before responding. "Being from Tibet, I am not of Han ancestry such as you. We are Buddhist, so we do not eat meat. We do not believe in killing any living creature."

Yi realized he had made an awful mistake.

"I'm so sorry, Sarah. Please forgive my ignorance. I didn't mean to offend you or your culture," Yi sincerely offered his apology.

Sarah smiled warmly. "I am not offended, Yi. Don't worry about it."

Yi was relieved but eager to move to a safer topic. "The judges' directory says you have an interest in Tibetan antelope."

"That I do," she perked up. "I care a lot about the animals in Tibet but especially the antelope because they have been hunted illegally to the point of near extinction. I've seen it for myself. My hometown is near where they would come each year in the summer, after traveling north to the area of lakes to give birth to their young. They make the return trip in August with their new babies, to the Nyainquen Tanglha Mountains where my family lives. I loved to watch for them. But each year their numbers became fewer and fewer."

"I don't understand," Yi said. "If they are endangered, why doesn't the government do something to stop the poaching?"

"Because many of the local officials are paid well to do nothing," she responded, lowering her eyes to hide the emotion in them. "The antelope's fur is so thick and soft that the *shahtoosh* shawls made from them sell for about ten thousand dollars each in some Western markets."

Yi's eyes widened. "You're kidding! Ten thousand dollars?" He was genuinely surprised.

Sarah nodded. "That's why I became a judge. Such useless killing and the corruption allowing it must be stopped. I myself could not be bribed to look the other way!" Realizing their conversation had escalated in volume, they both glanced around the room. Tan Yang was glaring at them. As if displeased by the distraction, he got up and left.

"Sorry," she said softly, embarrassed for having disrupted a fellow judge.

Yi was glad to see Tan Yang leave.

Since they were alone again, Yi leaned in and spoke softly. "Sarah, I had the opportunity to spend some time in Hainan recently, and, I must say, I saw some rather unusual things in a culture village there—one of which was the female leaders with tattooed faces. There were two such women in the village, but I wonder if there could be others . . . particularly outside the village. And there was a very modern-looking logo on a computer there. I was wondering if you could tell me something about it."

"I thought the purpose of a culture village was to demonstrate a primitive lifestyle," Sarah said, confused. "Why would they even have a computer?"

"I know," Yi replied. "That's why I thought it was strange. But what I'm most curious about is the symbol. I think it may be the same one on the letter the Stillmans talked about at lunch the other day."

"You mean the one from the strange woman with facial scars?" Her eyes opened wide as a thought came to her. "You don't suppose those were tattoo marks, do you? Do you think Stillmans' visitor was one of those tattooed women from Hainan?"

"Well, that's what I want to find out. I was hoping you could answer some questions for me about Hainan and the culture village there."

Sarah suddenly looked crestfallen. "Oh, Yi, I wish I could, but I'm afraid you know more about Hainan than I do. My assignment as a

CHAPTER 22

Evenings of karaoke, dancing, and drinking were becoming a regular weekend diversion for the judges. Occasionally, even the foreign teachers participated. The judges enjoyed showing off their skills in singing Chinese as well as American songs, and many of them knew Western ballroom dances. After a few drinks of alcohol, their shyness melted away and the foreign teachers got to see a totally different side to them. Instead of the serious and competitive students they saw in class, they were jovial, boisterous comrades, dancing and singing at the top of their lungs.

The younger foreign teachers enjoyed the folly and would join in, but the Stillmans preferred a quieter environment. On this particular night when Yi noticed them get up to leave early, he knew it might be his only chance to speak to them in private. He waited a moment so as not to be obvious, then he followed them to their apartment.

Frank answered the door.

"May I take a few minutes of your time, sir?" Yi asked.

"Of course, Yi," Frank replied warmly. "There isn't anything wrong, is there? You should be at the karaoke party."

"No, no, there's nothing wrong," Yi said. "And I apologize for the late hour. But this is the first opportunity I've had to speak with you without the others. I hope you don't mind."

"Not at all, Yi. Come on in."

After Frank had closed the door, Yi said, "I wanted to follow up on something you mentioned in conversation a few days ago."

"Okay," Frank replied, gesturing for Yi to sit down.

Sylvia entered the room. "I thought I heard someone. Hi, Yi! This is a pleasant surprise."

"Good evening, Mrs. Stillman. I was about to ask Mr. Stillman about the symbol you described at lunch the other day." Turning to Frank he said, "I was wondering if I might see it—if you still have the piece of paper."

Frank took a deep breath and exhaled. "I'm curious, Yi, about why you're interested. Do you know what it means?"

"Well, no," Yi replied. "But I believe I've seen the symbol before."

"Really? Where?" Frank asked, genuinely surprised.

"I'm not exactly sure," Yi lied, "but I think it was in some old family documents. I think there could be a connection with my ancestors. Maybe the woman used it on the letter like a chop—a signature block—representing her family name."

"In which case you'd be related to a crazy woman," Frank teased.

Yi laughed. "Maybe so. Anyway, I was curious about it and thought I would try to find out where the woman had gotten it and what it meant."

Frank hesitated, so Yi added, "It's vitally important to me if I can identify a piece of my family's history. So much of it was destroyed during the Cultural Revolution."

Frank nodded. He knew how important family was to the Chinese. He didn't see how he could say no. And if he did, it might appear as if he were hiding something. He looked at Yi with complete seriousness. "If I show you the piece of paper, I have to clarify that the woman made some pretty wild accusations in her letter. We had no involvement with her other than her showing up at our door uninvited."

"At the time, we didn't even read the whole letter, only the first little bit," Sylvia added. "But I know my face must have looked as shocked as Frank's. We were both having mixed feelings about whether she was mentally stable or not. We certainly didn't want to do or say anything that might agitate her more."

"It sounds like you did the right thing," Yi replied then added with a half-hearted chuckle, "but now you've piqued my curiosity. What did the letter say?"

Sylvia responded before Frank could say anything. "Basically, it said she was an editor of a news magazine in Beijing, reporting on the

Israeli/Palestinian war, and she knew of terrorist groups here in China. She went on about one in Hainan . . . with plans to attack Americans, that local officials were involved, and . . ."

Frank interrupted, "For the record, Yi, we assumed the letter was a crazy woman's delusion, so we don't want to cause her or anyone else any trouble with authorities here. At most, I figure it was a fabrication to gain attention from some foreigners—totally harmless."

"I understand. And you're probably right. I'm sure it's not the first time foreigners have been approached in such an unnerving way," Yi replied with a nod of his head. "I can assure you I am only interested in the symbol for family reasons."

Frank thought for a moment. "Well, okay." He then turned to Sylvia. "Any idea which box the letter is in?"

She thought for a moment. "I think I put it in the photo album we kept on the lamp table at Peking University. I believe the album is packed in one of those boxes." She pointed to three cartons sitting in the corner.

Frank left the room to find a pair of scissors while Sylvia kept up the conversation.

"It's really silly about that letter, but the more we thought about our strange late-night visitor, the more our imaginations ran away with us. I'm sure that's all it was." She chuckled, shaking her head as if a little embarrassed. "And when we mentioned it to our neighbor, a young teacher from Ireland who was also teaching at the university, she remembered seeing a woman who fit the same description wandering around the outside of the foreign expert hotel a few days earlier. She said the woman had asked her if she was from America. We wondered if we should tell someone. But who? We were probably being paranoid, but when you're a guest in a foreign country, you want to be extra careful."

Yi nodded politely but had to laugh to himself. *If they only knew!*

Realizing that their conversation could be overheard, Yi scanned the room for any indication of listening devices. An apartment for foreigners, especially teachers promoting American ideologies, was surely monitored.

His eyes stopped at a framed yet simple picture hanging on the wall. A feeling of sadness came over him. It seemed like such a long time since he'd had the opportunity to visit there: the Stillmans had hung a picture of the Washington DC Temple on their wall. After he had moved to Virginia, Yi had attended almost weekly before coming to China. He allowed his eyes to linger only a moment.

"Hey, I almost forgot," he said suddenly. "There's a program on the television I think you might be interested in. Do you mind if I turn it on?"

"Oh, sure . . . that would be fine," Sylvia replied with a puzzled look on her face.

"We can continue our conversation. I just thought you might like to see this program."

Sylvia turned on the television and handed Yi the remote.

"Let's see . . ." he said as he flipped through the channels. He hoped he could find something of interest. Thankfully, there was a travel program presented in English. Yi turned up the volume, nodded, and pointed at the television, indicating this was the important program he had wanted the Stillmans to see.

"Now, where were we?" he said and settled back into the sofa cushions. If the room was being monitored, the background noise from the television would help prevent them from being understood.

Sylvia continued talking as if there had been no interruption. "Luckily we were going to be traveling during Spring Festival. Then we moved here—thank goodness—on the other side of town. So I don't think we'll ever see her again."

Frank reentered the room with scissors in hand. He glanced briefly at the television then began opening the boxes.

"But we've often wondered about her—if she's okay," Sylvia rambled. "As silly as it seems, we still find ourselves looking at faces in the crowds of every tourist place we visit, watching to see if she reappears."

"I can tell you're both very caring people," Yi reassured her.

Sylvia got up from the sofa and joined Frank in looking through the boxes. She pulled out what appeared to be a picture album. Frank paused, his head slightly tilted as if puzzling over something, then said, "She had such an unusual face." He waved his fingers around his cheeks. "With those . . . pockmarks, I guess you'd call them."

Yi thought about the tattooed women in the culture village. *Could this woman be a leader from the Li tribe? Here in Beijing? How else would she know about the symbol on the computer?*

"Here it is," Sylvia said and handed a folded piece of paper to Frank. Frank unfolded it, nodded, then handed it to Yi.

"So, is it the same symbol?" Frank asked.

Before he looked at the paper, Yi hoped one more time that Frank and Sylvia were correct about the woman, that she was just trying to get some attention and that there was no connection to Hainan. That way Yi could put the symbol out of his mind and focus again on his work in the judicial training program.

Yi looked at the paper. A heavy feeling settled in his stomach. On the bottom of the page was the exact same symbol as the one he had seen on the culture village computer.

***

Tan Yang had watched from the hallway as Yi went down the stairs of the bar, through the darkened lobby, and outside. There were no street lights, so it wasn't long before Yang could barely make out Yi's silhouette. As he was about to step outside, Yi glanced over his shoulder. Yang had to quickly pull back inside the building. That was okay. He knew if Yi was going to the Stillmans' apartment, he could cut through the alley and still have a clear view of the entrance in time to watch Yi go in.

He didn't like Yi, and his intuition told him Yi, or whoever he was, could ruin operations in Guangzhou. Tan Yang took pride in being a senior court judge there. He had acquired the prestigious position at the unusually young age of twenty-seven. Now, with fifteen years of service behind him, there were few judges in Guangzhou with more seniority.

In the early years he worked hard to earn the recognition of his colleagues and the Communist Party. They regarded him well for his thorough understanding of Chinese law. And they appreciated his willingness to perform dirty little favors. Yang took every opportunity to carry out the wishes of his superiors, even if illegal, so they would be obligated to him. The unspoken rule was "I'll help you, if you help me."

Favors Yang accumulated over the years helped him acquire his own personal interest—money. When Guangzhou was declared an economic development zone, the opportunities for rapid growth gave unscrupulous officials, like Yang, lucrative ways to collect on unpaid favors. Companies with illegal business practices eagerly secured financial arrangements with Yang. His *guanxi* connections networked all the way to the top of Guangdong Province's bureaucracy. Unlike other officials, however, Yang's payback requests weren't always extreme. He often satisfied a favor simply by looking the other way. Yang's strategy was if the value of his request was less than that of the original favor, he could ask for another in the future.

But Yang didn't like to share. It annoyed him when he had to reduce his amount in order to pay off a lower official. For that reason, he finagled the additional administrative responsibility of approving all new judges hired in the Guangzhou Administrative Court. He wanted to make sure they knew his rules and played along.

Tan Yang viewed the judicial training program merely as a chance to socialize with his high-level friends in Beijing. He attended the program as a favor to the provincial party secretary, who had asked him to monitor the program for capitalist propaganda that the Americans would undoubtedly spread. Yang had no intention of putting into practice the rule of law or anything else the Stillmans taught. He wanted as little contact with them as possible.

At first Yang thought Yi was avoiding the Stillmans for the same reason. Now, he wasn't so sure.

His suspicions began from the moment he met Yi. First of all, Yang had not given his approval for Yi's hire. In fact, Yang wasn't even aware that a new judge was being hired. It was unnecessary, given the court's recent reduction in cases. Furthermore, his doubts were heightened when he overheard Yi talking to the Tibetan judge in the library. She was a legal fanatic on a quest to rid the world of corruption. If Yi joined that same crusade, he could destroy everything Yang had worked to establish.

That's why when he noticed Yi go after the Stillmans from the karaoke bar, Tan Yang followed. He arrived at the far side of the alley just as Yi entered the Stillmans' apartment building.

Yang considered waiting to see how long Yi stayed at the Stillmans' but decided to return to his room before his roommates came back from the party. He took out the business card Yi had given him the first day of the training program. He also located the judges' directory and studied the information on Yi Jichun, administrative judge from Guangzhou. He placed a call on his cell phone to a high-level official in Guangdong Province. Yang needed to cash in a favor.

"*Wei?*" the man answered in a startled voice, awakened from sleep.

"Ah, *ni hao*, this is Yang. Sorry to disturb you, but I need a small favor."

"Oh, Yang, of course. How are you? How is Beijing?"

"Fine, *hun hao*. I need you to check the background of someone from my court. His name is Yi Jichun."

"Let me write that down. One moment . . . Now, that was 'Yi Jichun' you say?"

"*Dwei, dwei*, yes. The information I have on him says he was born in Zhaoqing, Guangdong Province, in January 1971, and graduated from Tsinghua University with a bachelor's degree in law. I don't know the year but probably around 1993. He then supposedly served in the Beijing Haidian District Court before being transferred down to Guangzhou the beginning of this year. That's all I have."

"Okay. I'll call you back when I've verified the information," the man responded, half yawning.

"Oh, *xie xie, xie xie*," Yang replied most graciously.

"No, I should thank you. It is a pleasure to repay a debt, even an old one."

***

"It is the same symbol," Yi said, trying to sound jovial to Frank and Sylvia while a sickening realization spread through him. *If the symbol is real, are the woman's allegations also true?* Yi couldn't rule out the possibility.

He continued to study the letter. There was no letterhead at the top or signature at the bottom. No name or address of the person who had sent it. It was simply a plain white piece of paper with typing in English and the symbol copied at the bottom. There was nothing official looking about it. Under other circumstances Yi too would disregard the letter as a scam. But there was no mistaking the symbol. It was just like the one he had seen on the computer in Hainan. And if the marks on the woman's face were tattoo marks linking her to a leadership role in Hainan, then Yi couldn't ignore the possibility that what she had written was true.

The letter's structure was like a memorandum with *TO:* and *FROM:* at the top. It was addressed to *President of United States, White House.* A fax number followed with an area code of 202.

At least the area code's correct, Yi thought. *But if this fax had been received at the White House, why hadn't it been followed up? Or had it been, and it was determined to be a hoax?* That thought made Yi cringe. He did not want to jeopardize his cover by taking time away from his assignment to chase after a strange woman with a crazy notion that a terrorist group was operating from an island in the South China Sea. Yi shook his head. He couldn't believe he was entertaining such a ridiculous idea.

Thoughts poured through Yi's mind. *Maybe the fax didn't go through and the White House never received it . . . Not likely . . . Maybe I should contact Boyle back in DC and have him check it out through his White House connections . . . Definitely not before I know it's valid . . . Okay, so what if I follow up on the letter's theory and it proves to be false? I wouldn't have to report it. As long as I don't blow my cover for this program, what I do on my own time is my business. Besides Sarah, this letter has been the most exciting thing this program has had to offer. So why not? Checking out the possibility of a connection between the woman, the letter, and the Li-ren Culture Village on Hainan Island adds an amusing twist.* Yi weighed in his mind what the remainder of the program would be like without some form of diversion, especially since Sarah seemed determined to spend all her time studying. *What the heck. It's a chance to practice my investigative skills, if nothing else,* Yi rationalized.

"Uh . . .Yi?" Frank asked after watching Yi read for what seemed an unusually long time.

"Sorry," Yi apologized, realizing he had taken too much time studying the letter. He chuckled and shook his head as if in disbelief. "I have to agree with you, Frank," he said as he looked up from the letter. "I think this woman may be just a little crazy. Still, I would like to learn more about the symbol."

The *from* line of the letter gave a fax number.

"I see from the city code of this fax number that the woman is from Beijing, or at least faxed the letter from Beijing," Yi commented.

Frank nodded.

"She also gives an e-mail address in the letter," Yi continued, making a mental note of it.

"Are you going to contact her?" Frank asked. "She made it very clear to us that she would not talk to anyone Chinese—at least not about the letter."

"I'll try to e-mail her. I'll explain that I think the symbol has a family connection. Hopefully then she'll respond," Yi said.

Handing the letter back, he added, "Frank, can I ask a favor? Given the sensitivity of the contents of the letter, can I ask that you and Sylvia not mention my interest in the symbol? At least not until we know more about it."

"Absolutely. Sylvia and I certainly wouldn't want anyone to misconstrue how we came to be in possession of the letter," Frank replied with relief, as if involving a Chinese judge somehow minimized their accountability. "We would be interested in hearing if you make contact with her and what she says about the symbol."

"I'll keep you posted, then," Yi said. "Thank you for taking time out of your busy schedule to meet with me."

He stood to leave.

"Um . . . I appreciate the opportunity to practice my English."

"Our pleasure, Yi," Frank said. "Although, as far as your English is concerned, you speak it as if you were an American."

Yi beamed a warm smile and waved good-bye.

Standing in the light of the bare bulb above the entryway to the Stillmans' apartment building, Yi took out a small notebook and pencil from his jacket pocket. He wrote down the woman's e-mail address and fax number. He had memorized them before giving the letter back to Frank Stillman.

Yi sent a cryptic e-mail to the address on the letter. It read:

I am a Chinese-speaking American. I have seen the letter you left with the Stillmans at Peking University. They have not shown it to anyone else. They are my friends. I think I can help. I would like to meet you. Please e-mail me at JasonYi@hotmail.com.

***

"Excuse me, I need to locate the address of a business that sent me a fax a while ago," Yi told the telephone company's accounts clerk five days after sending the e-mail. "Unfortunately, they did not give their address or telephone number, and I need to contact them. It's very important." Yi gave the stern woman his most charming smile.

"What is the fax number?" the clerk asked.

"Let's see," Yi said as he opened the small notebook. "Oh, yes, here it is. The number is 10-5667-0113."

"The number is here in Beijing," the clerk stated. "It will take several days to trace it. You'll have to come back next week."

"There's no way I can get the address today?" Yi asked incredulously.

The woman laughed so loud it drew the attention of the people around them. Yi could feel all eyes upon him.

"Ms. Chen." Yi read the name tag the woman wore on her uniform. "I wish to convey to you how important this business transaction is to my company and how confident I am that you can help me find the address as quickly as possible."

The woman scowled. "Do you have any idea how many telephone numbers there are in Beijing?"

"No, I guess not. And I'm terribly sorry to have bothered you. If you'll please research the number, I'll come back next week as you have directed," Yi said, somewhat embarrassed at the commotion he had caused. He turned to leave.

"If you want to leave your name and telephone number, I'll call you with the address as soon as I find it. That's the best I can do." The woman's demeanor had softened slightly.

"That would be fantastic!" Yi returned to the counter and gave her his name and telephone number.

"You know," she added as an afterthought as Yi was walking away, "if you're in such a hurry to get the address, why don't you just send them a fax and ask them for it?"

Yi turned and smiled at the woman. "That's a great idea. I'll do that. But I'm also coming back next week to get the address from you if you don't call me. It's my excuse to come and see my favorite telephone company accounts clerk." Yi gave her a big smile and winked. She laughed and blushed.

Yi needed her to be successful in finding the address because the telephone company had been his last resort. He had tried sending a message to the strange woman's fax number. But, like his e-mail, there had been no response.

CHAPTER 23

Sounds of voices and clanking utensils filled the air of the Judges College faculty cafeteria. The forty judges scurried to fill their metal lunch trays. No one queued up or waited for anyone else at the buffet cart and food table—it was each man for himself. And once they filled their trays and sat down at one of the Formica-topped tables with attached plastic chairs, they ate with the same speed and gusto with which they had filled their trays.

Yi scooped some egg with tomato, garlic celery with small shrimp (head, shell, and tail still on), white rice, and three fried dumplings onto his tray. He then picked up a bowl of spicy Beijing noodles and went to sit down at the table where Sarah was sitting. Three other female judges sat with her.

". . . and this is the faculty cafeteria! Can you imagine how bad the student cafeteria food must be?" Sarah said to the women as Yi reached the table.

"I can recommend a good Sichuan restaurant downtown," Janet, a judge from Chengdu in Sichuan Province, told the others at the table. "And it's reasonably priced."

"That sounds good to me. The food in this cafeteria is awful!" one of the ladies replied.

"I've certainly had all I can stand of this flavorless slop," another chimed in.

"I kinda like this flavorless slop," Yi said jokingly as he sat down next to Sarah.

"Ugh!" they all replied in unison.

"Some people have no taste," Sarah said, eyeing the tiny shrimp on Yi's tray. "How can you eat that stuff?" she said with a grimace on her face.

"You know, we Cantonese eat anything that flies except an airplane, anything in water except a boat, and anything with four legs except a table," Yi answered with a big grin.

The other female judges burst out giggling, while Sarah merely shook her head.

Yi put one of the shrimp—head, tail and all—into his mouth and began crunching and chewing, exaggerating his enjoyment in order to tease Sarah more. He hadn't eaten whole shrimp with the head and shell on since he was a child. His mother had told him the shell was the most nutritious part because it had lots of calcium. Even so, he still preferred shrimp headless and peeled. But eating them whole now was worth it since it gave him the opportunity to tease Sarah.

"That's disgusting," Sarah said and turned back to face the other female judges. "So how about if we try out that Sichuan restaurant this weekend?"

"I'm ready for a change," Janet replied.

"Me too," another said.

Yi feigned surprise. "None of you charming ladies have plans for the long weekend? I'm shocked."

"We plan to study, as usual," Janet said with a shrug.

"How boring!" Yi teased and then added, "Well, count me in—for dinner, anyway."

Sarah looked at him in surprise. He had been so preoccupied lately that she didn't think he would take the time for something as frivolous as dinner out with a group of female judges, especially on a three-day weekend.

"In that case, how about if we go to a new vegetarian place I've wanted to try?" Sarah said half jokingly. She didn't think Yi would agree to it. "It's kind of expensive, but I hear it's worth it. They have all these meat dishes, like Peking duck, and fish in orange sauce, but they're made entirely from tofu and vegetables—totally meatless!" Sarah said enthusiastically.

"Totally meatless meat dishes . . . hmm . . . that sounds pretty irresistible to me." Yi's sarcasm was deliberate. "Any chance they'll have roasted yak on the menu?" he added, putting the emphasis on *yak* to annoy Sarah. She hadn't let him forget his faux pas in their first private conversation together, and he hadn't passed up an opportunity to tease her about being a vegetarian.

"I'll call ahead and request it just for you!" she replied, having gotten used to his teasing.

"I'm willing to give the restaurant a try, even if it is kind of expensive," one of the other female judges said.

"I'll go if Yi goes," Janet added, hoping a little peer pressure would help.

They all looked at Yi.

Yi turned to Sarah and said with utmost seriousness, "If it'll make Sarah happy, I'll go."

The ladies began to giggle again, and Sarah's cheeks turned bright red.

"I think it would make Sarah very happy," one of them replied.

Returning to his teasing mode, Yi smiled and placed another juicy whole shrimp into his mouth and crunched down on it with his teeth, causing Sarah to cringe. As he did so, his cell phone rang. He removed it from his pocket and flipped open the cover.

"*Wei,*" Yi responded, his mouth still full of shrimp.

"Is this Mr. Yi?" the voice asked.

"Yes, this is Yi Jichun," Yi said, trying to quickly empty his mouth of the shrimp. He didn't recognize the female voice on the other end of the line.

"I've located the address for that fax number, if you still need it," the telephone company accounts clerk said in a surprisingly pleasant tone.

"It's only been one day. I'm impressed, Ms. Chen. Thank you. Let me get something to write with." He put down his chopsticks and took a notebook and pen out of his backpack.

"Go ahead, Ms. Chen," he said.

"The address is in the name of Mr. Liu Yan Feng at 44 Dong Xiao Lu, Gaobeidian, Beijing. I hope this information is of help to you, Mr. Yi."

"Very much so, Ms. Chen. Thank you again."

"It is my pleasure, Mr. Yi. *Zaijian.*"

"Xie xie, Chen tai tai. Zaijian," Yi replied politely.

After disconnecting the call, Yi thought about the address Ms. Chen had given him. *Gaobeidian is near here,* Yi calculated in his mind. *There are signs for that area off the Jin Tong Expressway coming back to the college from downtown . . . Tomorrow's Friday . . . That should be a good day to check out the address. If the woman works or goes to the market, she'll probably leave between 7:30 and 8:00 in the morning . . .*

Sarah and the other judges waited for Yi to rejoin their conversation, but he seemed distracted once again.

"Something important?" Sarah asked.

Yi shook his head and smiled as he put the notebook back in his bag and began to plan his visit with the strange woman.

***

Gaobeidian was a small industrial area on the eastern outskirts of Beijing. Economic expansion into Beijing's outer areas, beyond the government and shopping hubs of the immense downtown center, had been rapid— maybe too rapid considering the number of unfinished commercial buildings there. Many of the unfinished structures—most of them with no side walls, only exposed rebar-reinforced concrete columns and slab floors—were embarrassing monuments to overzealous foreign businesses whose funds had been skimmed to the point of bankruptcy by local partners. Some of the unfinished buildings along the Jin Tong Expressway had gone without work for so long that squatters had taken up residency, hanging thick military-green padded quilts where walls should have been in a feeble attempt to block out the biting wind and freezing cold.

Numerous small metalworking shops lined the streets below the expressway, one right after another, displaying ornate metal archways and gates. Since these shops also served as the owners' residences, many of the men had already begun their workday, wearing their welding helmets and operating torches that sprayed blazing sparks as they worked the metal.

Here and there Yi saw women outside the makeshift dwellings, sitting on tiny wooden stools not six inches off the ground, cutting up breakfast vegetables by the morning's faint light. Near one of the women, a young toddler in split-bottomed quilted pants with his bare buttocks exposed to the cold morning air squatted and played with a stick. As Yi walked along the street below the noisy expressway, he marveled at the sights and sounds of Beijing's working class on this sixteenth day of March.

Not quite sure which direction to take to get to Dong Xiao Lu, Yi asked a group of men who were admiring a new billboard in their small neighborhood. It advertised women's lingerie and had a picture of a scantily clad blonde woman.

"You have to go to Xiaowu Qiao bridge and turn right," one of the men said.

"No, no, that's not right. It's over by the eastern train station," another said.

"Yes, stay on this road for about two kilometers and then turn left when you see the signs for the train station. It's a few blocks from there," the third man said.

Yi thanked the men and left. They went back to admiring the billboard.

Yi arrived at 44 Dong Xiao Lu at 7:38 A.M. A dim light shone from a window on an upper floor. No one answered when he knocked on the door, and when he pushed on it, it was locked. There were no business signs, and the street-level windows were broken and boarded. Cheap posters pasted to the side of the brick building advertised a news magazine, which looked to Yi to be a controversial one. He guessed he was at the right place.

Yi leaned against the building and waited to see if anyone came or went from the address. Rubbing his hands together and blowing on his fingers, he wished he had worn gloves. In addition to the bitter cold weather, the tiny bits of coal ash that filled Beijing's gray sky stung Yi's eyes. Even squinting, however, he was sure he would be able to recognize the strange woman from the marks on her face.

At a few minutes past eight o'clock, a tall, slender woman in a brown coat stepped out of the building. She removed several locks from an old, thin-tired bicycle and placed a cloth bag in the wire basket attached to the rusted handlebars. Yi walked up beside the bicycle.

"*Ninen hao, peng you.* May I request a small favor?" Looking at the woman's face, Yi saw the faded traces of blue dots along the woman's cheek line and temple. He saw the weathered wrinkles and aged lines of a woman who had known hardship. A permanent frown creased her brow.

"I am not your friend. Now leave me alone. I have nothing to give you," the woman responded, not looking at Yi.

"I'm not a beggar. I wish nothing from you but a moment of your time. I am a friend of the Stillmans," Yi said, placing a hand on the handlebar of the bicycle.

The woman quickly turned her head to face Yi. A look of terror filled her eyes.

"Didn't you receive my e-mail and my fax? It is most important that I speak with you," Yi said.

"I don't know what you're talking about. I know nothing."

"I've read your letter."

The woman let go of her bicycle and turned to run away. Before she could, however, Yi slipped his hand around her thin arm. Feeling his strong grasp, her shoulders slumped in the realization that she was trapped.

She looked at his clothing for any indication of an official uniform. There was none. Yi was dressed in casual clothing.

"Who are you? A government crony? I will tell you nothing."

"I am not with the Chinese government. How can I make you trust me?"

"You can't," she said as she pulled her arm from his grasp and started to walk her bicycle. Yi walked alongside.

"I'm not from China," Yi said.

She stopped and looked at Yi then continued walking. "You look Chinese. That's good enough for me," she said. "I will tell you nothing."

Yi thought of the danger he faced if he confided his true identity but decided he had no other choice. "Look, what I'm about to tell you could cost me my life. But I'm willing to trust you. Maybe then you'll trust me."

He leaned forward and whispered, "I'm an American."

The woman laughed. "And that should make me trust you? Stillman didn't want to help me. Why should I trust you? You Americans are all the same," she said and spit on the ground.

"The Stillmans are only teachers here. They couldn't help you," Yi explained.

"And what are you? CIA?" She hacked and spit again.

Yi ignored her question. "That symbol you put on your letter, I saw it on a computer in the Li-ren Culture Village on Hainan. I was there in January."

She stopped and turned to face him. He had honest eyes.

"I know you are a leader from the Li tribe in Hainan," Yi said.

"Me, a leader? Hah!" She laughed. "Look at me. I am not a leader. Now leave me alone."

Yi could see the pain in her eyes.

"I know you're a leader because of the marks on your face. I was in Hainan. I know the culture there. What I don't understand is why you left your tribe in Hainan and why a computer in such a primitive island village has the same symbol as the one on your letter—a letter in which you identify foreign terrorists in South China. Are you suggesting the Li tribe has something to do with these terrorists? Is that why you left?"

"It's a long story," she replied, giving in to talking with this stranger.

Yi pointed to the building. "Can we go in and talk?"

She shook her head. "Those walls have ears."

"Would you at least tell me your name?"

Reluctantly, she said, "Meijuan."

They took the subway train from the Gaobeidian station to Ritan Park. A pottery exhibition was going on, and people crowded around the display areas. The paths and pavilions in the park, however, were practically empty. Yi and Meijuan located a bench out in the open yet away from any people walking nearby. Only after she was sure no one was within listening distance did Meijuan begin to tell Yi about her life on Hainan.

"I must start at the beginning . . . so you will understand my family," she said, hesitating as if Yi wouldn't be willing to hear everything she needed to say. "This will take some time."

Yi smiled and patted her hand, which was gripping the bench's edge like it might jump out from under her. "My time is yours."

She nodded then took a shallow breath and began. "The women of my family have been leaders of the Li tribe on Hainan Island for many generations. My father, however, was not of the Li tribe."

Yi looked surprised. "Where was your father from?"

Meijuan shook her head. "I don't know. But he carried very bad seed. My mother wouldn't talk about it, but others who knew the story told me. I came as a result of the final battle of the women's army of Hainan."

Yi remembered the history. "You mean the Emissary Company, Second Independent Regiment of the China Red Army—formed in 1931?"

"Yes, that is correct," Meijuan continued. "As a matriarchal society, 103 women on Hainan left their families and took up guns to fight against the traditions of feudalism, seeking equality in the government's eyes and hoping to end the local Kuomintang's unfair practices. Most of the women were between fifteen and thirty years of age. My mother, Shi Lin, was one of them. She was only seventeen."

"So your mother fought with the women's army?"

"She not only fought, but she was one of their leaders. She brought valuable skills taught to her by the older leaders of the Li tribe. For instance, she knew the labyrinth of caves on Hainan and the provisions stored there by the Li people during storms. This knowledge helped greatly in the success of the women's army.

"At first the government didn't take the women seriously. But as they honed their fighting skills and stood stalwart against local officials, the government became outraged. They sent two hundred soldiers to Hainan to put an end to the women's army. But the women held their ground. And over the course of the next year, they fought eight glorious battles. In February 1932, facing the more powerful government army at Wenkui Hii, my mother taught the women to dig deep pits and chop off sharp bamboo poles, setting hidden traps. When the enemy's aircraft bombed the area, the women stayed safe in the hidden caves. Then they lured the soldiers closer, and by strategically placing grenade blasts, they were able to maneuver the enemy into their traps, causing great losses to the government.

"More soldiers were sent and eventually half of the women were killed. In February 1933, the women's army retreated. Many of the remaining members sought refuge with villagers until the government troops finally left the island."

"It is a history to be proud of," Yi said. "But I don't understand what it has to do with your father."

Meijuan hesitated before continuing her story. "One tribal member who was a close friend of my mother and who served with her in the women's army told me of the last battle and how I came to be. She felt it was important that I know what my mother had endured out of love for her fellow soldiers and for the daughter she would later bear. She told me that although they were courageous, they were still women who were looked down upon by the male government. They could hear the enemy soldiers in their camps at night, laughing and boasting of the tortures they planned to carry out on the women." Meijuan paused. "They did horrible things."

Yi could tell Meijuan was uncomfortable talking about this part of her history. "Your mother must have been a very courageous woman," he reassured her.

Meijuan nodded. "With so many of her comrades being slaughtered in that final battle, my mother charged the enemy with only a sword in her hand. Although she was able to kill many of them, they eventually overpowered her. They saw the tattooing on her face and recognized that she was a leader. So they tortured her and left her for dead. At first, she wished she had died." Meijuan paused again. "I was born nine months later."

Silence hung in the air.

"Despite the painful memories, my mother loved me," Meijuan added with a sigh. "And the Li tribe accepted me, even with the bad seed."

Yi nodded. "They made you a leader."

"Yes. Like my mother and her mother before her, my face was tattooed, marking me a leader. It is an honor, but one that comes with great responsibility."

They both sat in silence. Yi wasn't sure where to direct the conversation.

"Did you marry?" he asked.

"Yes, to a wonderful man named Bao Liang. We were married in 1951 in the traditional Li fashion. The next year I gave birth to our only child—a son. My husband named him Bao Jiaoshi—the characters meaning "reef"—because he knew of my great love for the ocean and Wild Boar Island. Unfortunately, my husband died during the Cultural Revolution."

"I'm sorry. And your son?" Yi asked.

Meijuan shook her head. "I'm afraid he is of the bad seed. My mother and I tried to raise him well, to teach him integrity and the righteous ways of our ancestors. But he was a troublesome child, and life became difficult for him. My mother died when he was nine years old, and the Cultural Revolution took away his father. Jiaoshi and I were required to work in the rubber tree forests on Hainan during that time. It was grueling labor, especially for a young boy. As Jiaoshi grew, so did his bitterness toward the life he had been dealt by the government, having to give up the prestige of our family's high position on Hainan, the conveniences it afforded, and the loss of his father. The Cultural Revolution finally ended in 1977 when Jiaoshi was twenty-five years old. But his damaged character had already taken hold."

Yi sighed. "I am touched by what you and your family have endured."

"Thank you." Meijuan looked down then continued. "My family was given the best land on Hainan—the coastal area of Yalong Bay and the small island known as Wild Boar. That island was my favorite place as a child. Besides its natural beauty, I loved it because it was the one place where I could be alone with my mother. Unlike Hainan's many caves, Wild Boar Island has just one cave—a large, hollow cavern at the end of a narrow, twisting tunnel. In our years of exploring the island together, my mother and I discovered that there was just one entrance accessible from above the water. We kept it well hidden with rocks and scrub brush. Inside the cave, I could enjoy my mother's company without the frequent interruptions that came to such an important leader. There she taught me much about honor and bravery."

A moment of silence passed.

Yi didn't want to offend, but he still didn't have the answers he needed.

"Meijuan, how do you know the things you wrote in the letter are true?"

She breathed a heavy sigh before continuing her story. "Because of my family's high standing in Hainan, after the Cultural Revolution, my son was appointed mayor of Sanya, the capital of Hainan Province. At first Jiaoshi was a good leader, but over time the effects of the revolution's hard labor and sacrifices plunged him into an obsession for money. I'm afraid he has become a very corrupt man. He arranged an agreement with some foreigners who wanted a secret hiding place in the South China Sea to base their terrorist activities." Meijuan dropped her head as if she were responsible for her son's unscrupulous activities. "I tried to stop him. I tried. But he would not listen to me. I told him I would go to the authorities, but he laughed at me because many of the authorities are involved with him. No one can be trusted. If they knew I tried to stop them by contacting American authorities—even my talking with you now . . ." Meijuan paused and looked around. Yi could see tears running down her cheeks.

"Who are these foreigners, Meijuan?" Yi interrupted. "Do you know where they come from?"

"I don't know for sure. My contacts with counterrevolutionary groups around China believe this organization—called the Hainan Net—is made up of international mercenaries. Their symbol has Arabic characters in it, but they pay our officials in US dollars. My son has accumulated quite a fortune in funds held in an international bank somewhere in Europe—Switzerland, I think."

"Have you tried to report this to officials here in Beijing?" Yi asked.

"My son has connections, even in Beijing. Many officials know who I am, especially because of my involvement with the news magazine."

"You know, Meijuan, the magazine can't protect you from your son or this group," Yi said, genuinely concerned.

"No. If my son thought I was about to expose them, his cronies would have me killed. Of that I am sure." She eyed Yi guardedly. "I only hope my conversation with you does not prove to be a mistake."

"I assure you it is not, Meijuan," Yi responded warmly, folding his right hand over his left fist and rocking his clasped hands close to his chest as a gesture of respect.

Meijuan nodded, accepting the fact that she would have to trust Yi.

"Meijuan, can you tell me what the symbol means?" Yi continued questioning her.

"It is the symbol of their network, which supposedly reaches worldwide. I understand the Arabic characters in the center to mean 'power of the boar.' I believe it is because their control center is in Wild Boar Island."

"When I was there, I didn't see any structures except an old lighthouse," Yi commented. "The island appeared to be nothing but a hill of scrub brush."

"That is correct." Meijuan nodded. "My family left the area in its natural state."

Yi thought about the diving he had done there and the area of damaged coral he'd seen. "There was one unnatural spot near that island," he said. "While I was diving there, I noticed a large section of damaged coral a short distance out to sea."

Meijuan nodded her head. "Yes. That is because of the explosives they were testing. I believe they have since moved it to another location."

"Explosives for what?"

"I don't know," Meijuan said and shrugged her shoulders.

"So you're saying a terrorist group has set up a control center inside Wild Boar Island's secret cave so they can carry out activities—including bombings—in other parts of the world?" Yi was beginning to have doubts about Meijuan's story. "If the island is a control center, how do they communicate with other locations?" he asked.

"In addition to computer hookups located in the Li-ren Culture Village, they use satellite communications," she answered.

"That's impossible," Yi challenged. "They would have to position above-ground receivers and transmitters. There were none on that small island or in the culture village."

"It is true. There are none visible on the island. They use wireless transmitters and receivers hidden in sampans around the island," Meijuan replied.

Yi was stunned. "Those old fishing boats in the bay? How ingenious!"

"Most of them, yes. The fishermen are paid well to have the equipment on their boats."

Yi paused as he tried to absorb all that Meijuan had told him. Some pieces still didn't fit. Yet he hated pressing her for more details given her emotional state.

"Why would the Li people allow these foreigners into their culture village, Meijuan?"

"My son is of the Li tribe. He must have told them many lies. I'm sure they do not know the outsiders have evil plans to kill innocent people," she replied.

Yi felt there was more. "In addition to seeing their symbol on a computer in the culture village, I happened to see shipping documents under the name of 'Li-ren Culture Village Enterprises, Hainan' for shipments of herbal medicines to South America. Do you know anything about that?"

Meijuan shook her head. "The Li people have nothing to do with herbal medicines. Their business is entirely based on tourism at the culture village."

Yi continued. "The official who handled the export tax documents was murdered shortly after the documents were released to the cargo carrier. I assumed it was merely a coincidence."

Meijuan shook her head again. "There are no coincidences, Mr. Yi. Most likely he was caught doing something he wasn't supposed to do.

judge in Sanya doesn't begin until I complete this WTO training. The senior judges in Shanghai's courts recommended me for a promotion, but since no judgeship positions were available there, I was assigned to Hainan. I haven't moved there yet, and I haven't had a chance to study up on the history of the area. I'm so sorry."

"No, Sarah, that's quite all right," Yi said, hoping his disappointment didn't show in his face. "It's probably nothing anyway."

What you have said disturbs me greatly. I wasn't aware that the name of the Li-ren village was being used for illegal purposes. My guess is the foreigners are using it to launder money to support their heinous activities."

Yi nodded in agreement but recognized he would have to verify Meijuan's information before he could take any action.

"Meijuan, if I were to go back to Hainan, is there any way I could get access to the cave without being seen?"

Meijuan shook her head. "Not from above ground. I'm sure they have that entrance heavily guarded."

She thought for a moment then said, "You said you were diving there, correct?"

"Yes." Yi nodded.

"Then I will tell you how you can enter the cave from underwater. On the seaward side of the island . . ."

"The rocky side?" Yi interrupted.

"Yes. Near the western edge on the rocky side, underwater, there is a large boulder shaped like a bell lying on its side. Because the edges flair out, it doesn't look like there is anything behind the rock. However, just to the left you'll find a passageway leading directly into a small lake in the back of the cave. You won't be able to wear a scuba tank because there isn't enough room in the passageway. But you can make it if you take a really deep breath."

At that moment, for the first time, Yi saw Meijuan smile.

"I can tell you love Wild Boar Island and the Li people very much," Yi remarked, pleased to see Meijuan's happiness.

Meijuan nodded. "I want to see my island rid of the evil my son has allowed in."

"I will do everything I can. Meijuan, are there any other places on Hainan, or elsewhere in China, where these people may be located?" he asked.

Meijuan thought for a moment. "You know, Mr. Yi, now that I think about it, a newspaper colleague of mine in Ürümqi told me about a pharmaceuticals manufacturer there who produces high-grade heroin for shipping in herbal medicine packaging. Could it be possible the herbal medicine shipment to South America under the Li-ren Village name is, in fact, heroin?"

"You're the one who said there are no coincidences," Yi pointed out.

Yi wondered how far the Hainan Net's organization extended beyond Wild Boar Island and the culture village. "Meijuan, would it be possible for me to get a list from you of the people, Chinese and otherwise, whom you know to be involved with this Hainan Net or any of its activities?"

Meijuan hesitated before answering. "I will send you an e-mail. It will simply be a list of titles by location. No explanations."

"How about names and agencies?" Yi asked, doubtful Meijuan would go that far.

She shook her head. "Only titles and locations. No more."

"That's fine," he replied. He could live with that. But there was still one piece of Meijuan's puzzle that bothered him. "One last question, if you don't mind, Meijuan. I've been wondering how you know these foreigners are planning to attack Americans?"

She immediately responded. "Not only planning, Mr. Yi. They are attacking Americans."

"I don't follow you, Meijuan. I'm not aware of any recent attacks."

"You don't remember a month or so ago the airline flight that crashed into the South China Sea on its flight from Hainan to Guangzhou?"

"Do I remember?" Yi replied. "It was flight CS1322, and I was supposed to be on that plane. Thank goodness I managed to get an earlier flight."

Meijuan's face turned ashen gray. "I know for a fact my son received a large payoff in US dollars to arrange for a different pilot to fly that plane. Mr. Yi, it was no accident the plane full of American embassy workers and their families crashed into the sea."

Yi was so stunned by what Meijuan had told him that he didn't notice the man walking directly toward them. But Meijuan noticed and became alarmed.

"I'm sorry, Mr. Yi, I must leave now," she said as she hurriedly gathered up her things. She left in the opposite direction, her back to the man walking quickly toward the bench where Yi now sat alone.

"Well, Yi Jichun, what a surprise," the man said as he watched Meijuan scurry away.

Yi looked up to see Tan Yang standing in front of him.

"It's no surprise to me, Yang. This isn't the first time we've run into each other off campus. That's quite a coincidence in a city of fifteen million people, don't you think?"

"Yes, quite a coincidence. We must have the same interests," Tan Yang responded as he sat down on the bench. He took out a cigarette and lit it.

Yi waved away the smoke. "Somehow, I think it's more than that," he said as he got up to leave. "And, I have to say, Tan Yang, I find your following me quite annoying."

Ignoring Yi's accusation, Tan Yang asked, "Who was your friend?" as he tilted his head in the direction Meijuan had gone.

"The mother of an old classmate of mine, not that it's any business of yours," Yi said with a sharp edge in his voice, letting Tan Yang know the conversation was over.

Yi walked back to the entrance of the park and hailed a cab to the National Judges College.

***

Tan Yang kept a close watch on Yi. After seeing him in the library talking with the Tibetan judge and then meeting with the Americans alone in their apartment late at night, he began following Yi. He noticed when Yi went to class, who he spoke to, and where he went after class. He followed Yi when he left the college campus, such as on the day he went to the telephone company. He also became aware of Yi's fondness for American food after following him several times to Western restaurants. He wondered how Yi could afford such expenses on his limited judicial salary.

Tan Yang even paid a small amount of money to Yi's roommate, Henry, to search Yi's belongings for anything unusual, to apprise him of what Yi studied in his dormitory room and who he telephoned on his cell phone.

So when Tan Yang didn't see Yi go to breakfast with Jerry and Lincoln, he watched for Yi to leave the dormitory building. Then he followed him again. He watched as Yi talked to the men studying the billboard and then pointing toward the train station. He followed Yi to an old, rundown building and then watched him from inside a tea shop across the street. He saw Yi approach the woman with the bicycle and her attempt to run away. He followed them both when they took the subway to the park. Although he couldn't hear their conversation, he most definitely didn't believe the woman was the mother of Yi's old classmate. And he doubted Yi was a judge from Guangzhou.

The report he had received from his friend in Guangdong Province claimed Yi's records matched what he said. But no one remembered working with him at the Haidian District Court.

CHAPTER 24

Yi went straight to the makeshift law library on the second floor of the Judges College. He knew he would find Sarah there. She was sitting alone at a table with a stack of books opened in front of her. Busy reading and taking notes, she didnʼt notice him slip up behind her.

"Have dinner with me?" he whispered in her ear.

"Oh, Yi, you startled me!" She paused to catch her breath then whispered, "Where have you been? You werenʼt at breakfast or in class. Are you all right?" She sounded concerned.

"So you were worried about me, eh?" Yi teased.

"Yes, of course I was. Youʼve been missing a lot of classes. And besides, Iʼm not at my best if the competition isnʼt around."

"Ah, is that all I am to you—the competition?" Yi feigned feeling hurt.

"You know Iʼm teasing," she said with a grin.

Yi chuckled. "You had me worried there." He then added seriously, "So, Sarah, how about dinner?"

"Arenʼt we going to the vegetarian restaurant tomorrow with the group?" she inquired.

"Ah . . . I may have to reschedule that. But I need to talk with you today. Not here. Somewhere private."

"You sound so serious, Yi. I hope everythingʼs okay."

"Everythingʼs fine. But I am serious. I really do need to talk to you privately."

"Okay," she said as she started gathering up her things. "Do you want to leave right now?"

"Umm . . . not just yet. There are some things I need to do first. Let's meet at the front gate at five o'clock."

Yi went looking for Lincoln and Jerry, who were studying together in the dormitory.

"Hey, you're precisely the two people I was looking for," Yi said as he walked up and put his hand on Jerry's shoulder.

"No kidding?" Jerry replied. "It seems we hardly see you anymore."

"Yeah, where have you been?" Lincoln added with a smile.

"That's what I wanted to talk to you about. Something important has come up, and I'm going to be away for at least the long weekend, maybe a few days more."

"You've got plans for the long weekend? Anything exciting?" Jerry asked.

"No, just some work that can't wait until I finish here. Anyway, I wanted to follow up on our conversation about putting together that list, remember?"

"As a matter of fact," Lincoln said, "after talking to some of the other judges, we started making a list. I think it will be an interesting comparison when it's finished."

"And it's only provinces and titles, right?" Yi asked. "No names? And you're absolutely sure each one listed is involved in . . . you know . . .?"

"Definitely," Lincoln replied with a nod.

Yi patted Lincoln on the back. "That's great! Do you think it might be finished by this weekend?"

Lincoln shook his head. "Sorry, Yi. I'm going home to be with my family. I leave in an hour."

"Hey, don't apologize, man. That's the most important place for you to be."

"I can get it done by this weekend. But I thought you were going to be away," Jerry said.

"I am." Yi nodded. "I was hoping you could e-mail me the list so I could take a look at it over the weekend. I'll add my list, and then we can go over it together when I get back."

"Sounds like a plan. I'll e-mail it to you on Sunday," Jerry promised.

Next, Yi went to the Internet cafe outside of campus. He knew it was too soon to expect something from Meijuan, but he wanted to check before leaving town. And he needed to send a status report to Trenton Woodbury, although at this point, all he could tell him was he had some interesting leads and would get back to him shortly.

The final thing Yi needed to do was purchase a new camera—a sore subject as he thought about his first trip to Hainan and having his expensive camera equipment confiscated. He took a taxi to Beijing's largest Canon camera distributor and purchased a new, pocket-sized digital camera with a waterproof shield.

Hardly compensation for my old equipment, he thought. *But it'll do.* If what Meijuan said was true, he would need an underwater camera to establish visual proof of her allegations. Without pictures, it would be impossible to convince the people back in Washington DC.

Yi figured he could spend a few days in Hainan verifying facts while he waited for the lists from Jerry and Meijuan, assuming Tan Yang hadn't scared her into not sending it.

Yi and Sarah went to an early dinner at the Hundred Different Dumplings restaurant near Xichang'an Jie Street in the financial district of Beijing. They sat at a table in the loudest section of the restaurant. Sarah ordered cabbage, celery, and spinach dumplings. Yi ordered pork dumplings, spicy beef dumplings, and cold, sliced cucumber with garlic.

"Make sure none of your meat dumplings touch any of mine, okay?" Sarah joked.

"I have no intention of sharing. Not even the juices," he responded.

"And to drink?" the waiter asked.

Yi knew what Sarah's choice would be. "*Zhu hua cha. Xie xie.*"

"Yi, you remembered!" Sarah exclaimed. "Chrysanthemum tea is my favorite. Thank you." She waited for the waiter to leave before she shook her head. "Yi, you are so different from other men. Most wouldn't pass up a beer for anything, let alone herbal tea."

"I don't mind," Yi responded. "Really."

"In fact," Sarah said, tipping her head pensively, "I don't believe I've seen you drink any alcohol or smoke for that matter. That is very unusual, I think."

"Not particularly. More and more people are choosing not to smoke or drink." He leaned forward. "Sarah, would you mind if we spoke in English?"

"Not at all," she responded.

"There's less chance of us being overheard if we use English," Yi said, glancing around the restaurant. "This isn't a tourist spot, and most of the people here are older—less likely to have kept up a foreign language. So let's act as if we're students practicing our English, okay?"

Sarah looked puzzled. "We are students practicing English, Yi. What's going on?"

"Right, right," Yi responded, shaking his head. "Anyway, something has come up, and I have to be away for a few days."

"I didn't think you had plans for the weekend. Yi, are you okay? Nothing's wrong with your family, I hope," Sarah said with genuine concern in her voice.

"No, no, no, everything's fine. I was going to say it was work related, but that's not entirely true."

"Then where are you going?" she asked with a twinkle in her eye, as if Yi had some secret rendezvous planned.

"I'd rather not say," Yi replied before thinking.

Sarah's face showed surprised then a hurt look at the revelation that Yi would keep secrets.

"I'm sorry. That was thoughtless of me," Yi apologized. "It's just that I don't have a lot of answers right now."

Sarah was not appeased. She knew if Yi didn't have an answer, he usually had a clever retort to give instead. She guessed that something was bothering him. He had been preoccupied lately. And whatever it was, it didn't appear to be related to the training program because he had missed classes several times this week. Her feelings of hurt were replaced with curiosity. "Does this have anything to do with the telephone call you received at lunch yesterday? And why you weren't in class this morning?"

Yi hesitated but decided to tell Sarah the truth. "I missed class because I met with Meijuan this morning."

"And . . . who is . . . Meijuan? I'm confused," she replied.

"Meijuan is the woman who wrote the letter with the strange symbol. The one the Stillmans had talked about."

"You're kidding! How did you find her?"

"I convinced the Stillmans to let me see the letter."

"And was the symbol the same as the one you saw in Hainan?"

"Yep."

A crease began to form on Sarah's brow. "Were you able to find out from this . . . Meijuan . . . what the symbol meant?"

Yi shook his head.

"Well, what did the letter say? It must have had something to do with the symbol." Sarah's logic made perfect sense.

Just then the plates of dumplings arrived, and Yi popped a whole one into his mouth.

Sarah put down her chopsticks and waited for his answer.

"I don't know," Yi responded after he had swallowed, his chopsticks ready with the next dumpling.

Sarah was determined to find out why Yi was being so vague. "There must have been something pretty important in that letter to make you behave this way."

"What way?" Yi raised his shoulders as if he had no clue what she was talking about. He looked at Sarah as he dabbed his napkin at the corner of his mouth. She could be so persistent.

"Your evasiveness," she answered. Then, with her most charming smile, the dimple forming in her cheek and her wide-set eyes dancing with curiosity, she asked, "So, Yi, what was in the letter?"

Yi shook his head in amazement at her determination. "This is going to sound so completely ridiculous. I can't believe I'm telling you." He put down his napkin and leaned in close to Sarah. "Meijuan alleges in her letter that a foreign terrorist organization is operating out of a cave in Hainan, and they're planning attacks on Americans. Are you happy now?"

Yi was hoping Sarah would think he was joking, but her face became serious. "Do you think there's any truth to it?"

"The Stillmans believe she's a crazy woman trying to get some attention from foreigners. They're probably right."

Sarah stared at Yi, as if she could read his thoughts.

"You're going to Hainan, aren't you?" she confronted him.

"Only for a few days," Yi responded between chews, avoiding eye contact by focusing on the plates of dumplings before him. "It concerns me enough that I have to check it out. I'm telling you because I'll be gone for the weekend, so I'll miss our dinner plans tomorrow night."

Sarah sat quietly for a moment. Yi perceived her logical mind churning.

"How do you know this woman . . . Meijuan . . . isn't setting you up, Yi? Have you given any thought to that? You could lose your judicial license if the government thinks you are involved in subversive activity." She shook her head. "It's not a good idea."

"Sarah, the only reason I'm taking what she wrote in the letter the least bit seriously is because I know for a fact the symbol exists. I can't turn my back on the possibility that there may be at least some truth to what Meijuan wrote in her letter. Nevertheless, I can't go to the authorities without verifying her allegations. I've got to go and see for myself. Besides, Meijuan gave me some information that should help me check things out without being seen. I can come and go undetected."

"Sanya is a popular tourist area. How can you come and go without being noticed?" Sarah asked with skepticism.

"I was there as a tourist in January, remember? I know my way around . . . I'll be fine."

Sarah reached over and grabbed Yi's arm. "Yi, you're crazy if you're going to Hainan to check out a terrorist group. It's too dangerous!"

Her eyes suddenly got bigger, as if she'd had an important realization. "Unless . . ."

Yi studied her face, wondering where she was going with this sudden change in the conversation. "Unless what?" he asked, suspicion mounting.

"Unless I go with you."

Yi was dumbfounded. "That's totally out of the question!"

"No, Yi, listen to me. It makes sense."

"Absolutely not. If what Meijuan says is true, it would be too dangerous. And what about your study plans this weekend? You don't want to jeopardize your chance at the scholarship."

"You said yourself it would only be for the weekend, so we won't miss any classes. And I've studied the lesson materials enough to feel confident about the exams."

"You should. You study constantly," Yi quipped.

"And besides, this would give me a chance to visit the judicial offices where I'll be working in Sanya. I can do that on Monday before we return to Beijing. I think it's a great idea!"

"Well, I don't, Sarah."

"If I'm not along as part of your cover, you'll look more suspicious and be in that much more danger," she persisted.

"I don't follow you," Yi responded, not really wanting to hear her logic.

"Sanya is a tourist town, but this isn't the tourist season, Yi. The place is probably deserted. It would look a lot less suspicious if you had a female friend along with you because it would appear as nothing more than lovers on a special vacation."

"Lovers, huh?" Yi raised his eyebrows.

Sarah blushed. "You know what I mean. And you know I'm right!"

Yi thought for a moment. "True. But I still don't like the idea of putting you in harm's way."

"There's probably no validity to Meijuan's allegations. So nothing's going to happen."

"It had better not," Yi stated. Then, hoping to lighten the mood, he added, "I'm counting on you winning that scholarship to the United States so we can see each other after this is all over."

A puzzled look came over Sarah's face. She hesitated only a moment before commenting, "How would we see each other if I am in the US and you are in Guangzhou?"

Yi realized he was on the verge of blowing his cover. He liked Sarah very much, and he trusted her, but he couldn't take the chance of her learning his true identity just yet.

Yi shoved a whole dumpling in his mouth and shrugged, hoping to cover any nervousness. Taking his time to finish off the dumpling, he finally explained, "Well, of course, silly. I plan to be the other recipient of a scholarship to the United States. There are two of them, remember?"

"Oh, of course, that's right." She smiled. "And I would say you stand an excellent chance of winning one. That is," she paused for effect, "if you'd attend classes."

They both laughed.

"But, please, Yi," she added with seriousness, "just don't take my slot."

Yi grinned.

"There's no chance of that happening," he reassured her.

CHAPTER 25

The Beijing International Airport was crowded as usual. Yi stood behind Sarah in one of three slow-moving lines to pay airport taxes before proceeding to the departure gate. The long queues extended so far back that they blocked the main walking aisle of the airport. People had to maneuver around the queued travelers in order to pass through the terminal. As Yi stood there watching people coming and going, he noticed something peculiar. The points at which the people—men—were pushing through the queues were where a woman stood in line. As the line moved ahead, the passing point changed to where another woman stood in line. The men simply pushed through with no acknowledgment or apology to the women. They didn't even look at them. It was as if they didn't exist. Yi was surprised and disturbed at this display of sexual inequity, especially in a country that now purported total equality. And the women, even if knocked off balance, would merely lower their eyes and say nothing, as if their implied lack of existence were normal and accepted.

As Yi and Sarah moved forward in the line to a point where cross traffic was occurring, men began cutting in front of Sarah. She didn't seem bothered by it, but Yi was becoming increasingly annoyed. Without saying anything, he discretely slid his suitcase forward with his foot, just beyond Sarah's right side. Immediately the cross traffic began to shift to another woman in the line. Then, suddenly, a man carrying a briefcase, obviously in a hurry and not paying attention to where he was walking, stumbled over Yi's suitcase as he tried to cross in front of Sarah. Trying unsuccessfully to avoid falling to the floor, the man flailed his arms to regain his balance, swinging his briefcase in the air. People scattered to get out of the man's way. Others snickered at his clumsiness.

"You might want to watch where you're going," Yi said to the man politely, while extending his hand to help him up.

The look of puzzlement mixed with annoyance that the man directed at Sarah, as if it had been her fault, angered Yi even more. Surprised at his feelings, Yi realized how protective he felt toward her.

"Are you all right?" he asked her.

"Yes, I'm fine. I didn't realize the suitcase was there. I'm so sorry it was in the way," Sarah responded, looking down at the suitcase now lying on its side some distance away.

Yi retrieved the suitcase and set it beside him.

"I set it there because I didn't like the way men were cutting in front of you," he said. "And that man should have been watching where he was going."

"I don't mind the men crossing in front of me, really," Sarah said.

"Well, I mind," Yi answered matter-of-factly. "Women should be treated with honor and respect, not as chattel."

Once again, Sarah was surprised, albeit pleased, at the differences she saw in Yi from all the other men she knew.

CHAPTER 26

"Listen to this," Sarah said during the flight from Beijing to Hainan. True to her nature, she was spending much of the flight studying. This time it was a travel brochure about Hainan Island.

At least it's not a law book, Yi conceded.

"'Once home to China's most reviled exiles, Sanya has been transformed from a spot no one wanted to visit at the end of the world into one of China's most popular, most beautiful, and relaxed areas.' That sounds heavenly to me."

"I agree, Sarah," Yi replied and squeezed her hand. Under other circumstances, Yi thought Hainan Island would be the perfect place to bring Sarah on holiday. This trip, however, was not going to be a vacation, and Yi was already worried about her safety.

***

The airline flight to Hainan arrived on schedule. Yi and Sarah collected their baggage and exited the small terminal. Sarah closed her eyes, leaned her head back, and took in a deep breath of the clean, warm air.

"What a wonderful change from Beijing," she said.

"Just think, Sarah, soon you'll be enjoying this lovely weather year-round."

"That's very true. I can't wait."

"Well then, would you give up the opportunity to go to America on scholarship in order to move here sooner?" Yi teased.

"Uh . . ." Sarah hesitated for only a brief moment. "No. Definitely not!"

"That's good to know," Yi responded with a smile.

The resort's surroundings were more verdant than Sarah imagined. In one direction, beginning on the far side of the road, a steep mountain arched up, its dense covering of monsoon forest alive with the constant noise of cicadas, the humid air thick with the sweet smell of steaming vegetation. On the ocean side, garden walkways were edged with banana trees and tall coconut palms that swayed in the sea breezes.

Leaving Sarah standing with her mouth open as she gazed about, Yi picked up their suitcases and entered the hotel lobby.

"Sorry," Sarah said sheepishly as she rushed to his side.

The lobby was spacious and open, with a warm ocean breeze drifting through. Yi checked in while Sarah walked out on the patio to take in the view. It captivated her. She had never seen an ocean so turquoise. In contrast to the newness and elegance of the hotel, several time-scarred old fishing sampans bobbed out beyond the breaking waves. And the shrub-covered hill of Wild Boar Island loomed large above them. She watched the waves gently break along the beach, the rhythmic sound of the water being interrupted only by the occasional squeal of a seabird. She pondered the tranquil scene before her, contrasted with Meijuan's allegations. *What secrets do you hold?* As she looked across the bay to the benign-looking island, a shiver crossed her shoulders.

Sarah rejoined Yi as he finished signing for their rooms. The hotel manager came into the lobby as they were turning toward the elevator. He immediately recognized Yi.

"Mr. Yi, it is so good to see you again!" he beamed. He glanced from Yi to Sarah then back to Yi.

"This is my friend and fellow judge, Sarah Decker," Yi said to the manager.

"It is a pleasure to meet you, Miss Decker," he replied with a slight bow. Then turning to Yi he asked, "Tell me, Mr. Yi, were you able to recover your camera?"

"No, I'm afraid not," Yi responded, a little uncomfortable that the hotel manager had brought it up.

"I am sorry to hear that. The police were of no help to you?" He seemed surprised and persisted in asking for details, much to Yi's dismay.

Yi had not gone to the police because he hadn't wanted any scrutiny of his identification documents. Now he wished he and Sarah had booked rooms at a different hotel.

"It worked out for the best, really." Yi smiled and patted the manager on the back. "With the insurance money, I was able to purchase a much nicer camera."

"Well, I can assure you there have been no other incidents of the kind here," the manager stated emphatically. "You can be sure our security is the finest."

Yi didn't believe him, but he wished to end the discussion. "I have no doubt about that," he said. "Now I'd like to get my friend settled in her room. We've had a long trip."

"Of course, of course!" the manager said. "And welcome again, Mr. Yi. Please enjoy your stay."

"You had your camera stolen here?" Sarah whispered to Yi.

"It was a stupid mistake on my part—nothing to be concerned about," he assured her.

The bellhop deposited their luggage in their separate rooms, and Yi left Sarah to unpack.

He stood at his room's windows, arms folded across his chest, wondering what the next few days would unveil. The whole place gave off an air of solemn anticipation. The hotel grounds and beach area were practically deserted. *Probably for the best.*

Yi unpacked his things then went back to Sarah's room. He knocked lightly.

She opened the door with a big smile on her face. Yi had never seen her so buoyant. She was almost giddy.

"This room is absolutely incredible, Yi! I think I've died and gone to heaven. Thank you. It must be costing you a fortune. I know on my salary, I certainly couldn't afford it."

Then, suddenly, the smile left, replaced with a look of wariness.

"How can you afford this, Yi?" she asked, now somewhat skeptical of him.

She waited for an answer, but none was forthcoming.

"You're not involved in any corruption, are you?" she asked, studying Yi's face for any telltale signs of deceit.

He shook his head and looked at her as if she were crazy for thinking such a thing. "No, of course not!" he answered.

Unable to rationalize any other possibility, she went on. "You would have to be in order to afford this kind of luxury. But . . . you told me . . ." The words trailed off, and she shook her head as if everything she believed had now become a lie. "I can't believe I trusted you."

"Sarah, stop," Yi interrupted. "Just stop, okay?" he added tenderly. "It's not what you think."

Sarah looked at him with coldness in her eyes. "I think I need some fresh air."

Yi ordered fruit drinks at the bar, while Sarah went over to a quiet sitting area near the beach-side entrance of the lobby. The cozy groupings of soft sofas, wicker chairs, and coffee tables had a clear view of the ocean and Wild Boar Island.

Looking for something to keep her mind from dwelling on the possibility that Yi was not the person she thought he was, Sarah noticed Chinese chess pieces on one of the sitting area coffee tables.

"Do you know how to play elephant chess?" Sarah asked Yi when he brought over the beverages. She picked up one of the round wooden disks.

"That brings back pleasant memories," Yi responded. He set a drink down in front of Sarah and then sat across from her. She was studying the light blue plastic mat that was the chess game's playing field. "My grandfather taught me years ago. I used to watch him play in the park near our home."

"Then would you teach me?" she asked, still somewhat guarded.

"Well, it's been a while, but sure, I can teach you. I'm surprised you've never played it before."

"It's not a common pastime in Tibet."

"Oh, that's right. I keep forgetting you're not a local girl. Which color would you like, red or green?"

"Red's my favorite."

Yi picked up the wooden disks with green Chinese characters and instructed Sarah. "You take the sixteen disks with red characters and position them on your side of the mat the same as I do."

After positioning the pieces he said, "This line in the middle is the river. The generals, captains, and elephants cannot cross the river. Like Western chess, each piece has a certain direction in which it can move."

"Well, I'm not familiar with Western chess either, but I think I get the idea. Who goes first?"

"You can move first, but let me mention some strategies." Yi proceeded to point out the rules about each piece along with some standard strategic moves. As the game progressed, however, Yi could see Sarah didn't need any coaching. She was an aggressive and shrewd opponent. Yi liked that about her.

Sarah, on the other hand, was more interested in trying to figure Yi out than win the chess game. Still bothered by the incongruities in his background, she studied his face as he looked over the chess mat.

"My mother used to tell me, 'You must be clear-sighted in nature and in mind to avoid disasters,'" Sarah said.

"Uh huh," Yi responded, only half paying attention to Sarah's words as he intently studied the game.

She waited for more of a response but didn't get any.

She then added, "My mother also said, 'To smash foolish emptiness, you must be awakened to emptiness.' What do you think that means?"

Yi looked up for a moment then continued studying the mat.

"I suppose it means you have to know your enemy in order to defeat him."

Sarah answered, "I agree. And I think that philosophy applies in other things too—like stopping corruption. I think in order to eliminate corruption you have to have an intimate knowledge of it. Wouldn't you agree, Yi?"

"Uh huh," Yi responded, still studying the chess game and not seeing where Sarah was going with her line of questioning.

She continued. "Using that strategy could be dangerous, though. Even someone with the best intentions could easily succumb to the temptations of corruption."

Sarah watched Yi for any reaction in his expression. There was none.

"At least that's what I think," she added halfheartedly, worried that her persistence might offend Yi or make him angry. But she felt she had to say what was on her mind.

Without looking up, Yi responded, "And my grandfather used to tell me, 'If you are cultivating your conduct, subtle vapors escape when you open your mouth; but when you wag your tongue, trouble starts.'"

Sarah looked at him for a moment with a puzzled look on her face. "What does that mean?"

Yi thought for a moment then looked at Sarah and chuckled. "I have no idea."

They both laughed, and the tension that had been developing between them eased.

Yi regarded Sarah warmly, wishing he could tell her everything and assuage her fears. But he knew he could not.

They both seemed to lose interest in the chess game. Their eyes drifted to the peaceful scenery outside. The ocean reflected orange and pink as the sun began to set.

"It's too late to take a boat out on the water today, but how about a walk along the beach?" he asked Sarah and extended his hand.

She placed her hand in his, once again thinking how different he was from other Chinese men. A girl walking hand in hand with a female friend was common and accepted in Chinese society, but holding the hand of a male friend was a radically bold gesture indeed.

They strolled barefoot at the surf's edge. Yi's pant cuffs were rolled up slightly, and Sarah carried her sandals in one hand, stopping now and then to pick up a shell or interesting rock. The sound of the cicadas grew louder in the nearby trees as night began to fall. There was no one else on the beach. Surprisingly, they both felt comfortable enough with each other to not have to keep up a conversation. They walked in silence, except for the soothing sounds of the surf gently rolling up and occasionally covering their feet. A noisy quiet surrounded them.

Out of nowhere, a small Chinese man dressed in black swung down from the branches of a tree at the forest's edge and ran toward a small fishing boat near the water.

"That's a bizarre mode of transportation, don't you think—swinging through the treetops?" Sarah whispered.

"Oh, I don't know," Yi replied after the man had moved a little farther out of earshot. "It worked for Tarzan."

Sarah turned to look at him. "Who is Tarzan?"

Yi realized his American upbringing was showing again. Feigning shock, he stated, "You've never heard of *Tarzan of the Apes*—that great twentieth-century American classic where Tarzan lives in the jungle and swings through the trees? Where have you been all your life?" he gibed.

"Well, I certainly have never seen anyone swing through the trees before."

The man in black placed a folder-sized packet in the boat and pushed it out from the shore. He began to row toward Wild Boar Island.

Yi pointed at a bench under an arbor of green vines, secluded by palm trees. "Let's sit there and watch for when he returns," he whispered. "We can enjoy the full moon's reflection on the water while we wait."

"That sounds very romantic," Sarah replied with a smile.

After a while the strange little man returned in the boat, empty-handed, and stopped at the edge of the cluster of trees where he had descended. He glanced around and, not seeing anyone, climbed back up into the canopy and disappeared.

"Very strange," Yi said, contemplating what they had just witnessed. "I suspect he uses the trees to travel undetected." In a more somber tone he added, "I wonder what he's hiding?"

CHAPTER 27

SANYA, HAINAN ISLAND
MARCH 18, 2001

Yi had difficulty sleeping. He couldn't wait for the opportunity to explore Wild Boar Island. He had spent a good portion of the night going over in his mind his plan for getting inside the cave and what he would do if he found Meijuan's allegations to be true. As the sun cast its first rays of warm light through the partially opened drapes, Yi quickly showered and dressed then went to Sarah's room. He tapped lightly on the door. A few minutes passed before she opened it a crack and peeked out, her eyes squinting and her hair in disarray.

"Come on, sleepyhead, we've got a busy day ahead of us," Yi chimed with enthusiasm.

Sarah rubbed her eyes and opened them wide, trying to focus. Yi couldn't help but notice that even in her disheveled state of waking up, Sarah was beautiful.

"What time is it?" she asked, triggering a yawn and covering her mouth.

Yi looked at his wristwatch, not having thought about the actual time. "It's 7:40. Let's go!"

"I had no idea it was so late," she replied. "I guess I shouldn't have closed the drapes. They blocked out the sunlight, and I've lost all track of time. Wow, that's something I haven't done in a very long time, Yi." She beamed a radiant smile, now fully awake.

"I take it you slept well, then?" Yi asked.

"Oh, like a baby. This is the most comfortable bed I've ever slept in—firm but like sleeping on a pillow. And I didn't freeze all night like in the cold dormitories in Beijing. I absolutely love this warm climate!"

"Maybe what you need is someone to keep you warm at night," Yi said with a twinkle in his eye.

Sarah blushed. "Well, I guess I had better get dressed. Could you give me about twenty minutes?"

"Sure," Yi replied. "Just knock on my door when you're ready." He turned to go back to his room. "Take your time," he added, looking back at Sarah.

Sarah closed the door and rushed to get dressed.

At breakfast they planned their day: rent scuba gear and a boat, explore Wild Boar Island, return to the hotel to clean up and have lunch, then visit the Li-ren Culture Village in the afternoon. Depending on what Yi might find on Wild Boar Island, they would adjust their schedule accordingly.

Yi had no trouble renting scuba gear from the same place he had when he vacationed there in January. Renting a powerboat, however, was a little trickier.

"The boat owners don't want to rent their powerboats without going along to pilot them," he told Sarah. "Their idea is to take you where you want to go, not let you take their powerboats on your own. That's a service reserved only for the rowboats." He laughed. "I guess they're less likely to be stolen."

But Yi and Sarah needed to be able to get away quickly if necessary, depending on what he uncovered at Wild Boar Island. So he persisted and finally convinced one of the powerboat owners to let him take a small motorized boat out as far as the southwestern tip of Wild Boar Island for some scuba diving—"and to spend some private time with my girlfriend," he added to the boat owner with a wink. He assured the owner that the boat would remain visible through binoculars at all times, and they would have the boat back before noon. And, after all, it was the off-season, and Yi had sweetened the deal with a tidy sum of extra cash.

"I basically bought the boat," Yi said to Sarah after arranging the rental.

"Then let's hope it proves worth it," she replied.

They loaded their gear and set off for Wild Boar Island. Yi's watch showed the time as a few minutes before 9:00 AM. That gave him only three hours to locate Meijuan's underwater entrance to the cave, find out what, if anything, was inside the cave, and get out without being seen.

He had one hour of air in the scuba tank. The plan was that Sarah would stay in the boat and keep watch while Yi used the scuba gear to explore the area Meijuan described on the south side of Wild Boar Island. Once he found the entrance Meijuan had described to him, he would return to the boat, remove the scuba gear, and then gain access to the cave using his own air as Meijuan had instructed.

He looked at his watch. "One way or the other, I'll be back within the hour."

He then smiled and disappeared below the surface of the water.

Sarah occupied the time taking pictures of the island and of the resort beach in the distance. A few fishing sampans still bobbed about as their occupants threw out their nets one last time before turning back to shore. Several times Sarah glanced at her watch and wondered what Yi might be discovering. The last time she looked, a feeling of concern began to set in because the hour was almost up and she had not seen any sign of Yi. But just at that moment, he surfaced and removed the regulator from his mouth.

"I can't find it," he told Sarah, an edge of frustration in his voice.

"Are you sure?" Sarah asked sympathetically. "Maybe we need to get another tank of air and try again."

"I don't know," Yi shook his head as he hefted himself out of the water and into the boat. "I'm beginning to think this is all a figment of Meijuan's imagination."

CHAPTER 28

"Maybe we'll find another entrance or at least some clues that would support Meijuan's allegations," Sarah suggested. She knew Yi was disappointed. And since there was still some time left on the boat rental, she thought they ought to explore the surface of Wild Boar Island.

"It's worth a try," Yi replied, trying to sound optimistic but not feeling convinced.

Sarah reached over and placed her hand on his.

"At least it will be fun to explore the island together."

The next hour passed quickly, and although they enjoyed exploring the island and taking in the spectacular view, they could not find an entrance to a cave or any trace of activity. The only incongruity was the old lighthouse, which didn't appear to be in use, even though it had what looked like a new chain-link fence around it with No Trespassing signs.

"Do you recall seeing this lighthouse lit up last night? Because I sure don't," Yi commented to Sarah. "Why would they have new fencing around a lighthouse no longer in use?"

"My guess is the old structure is dangerous and the government doesn't want the liability of tourists getting injured in there," Sarah speculated.

"You're probably right."

They returned to the resort, turned in the boat and scuba gear, and cleaned up. Although the morning had been fruitless, they decided to continue with their plans to have lunch and then visit the Li-ren Culture Village. Maybe there they could uncover a solid lead or at least finally put to rest Meijuan's fabrications.

Lunch proved to be as much of a disappointment as the morning had been. Seated at a restaurant table on the resort's patio, Sarah watched as a chef in a starched white jacket and tall round cap grilled beef steaks and chicken on an open barbeque. Then with horror she watched as the chef picked up a live crab out of a seafood bucket and carried it with long metal tongs, its claws and legs waving slowly, over to the flaming grill. As soon as the chef placed the crab on the hot surface, it became agitated and tried to scurry off. Each time, however, just before it reached the grill's edge, the chef would catch one of its back legs with the metal tongs and pull it back into the flame until finally the crab succumbed and died.

"Now I truly am going to be sick!" Sarah cried. "I can't stand to watch something suffer like that—I've got to get out of here."

In the hotel lobby, Sarah took a deep breath. Covering her ears as if to block the sound, she said, "I swear I heard that crab scream."

"I'm sorry," Yi replied. "I had no idea that would happen. Can I get you something else?"

"No, Yi. Thanks. I'm afraid I've lost my appetite. But, please, you get something to eat."

"Actually, after seeing that back there, I'm not very hungry either." He smiled at her and added, "Perhaps you're having a greater effect on me than I thought."

Yi negotiated for a black town-car taxi to take him and Sarah to the Li-ren Culture Village. He was not going to subject her to a ride like he had experienced in January—bumpy and choked with exhaust fumes. It was important to him to provide the very best for her.

The landscaped gardens and modern roads of the resort area quickly faded into the rural scenery of rice and taro paddies separated by ridged dirt pathways. The mounds stretched out from the road in all directions. In the distance, tiny concrete farm villas with orange-tiled roofs looked like little boxes in neat rows along the base of the terraced green mountain. The countryside still looked the same to Yi as it had in January, but this time he was seeing it through Sarah's eyes, taking in Hainan's lush tropical splendor in contrast to her mountainous homeland of Tibet and the commercial metropolis of Shanghai.

They watched in fascination as Hainan's rural life unfolded. The farmers in the rice paddies worked the crops the same way their ancestors had, with pants rolled to the knees, tromping in the mud behind a water buffalo and small wooden plow. Other workers, probably family members, stood bent over at the waist, shin-deep in muddy water. Even with cone-shaped woven hats to block the intense sun, the reflection off the water left them darkly tanned and leather skinned. Some walked with bamboo poles across their stooped shoulders, bent from the weight of the rice balanced in woven baskets on each end.

"Where are you from?" the taxi driver asked, breaking the reverie.

"Uh . . . Guangzhou," Yi responded, slightly guarded.

"We are quite proud of our farmland here on Hainan. These fields produce three times each year instead of two, as in Guangzhou," boasted the taxi driver, acting as tour guide. "The officials of Sanya provided well for our farmers when they moved them to this location," he added.

"It truly is beautiful," Sarah said with awe.

"Where was their land previously?" Yi asked the driver, remembering a senate report he had written on the subject of government-requisitioned land for China's economic development.

"Near the sea at Yalong Bay," the driver replied.

"So these farmers were assigned land closer to the mountains and provided with new villas to live in. The government certainly was generous," Yi said diplomatically yet thinking how inadequate it was as compensation for prime beachfront property.

From the sandy shore of Yalong Bay, through Hainan's fertile farmland, then up the steep curves of the forest-covered mountain, the drive to the Li-ren Culture Village surprisingly took less than an hour. As they got out of the car, Yi chuckled out loud, remembering his first encounter with the village's customary greeting of earlobe rubbing. He couldn't wait to see Sarah's reaction.

"What's so funny?" she asked.

"Nothing, really," Yi replied, not wanting to forewarn her.

As expected, when they walked through the bamboo archway, Sarah jumped when a hostess touched her ear.

"Oh!" she said with a start and then giggled when she saw what was happening. "That tickles," she laughed.

"Welcome to Luhuitou, a special place for lovers," the hostesses announced as they gently rubbed Sarah's and Yi's earlobes.

"So it's a welcoming gesture then—like shaking hands," Sarah commented. "How charming!"

Even though Yi was eager to return to the area where the computer was located, he wanted Sarah to have the opportunity to see the village. They joined with a few other tourists, and soon a young female guide began telling them about life in the village. She was clothed in a bright-red, full-length dress and a colorful checkered apron tied around her waist. She explained that each girl wove her own apron as part of their tradition.

"We are a matriarchal society," she began. "You can recognize our leaders by their tattooed faces."

"I see now what you meant by a pattern of dots," Sarah whispered to Yi after an elderly woman with a tattooed face walked by. "Is that how Meijuan looks?"

Yi nodded. "Meijuan's tattoos have faded some, but you can still see the pattern."

"And here," the guide pointed to one of the huts along the well-marked tourist path, "you see our homes are three sided, with dirt floors and walls made of woven grass or grass-encrusted dried mud. You are welcome to visit any of our homes along this path. The large one on stilts is the home of our village chief," she added proudly.

"They don't look like they would provide much shelter in a storm. Where do your people go when typhoons hit?" a tourist asked.

The guide explained, "In years past, when the typhoons came, the villagers used nearby caves for shelter until they could rebuild their homes."

"So there are caves here?" Sarah questioned for confirmation.

"Yes. This island has quite a few," the guide answered.

"Are any of them still in use?" Yi asked.

"No. No one goes there anymore," she responded. "Now when the villagers are not here, they live in concrete houses provided by the government."

Walking with the tour guide through the village, Yi recognized the place where, in January, he had followed the children and stumbled upon the computer.

"Let's wait here a minute," he said, gentling grabbing Sarah's arm to pull her back from the group. When the tour group was quite a distance ahead and no one was looking, they quickly slipped out of sight.

Maneuvering around several grass huts, they finally located the plastic tent. The computer system was still there, but this time there were two men: a Chinese man dressed in Li village attire and a dark-complexioned man with a beard, dressed in the nonstandard military fatigues Yi had been unable to identify in January.

There is a connection! Yi thought.

The Chinese man turned toward them. Instinctively, Yi grabbed Sarah in a romantic hug and began kissing her neck and moving his hands up her back. She let out a startled squeal, and the soldier in the tent stood up.

"I can't keep my hands off her," Yi explained, sheepishly. "We were just looking for a little privacy. Sorry to have bothered you, gentlemen," he added.

Sarah straightened her shirt and smiled shyly at the men. Yi took her by the hand, and they quickly walked away.

"Stupid tourists!" Abikar, the bearded soldier, said to Wahid, who had a puzzled look on his face.

"What's wrong?" Abikar asked.

"I think I've seen that man before," Wahid said as his mind raced to make the connection. After only a moment, he remembered. "That's the one who was here in January and took pictures of the computer." Confused more than ever he muttered, "But how can that be?"

"What? Why did you fail to mention this before? You fool!" Abikar shouted.

"I . . . I followed him back to his hotel and took his . . . his camera. He's . . . He was supposed to be on . . . the plane that crashed. I saw his plane ticket. I . . . I thought that took care of him."

"At any time did the man see you?" Abikar asked, hoping to piece together what had happened and assess the impact.

"Well . . . yes. We . . . we rode the elevator together at his hotel. But I was very careful."

"Well, what did you do with the camera? Let's see the pictures."

Shamefaced, Wahid answered, "I sold it."

Abikar contemplated how to handle the situation. "You're sure it's the same man?"

"I don't see how it can be, but, yes, I believe he is the one."

Abikar shoved Wahid out of the hut. "Hurry! Follow him and see where he is staying. Get his name from the hotel. Then go to the airport and find out if anyone who planned to be on that flight changed to another plane. Bring me the list. We'll see if he is the man who took the pictures."

***

"That was close!" Sarah said after they moved out of earshot from the computer hut.

"Yes, but did you notice the packet on the table?" Yi asked her.

"Not really. You grabbed me so fast I didn't have a chance to see anything." Sarah blushed as she realized the boldness of his public display of affection and how much she had enjoyed the moment even if it had been staged.

"It was exactly like the package the man in black carried down to the boat last night," Yi remarked. "And the uniform that bearded man was wearing is not from the People's Liberation Army. I noticed their encampment near our hotel when I was here in January. There's definitely a connection between the culture village and the military group on the beach."

"Do you think those packages are their means of communicating?" Sarah asked.

Yi thought for a moment then shook his head. "The man in black didn't go in the direction of the military camp. He went for the boat, remember?"

***

At dinner that evening Sarah brought up a point that had been nagging her since they had returned from their visit to the culture village. "Don't you think it's unusual that the man in black would carry a parcel to an uninhabited island at night and return empty-handed? Where did he leave it and why? And what was in the parcel? It doesn't make sense, Yi, unless there's something going on someplace on or *in* that island. My instincts tell me there is, and I think we need to go back first thing in the morning and try again to find the underwater entrance."

"Except we don't know for sure that the man in black went to Wild Boar Island," Yi interjected. "Yes, he headed in that direction, and, yes, he returned from that direction, but we don't know for a fact that he left the package on the island. Maybe another boat met him."

"True," Sarah mused, sipping her after-dinner chrysanthemum tea that Yi had thoughtfully ordered for her. "Although, we didn't see any other boats in the area."

"Maybe that was because it was dark," he answered with a slight hint of sarcasm.

"I beg your pardon. There was a beautiful full moon, and I could see quite well, thank you very much," she said boldly, her broad smile causing her eyes to squint.

Yi looked out the restaurant's window.

"And it is still a beautiful full moon this evening. Let's go for a walk," he suggested.

Instead of strolling in the surf tonight, they walked along the dimly lit path winding through the green archways and floral gardens around the resort grounds. The palm trees rustled softly overhead from the night breeze. They were alone. Sarah's arm intertwined with Yi's, and once again the conversation drifted into comfortable silence.

Since arriving in Hainan, Yi's full focus had been on locating the Wild Boar Island cave and ascertaining the full extent of what Meijuan had alleged. But tonight his focus shifted to the beautiful woman beside him.

He stopped and turned to face Sarah, whose eyes drifted to the ground, a slight pink coming to her cheeks. Gently, he lifted her chin until their eyes met, and then he kissed her. Her response was eager yet timid. Yi felt the trembling of her delicate body as he held her close. Touching her long flowing black hair, feeling the silky strands between his fingers, he marveled at her exquisite beauty. Physically, he wanted her. Yet he sensed this incredibly alluring and intelligent woman was also inexperienced in love. His desire to protect her grew stronger, and he realized he had never felt such emotion before. Beyond the passion, he felt a bonding of their souls—a cherished moment of oneness. He realized if he were to hurt her in any way or lose her, the pain in his heart would be more than he could bear. And it scared him.

CHAPTER 29

SANYA, HAINAN ISLAND
MARCH 19, 2001

"So you're going to visit the judicial offices this morning, is that right?" Yi confirmed with Sarah at an early breakfast.

Sarah seemed somewhat subdued—not her usual cheery self.

Putting down his chopsticks, he asked her, "Are you okay?"

"Yi, I've been thinking . . ."

"That scares me," he interjected with a warm smile. He loved to tease her.

"Seriously, Yi, I'm willing to forego visiting the judicial offices if you want to try again to find the cave entrance."

Yi rubbed his hand across his chin as he thought about her offer. "Actually, Sarah, I need to find an Internet cafe and check my e-mails this morning. I'm expecting some important documents, and since I'm not at the Judicial College as my colleagues expect, I think I had better check in. And besides, I'm afraid we wouldn't find anything anyway. You, however, need to visit your future office," he added with enthusiasm.

Sarah studied his face. He seemed set in his decision.

"Okay then, I'll go into town," she said. "Should we meet back here for lunch before checking out?"

"Sure. But there's no rush. I arranged for late checkout since our flight isn't until nine o'clock this evening. We can keep our luggage in the rooms until we leave."

As Yi walked Sarah to the taxi area, he asked the concierge in the resort's lobby, "Where might I find an Internet cafe nearby?"

"The Green Palms Resort has one. It's a short walk from here," the concierge replied and pointed up the road.

"Thanks," Yi said.

After arranging a taxi for Sarah, Yi kissed her lightly on the cheek and waited for the taxi to drive off. He stood there, thinking about all he needed to do. He was eager to check his e-mail. Jerry had said he would send a list yesterday. Hopefully, there would also be an e-mail from Meijuan with her list. Then he could start compiling his report for Trenton Woodbury.

Seeing Yi still standing at the curb, the concierge walked up to him. "There should be a sign in the Green Palms lobby, but if not, I believe the Internet cafe is on the first floor, near the stairs. Is there anything else I can do for you today, Mr. Yi?"

"No. You've been most helpful," Yi replied warmly then turned to walk up the road.

"Taxi?" one of the taxi drivers called from the row of red *Xiali* taxis. "I give you good price," he added.

Yi recognized the man as the one who had taken him to the culture village back in January. *Not on your life!* Yi thought. He was relieved he could walk to his destination. He smiled, shook his head, and waved the man off.

***

The Internet cafe was open. Yi chose a computer near the row of printers in the back. He paid the attendant then eagerly logged on to his Hotmail account. As he had hoped, both e-mails were in his inbox and both contained lengthy lists of titles and locations. Yi planned to print them out to review back in his room. Glancing briefly at Meijuan's list, Yi was not surprised by the first entry. It was the mayor of Sanya.

***

Sarah located Sanya's administrative and judicial office building. It was smaller than she had expected, but the offices looked clean and well kempt. The large windows and decorative green plants gave it a warm, open feeling. Sarah immediately felt she was going to enjoy working there.

"Mr. Bao, I would like to introduce you to Miss Decker, one of the new judges who will be working here after her judicial training in Beijing," the secretary said to a distinguished-looking man as he walked by. Turning to Sarah she added, "This is our honorable mayor, Mr. Bao."

The man appeared annoyed at the interruption until he looked at Sarah. His countenance immediately changed to a warm smile.

"This is an unexpected pleasure, Miss . . .?"

"Please, call me Sarah," she replied.

"Well, Sarah, I am happy to make your acquaintance."

Directing her to a large set of carved double doors, he added, "Come. I have a few minutes. I want to hear all about your visit to my lovely town."

He opened the doors and preceded her into the spacious room.

"Sir, I don't mean to take up your time. I'm sure you must be quite busy."

"Not at all. Please sit down."

"I stopped by to introduce myself and see the offices where I'll be working," Sarah said, a little embarrassed that she had interrupted such a busy man's day.

"I always have time for a lovely lady such as yourself."

Sarah could feel his eyes move up and down her body.

"So," he continued, "will you be starting work here soon?"

"Oh, no, sir. I have another six weeks before the judicial training is completed," she answered.

A puzzled look crossed his face.

"The college let you leave before the end of the program? Then tell me, what is so important here that causes you to interrupt your training?"

"Important? Oh, nothing really." Sarah realized she had to be careful how she answered him. Trying to change the subject, she glanced around the room.

"You have a lovely office, sir," she added.

Something caught her attention. It looked vaguely familiar, and yet she couldn't quite place it.

"That's an interesting plaque on your wall, Mr. Bao," Sarah commented, hoping the mayor's response would help her remember why it was so familiar to her. "I don't believe I've ever seen such a unique symbol."

"Yes, it is one of a kind," the mayor responded, not offering any further information but asking again, "You didn't answer my question as to what brings you to Sanya?"

"I'm sorry. But may I ask what the symbol means?" Sarah gently probed.

"It's Arabic. The characters in the center mean *boar*. It's the logo of an important business that operates here in Sanya. The director is an extremely wealthy personal friend of mine. He's a foreigner, so I helped him establish his operations here—hence the plaque acknowledging his deepest gratitude."

"That is quite an honor, Mr. Bao," Sarah said with a smile. But it immediately began to fade as she realized the symbol on the plaque matched the description of the symbol on Meijuan's letter.

She quickly stood to leave.

"I shouldn't take any more of your time, sir. It has certainly been my pleasure to meet you." She continued, trying not to stammer. "I happen to be in Sanya for a few days helping a friend with an investigation, and I thought this would be a wonderful opportunity to see my future office and become acquainted." She bowed slightly in recognition of his higher position. "I look forward to working with you upon completion of my training," she added.

"An investigation?" the mayor asked, intrigued.

Sarah realized she had chosen the wrong word.

"Oh, I mean research. My friend is researching the economic potential of tourist resorts in China." She hoped she sounded convincing. As an afterthought she added, "This is, after all, a wonderful economic growth area for China, isn't it, Mr. Bao?"

"Yes," he replied. He began to wonder if she had told him the truth, and if not, why she would lie. He stood and followed her out of his office.

At the street curb, he watched her hail a taxi then waited to hear her destination.

"Where to, miss?" the taxi driver asked.

"Yalong Bay Resort," she answered.

CHAPTER 30

"Yi! The characters in the center of the symbol mean *boar*." Sarah couldn't get the words out fast enough.

"What are you talking about?" Yi asked, stepping aside as Sarah rushed into his room.

"The symbol on Meijuan's letter." She had to pause to catch her breath. "The characters in the center are Arabic, and they mean *boar*, like Wild Boar Island. I saw the symbol in the mayor's office today. Yi, we have to get inside that cave."

"No, *we* do not," he quickly responded then grabbed Sarah by the shoulders. "You saw the symbol in the mayor's office?"

"Yes. It was exactly as the Stillmans had described that day over lunch."

"I don't understand. How did you come to see it in the mayor's office?"

"It was on a plaque," Sarah replied as she sat down in one of the chairs in the room's sitting area. "It was unbelievable, Yi. I'm sitting there having a conversation with the mayor and . . ."

"You're what?" Yi couldn't believe what he had heard. "Sarah, the mayor is Meijuan's son. Do you have any idea how dangerous it is for you to talk with him? I thought you were going to check out the judicial offices."

"I was. But the offices are in the same building. When the mayor happened to walk by, the secretary introduced us."

"And he just happened to have some spare time, so he invited you into his office for a little chat?" Yi couldn't help showing his skepticism.

"Yes. He was very nice," Sarah replied innocently.

"And the topic of the symbol just happened to come up in conversation? I don't believe this!" He sat down in the chair opposite Sarah.

"Yi, the plaque was on his wall, in plain sight. I merely commented on the unusual design and asked him about it," Sarah said, trying to calm him down.

"Does he know you recognized it?" A worried look crossed Yi's face.

"No. In fact, I didn't recognize it at first. I asked him about the plaque and what the unusual symbol meant. He was quite chatty about it. He said it had been given to him by a wealthy friend—a foreigner, I think he said—in gratitude for helping him set up his business here."

They both stared at each other.

"Don't you see, Yi?" Sarah said breaking the silence. "The symbol links the culture village to Wild Boar Island. Meijuan's story must be true."

"I've got to get inside that cave," Yi said then looked at his watch.

"We have plenty of time before our flight," Sarah stated. "What I'm concerned about is the overcast sky. It's getting quite dark out there. Do you think you'll be able to see well enough in the water?"

"I can rent a headlamp with the scuba gear just in case."

"And let's not forget the waterproof camera," Sarah added.

Yi frowned at Sarah and shook his head. "You're not going."

"Somebody has to stay with the boat, unless, of course, you would prefer a nosy boat captain watching your every move."

Yi didn't hesitate to respond. "Once again, you're exactly right. Let's go!"

They rented the scuba gear and boat without any difficulties. The boat owner they had rented from before was more than happy to rent his boat to them again under the same terms and for the same price.

They positioned the boat near the southwest corner of Wild Boar Island, like they had done the first time, and dropped anchor. The tide was high so the water was choppy, causing the boat to rock back and forth. Yi suited up, this time with headlamp and camera, and swung his legs over the side of the boat. He then turned to Sarah.

"Are you going to be okay out here?" Yi asked. "The water's kind of rough."

"I'll be fine, Yi. Just hurry back."

He kissed her on the cheek, put the regulator in his mouth, and slid into the water.

Sarah pulled her sweater more tightly around her body and took a deep breath then slowly exhaled. She looked at her watch to calculate exactly when Yi's air supply would run out.

Please be careful, Yi, she thought, hoping in her heart he would find the opening to the cave yet fearing what he might find inside.

The stormy motion of the water stirred up sand from the ocean floor, making visibility difficult and casting shadows all around. Yi feared he wouldn't have any better luck finding the cave opening this time than the last. Precious minutes passed as he recognized the same areas he had searched before.

Father, I can't do this on my own. Please help me.

A thought came into his mind, as if his grandfather had whispered the words into his ear:

Open your eyes, suner; *just open your eyes.*

Yi quickly turned on the headlamp. The fine grains of suspended sand shimmered like tiny diamonds before his eyes. Straining to see the rock formation just beyond his view, Yi could faintly see a shadow cast from the headlamp's bright beam against the jutting rock. It looked like a bell on its side—exactly as Meijuan had described.

Thank you, Lord!

He moved quickly to the other side of the outcropping. There, sure enough, was a small opening to what appeared to be a dark tunnel. Yi removed the camera from the netting bag attached to his belt and took pictures to show exactly where the opening was located.

Meijuan was right—it's not big enough for an air tank, Yi thought with dismay.

Then another thought came to him.

If I return to the boat now to leave the equipment, I may not find the opening again.

He wasn't willing to take that chance.

Slipping out of the air tank, Yi breathed deeply through the regulator and filled his lungs with air. He then anchored the air tank against the rocks and swam into the tunnel. With the headlamp still on and kicking forcefully with his fins, he propelled himself swiftly along the tunnel.

At the point when he felt his air would run out he switched off the headlamp. In the darkness of the tunnel a faint blue light began to come into focus. He swam harder. As he cleared the inner edge of the tunnel he let his head break the surface of the water enough to catch his breath. The roar of the pounding surf against the outer rocks echoed inside the cave, covering the sound of his gasps. It took Yi a few moments to filter out the sound of the surf so he could concentrate on any other noises. The only detectable sound was the hum of machinery.

***

Sarah looked at her watch again as more clouds darkened the sky. Forty-five minutes had passed. The winds were picking up, rocking the small boat even harder. Sarah was anxious for Yi to return. As she looked across to Wild Boar Island, she gauged the boat to be farther out to sea than it had been when he had entered the water.

The anchor must be drifting, she thought, her feelings of uneasiness moving to panic.

She scanned the surface of the rough water for any sign of Yi. There was none.

***

Yi pushed his mask to the top of his head and blinked the water from his eyes. A faint blue light reflecting off the water cast dancing shadows around the walls of the dark cave. The lake into which the tunnel emptied was edged with columns of stalagmites, some of which had joined with the stalactites that dripped from above. Beyond the columns, a wall with a door had been constructed. Above the door glowed a blue lightbulb inside a wire casing.

Yi eased himself out of the water and onto the cave floor near the door. He noticed numerous crushed cigarette butts on the ground.

Somebody obviously comes out here, Yi assessed. *Good. Less likely the door is alarmed or locked.*

After removing his fins, he quietly stepped to the door and leaned up against it with his ear. The hum of machinery was louder on the other side. Yi placed his hand gently on the doorknob and began to turn it slowly. The slight click of the latch seemed to echo loudly. Yi flinched but maintained his grip on the knob. He waited a moment before applying pressure to open the door. The only sounds were the increased hum of machinery and the roar of the surf.

Yi eased the door open just enough to see inside. The room was dark except for the glow of several computer monitors, a green radar screen, three black-and-white security camera monitors that switched between scenes about every thirty seconds, and floor-to-ceiling racks of equipment with tiny red and yellow blinking lights. Facing the monitors with his right side to Yi, a bearded man sat wearing camouflage green military fatigues with a black holster and 9mm handgun strapped to his waist. Yi froze. It was the same man he and Sarah had seen at the computer in the culture village. Holding his breath, Yi wished his heart would stop pounding.

The bearded soldier appeared to be reading a manual. A desk lamp shone down on an open binder on the desk. Yi carefully and silently released the doorknob, removed his scuba mask, and wedged it between the door and the frame, keeping the door open enough so he could watch the man's movements. Then he waited.

As he had hoped, within a few minutes the bearded soldier got up, turned off the desk lamp, and left the room by way of a door opposite to where Yi was standing.

Yi quickly entered the room, repositioned his mask in the door frame, and took out his camera. He took pictures around the room, including the painted red Arabic characters on the door through which the bearded man had exited, a hallway to the right of the door that led to the bottom of a circular stairway, the racks of communications equipment along the side and back walls, the ventilation ducts along the ceiling, and the communications console.

He then went to the desk, turned on the lamp, and began taking pictures of each of the pages of the manual, which were written in Arabic and contained numerous drawings and diagrams. Guessing his time was limited, Yi wiggled the computer mouse to activate the screens. On one of them were maps of the Panama Canal and US seaports. On the other was what appeared to be a web page written in Arabic. And at the bottom of the page, centered, was the spiderweb-like symbol.

Yi finished taking pictures of the screens, turned off the monitors, and exited the back door. As he was pulling the door closed behind him he noticed a serious mistake he had made. He had left the desk lamp on! As he started back in to turn off the lamp, however, the opposite door opened and the bearded man walked in.

That was close! Yi watched through the crack in the door to see if the man suspected anything.

The soldier tossed a folder onto the desk and sat down with his back to Yi.

Yi silently closed the door, gathered up his fins, and slipped into the water. He quietly maneuvered behind one of the stalagmites. Hopefully the bearded man hadn't suspected anything because if he were to come out the back door, even if he didn't notice Yi hiding behind the rock formation, the water puddle on the cave floor would show someone had been there and had entered through an underwater entrance.

Yi took a deep breath and swam back into the tunnel.

Once through to the other side, he located his scuba gear and filled his lungs with air from the tank. Then contemplating for a moment the full ramification of what he had just discovered, he took out his diving knife and cut a marker into the rock.

One hour and eighteen minutes. That's how long it had been since Yi entered the water. With only one hour of air in his tank, he knew by now Sarah would be either worried that something had happened to him or fuming mad at him for not returning to the boat when he had found the tunnel opening. Either way, facing Sarah was not going to be pleasant. He only hoped she hadn't returned to the resort without him.

His head broke the surface of the turbulent water. Startled at how much stronger the winds were, Yi quickly turned in the direction of the boat. His heart sank. It was no longer there.

"Yi!" Sarah called out when she saw the light from his headlamp. Overcome with relief, tears begin to flow down her cheeks.

She hoisted the anchor, started the engine, and maneuvered toward him.

"I didn't know what had happened to you," she sputtered between sobs, trying to control her emotions and at the same time trying to help Yi into the boat and out of his scuba gear.

"I'm okay, and I'm sorry to have worried you," Yi said, wrapping his arms around her. "There was nothing else I could do."

As the adrenaline began to drain from her body, Sarah shivered from the cold wind.

"We need to get you back to shore," Yi said with concern.

She pulled away from his grasp, practically yelling to be heard over the increasing wind. "But what did you find?"

Yi ignored her. He turned the boat around and increased the speed on the engine.

"Yi, what did you find down there?" she asked again.

He hesitated, assessing how much he should tell her.

"Obviously you found the cave because you were gone longer than you had air in your tank," Sarah responded to his silence. "What was in the cave, Yi?" she asked again, this time with annoyance at his reticence.

"I found the cave." Yi nodded.

"And?"

"And there was communications equipment inside," Yi answered, deciding not to tell her about the soldier with the gun. "Sarah, we need to get back to shore. Correct me if I'm wrong, but I think there's a major storm coming in," he added with a hint of sarcasm.

"Yi, if there's communications equipment in that cave, we need to notify government officials—ones who are high enough in command to be trusted."

"And tell them what, Sarah? There may be a legitimate and legal reason for communications equipment to be in that cave. Meijuan could have made up everything else in her story."

"I don't believe you. So you're just going to walk away?"

"No, I'm going to give the pictures to the proper authorities."

"Which ones, Yi?" Sarah queried with skepticism in her voice. "If there is illegal activity going on here—and I suspect there is since you're not telling me everything—how will you know for sure who you can trust?"

"I'm going to send them to an agency back in the United States. Now, no more questions, Sarah, please," Yi said as he guided the boat to the dock.

"I have a right to know, Yi," Sarah persisted. "You must think the activity is illegal or you wouldn't send pictures to the United States. But how are you going to get American officials to take this seriously since Meijuan apparently wasn't successful at contacting them?"

Yi thought about the mistake he could be making by telling her his true identity. Nevertheless he knew, at this point, she wasn't going to believe anything but the truth.

"Because I work for them, Sarah."

Stunned, Sarah sat in silence.

"You work for Americans?" She paused as the full impact set in then slowly added, "You're an American?" Staring at him, confused and disheartened, she waited for his reply.

"Yes."

Her confusion was replaced by anger as she blurted out, "What are you, Secret Service or something? How dare you come here and spy on us!"

"No, Sarah, I'm an attorney from Washington DC. I was asked to participate in the judicial training program to help identify corrupt officials who would try to prevent the implementation of the rule of law."

"Asked by whom?"

"The WTO Legislative Committee, in cooperation with the government of China."

Sarah sat and stared at Yi, shaking her head.

"That explains a lot," she finally said, relieved but still full of emotion. She was glad Yi wasn't involved in corrupt activities, but just as quickly as that relief had come, she felt a knot form in the pit of her stomach as she realized she had fallen in love with an American spy.

The boat owner stood at the dock, his hands on his hips, annoyed at their late arrival back with his boat.

"There's someone here to see you," he told Sarah as she stepped out of the boat.

Yi and Sarah exchanged looks of confusion and uncertainty.

The boat owner pointed toward the boathouse. Just inside the doorway, with binoculars in hand, was the mayor of Sanya.

"You had us a little worried out there, Sarah," the mayor said.

"We're fine," Yi replied as they walked past him.

"Did you find what you were looking for?" the mayor asked Yi. "It must have been important, diving so late in the day with a storm coming in."

Yi's heart skipped a beat as he turned to face this stranger whom he surmised to be the mayor.

"If you must know, I lost an expensive watch when I was diving a few days ago. Unfortunately, I didn't find it, and we're scheduled to leave later this evening."

The mayor looked up at the blackened sky. "I don't think any planes will be leaving tonight in this storm."

Yi could see Sarah's spirits start to plummet at the realization that she might miss the judicial training class in the morning. "Then we'll be on the first flight tomorrow morning."

"It's a pity you must leave so soon. I was hoping to learn more about your investigation . . . ah, I mean research . . . Sarah was telling me about."

Yi looked at Sarah, puzzled.

"Yes," Sarah interjected quickly, "I was telling the mayor about your research on the economic advantages of luxury resorts such as the one here in Sanya."

Yi nodded his head in understanding. "That's right, mayor," he said with a smile. "I'm from the administrative offices in Guangdong Province. We're considering a similar resort area on an island near Shantou."

"You're from the administrative offices in Guangzhou?" the mayor asked, raising his eyebrows. "Then you must know my dear friend, the senior judge, Mr. Tan Yang."

Hearing the name sent a chill through Yi.

"Yes," Yi replied with a smile. "I'll tell him you said hello."

Before the mayor could continue the conversation, Yi and Sarah ran for the hotel as rain began to pour.

CHAPTER 31

"Sarah, I'm sorry the flights back to the mainland were cancelled last night. We'll get you on the first flight this morning. You'll be back in Beijing by early afternoon, I promise."

He waited for a response from her, but none came.

"I'm afraid I will have to stay here a while longer, however," he added. She only nodded.

"May I ask a favor of you?" he asked hesitantly, worried at how Sarah had taken the truth about his background. She had immediately gone to her room upon their return yesterday and had been quiet all during breakfast.

"I suppose so," she answered, staring at her untouched food.

Yi realized he first needed to address the tension that had developed between them. He spoke as tenderly as he could. "Sarah, I apologize if I've offended you or hurt you in some way. I would never intentionally do anything that would cause you pain."

"Except lie to me," she answered as she pushed food around her dish, not wanting to look at him.

"I have been as honest with you as I possibly could—even to the point of jeopardizing my assignment here."

"But how much more about you is a deception, Yi? Is that even your real name?"

"Yes, it's my real name, and you know me. All the things we've talked about at the Judicial College, and here, everything we've shared together, have been real. I've not misled you in that way." Yi thought for a moment then continued, hoping she might see some humor in the situation. "Except maybe regarding my knowledge of American law. I have to tell you, Sarah, sitting through those boring introductory American law and basic legal English classes, having to pretend I didn't know anything, was really unbearable."

Yi could see the corners of Sarah's mouth start to turn up.

Then he added with honest sincerity, "The only thing that brightened up the days for me was being with you."

Finally Sarah looked at him and smiled. The tiny dimple Yi loved appeared in her cheek.

"I can imagine sitting through those classes would be pretty awful for an American attorney." Building on the humor she added, "And I have to say I am relieved to know you're no longer my competition."

They both laughed.

"That's for sure. I've been through enough legal training," Yi said.

"So, where did you go to law school?" she asked.

"Georgetown University in Washington DC."

She shook her head in wonder. "I feel I know nothing about you, Yi."

"I assure you that you do. You're only missing a few of the early details—like I passed the bar exam four years ago and have worked for a US senator since that time. My legal expertise is in international law and, of course, my specialty is US-Sino relations." He then added with emphasis, "And I firmly believe in this program, Sarah. I want to see China blossom into a world power. And if my coming here to help stop corruption is required for that to happen, then I'm willing to pay the price."

Sarah nodded in understanding.

"Do you have a family back in the States?" she asked, afraid of the answer Yi might give her.

"You mean, am I married? No, of course not. If I've conveyed nothing else, Sarah, I hope you know I'm a man of principle."

"Yes, absolutely, Yi," Sarah nodded. "I'm sorry. I guess I'm just really confused right now."

Sarah looked at her watch. "You can imagine I have a hundred questions for you . . . but I wonder what the favor is you wanted to ask me."

"Yes . . . the favor." Yi seemed to be searching for the right words. "When you return to the judicial training program today, I need to ask you to please keep my background and this trip to Hainan a secret."

Sarah chuckled sadly to herself at the paradox of the situation. "I'm not going back to the program, Yi. At least not just yet," she replied. "I leave for Tibet in a few hours."

Yi's jaw dropped. "But what about the training program? The scholarship?"

Sarah had to work hard to keep her emotions in check. "I don't know anymore, Yi. I don't know whether I want to go to America. I don't even know if I want to serve as a judge here in Hainan. Either place will bring painful memories . . . I just need a little time to think things through."

"Oh, Sarah, that is not how I wanted this weekend to turn out. I'm so sorry," Yi said, looking down at his hands.

"No, Yi, I'm okay with this." Sarah tried to sound cheerful. "I understand the importance of your work here, and I admire you for it. Anyway, it's for the best. I've decided to visit my family in Tibet. It's been a long time, and they are eager to see me. Then if I decide to return to the Judges College, I'll fly back to Beijing Sunday evening."

She reached over and squeezed Yi's hand. "Of course, I will keep your secret."

Realizing for the first time that she may never see him again, she added, "Does this mean you're going back to America soon?"

"No. I need to complete my report here. And until a strategy can be developed on how the United States will deal with this situation, my bosses will probably want me to stay and observe."

For the first time, there was an awkward silence between them.

"I don't know what to say," Sarah made an attempt to smile and then shrugged her shoulders.

"Sarah, don't give up on the judicial training program," Yi begged. "Promise me you'll reconsider."

Looking at her watch again, she said, "I had better leave for the airport soon."

"Would you mind if I rode out there with you?"

The tiny dimple reappeared in her cheek as she smiled. "I would like that."

At the airport, Yi helped Sarah check her bags then walked with her to the gate. He took her in his arms and kissed her.

"I want you to know I would give anything to see you in Beijing before I return to the States. Will you call me and let me know what you decide?" he asked.

"I won't have good phone reception in the mountains, but I'll call you from Beijing if I decide to go back."

"I'll be expecting your call," he said, kissing her on the forehead.

"Please be careful here, Yi."

After handing the attendant her boarding pass, Sarah glanced back at Yi, smiled, and waved good-bye.

With a big grin he called to her, "Tell your family hello for me!"

She smiled even bigger as she turned to board the plane.

***

Sarah's untimely departure and the realization that she might drop from the judicial training program weighed on Yi's mind. As a result, it took him all afternoon to prepare his report for Trenton Woodbury. He needed to be prudent in his selection of words because of Internet monitoring, yet he had to be specific enough to convey the essential information. As he had been instructed in his undercover training, for security reasons he would need to divide the report into pieces and send them in separate e-mails. He would have to do the same with the pictures.

Yi was eager to get the report sent off so Woodbury's office could research the full extent of the Hainan Net's operations. No doubt Woodbury would have his intelligence officers translate the manual and computer screens from the pictures Yi had taken as well as gather other intelligence on the group—if they didn't have something already. Yi hoped it wouldn't take too long for them to provide a detailed explanation and, more importantly, to advise him what the United States or China planned to do about it.

After he got the initial information sent, he also sent his compiled list of titles of officials suspected of corruption activities.

That will keep the CIA busy for a while.

CHAPTER 32

"Good morning, Mayor Bao, may I help you?" the hotel clerk said when she looked up from her work at the reception desk.

"Yes, good morning. There was a businessman by the name of Yi staying here doing research on luxury resorts. I met him a couple of days ago, but I didn't catch his full name. I was hoping you could give it to me."

"Of course, let me look," she said as she began scanning the hotel registry. "Yes, here it is. His name is Yi Jichun. From Guangzhou. He's staying in room 210. Would you like me to ring him for you?"

"Oh, no, no. That isn't necessary." *So, they didn't leave after all,* the mayor mused. As an afterthought he added, "And the woman with him, Sarah . . . Decker, I believe is her name. Is she in the same room?"

Once again the clerk began to scan the registry.

"No, sir. She was in room 208."

"What do you mean *was*?" Bao responded.

"She checked out yesterday," the clerk replied.

"Oh, I'm disappointed to hear that. But Mr. Yi is still here?" the mayor asked.

The clerk nodded. "Yes, it appears so."

"Thank you for your help, Miss . . . Guo," the mayor said, looking at her name tag. He then left the hotel lobby.

Once outside, he took out his cell phone and dialed the office number of Tan Yang, his friend from the Guangzhou Administrative Courts.

"Good morning, this is Mayor Bao from Sanya," he said to the secretary on the line. "I would like to speak with Mr. Tan Yang."

"Good morning, sir. Mr. Tan is out of the office for several months. He is in Beijing for judicial training," the secretary informed him.

"Oh, yes, of course." Bao nodded.

"Would you like me to telephone him for you?" the secretary offered.

"No, that won't be necessary. I have his cell phone number. I'll telephone him directly. Thank you," Bao replied.

"You're welcome, sir. Have a nice day," the secretary said before ending the call.

The mayor dialed Tan Yang's cell phone. After a few rings, Tan Yang answered.

"Well, well, Tan, how's Beijing this time of year? Certainly not as nice as Sanya!" the mayor gloated.

"Mayor Bao, this is a surprise. To what do I owe a phone call from you?"

"I had the pleasure of meeting someone here this week from your administrative offices," Bao replied as if he had a juicy piece of information.

"I'm not aware of anyone from my office having business in Sanya," Yang replied, sounding a bit annoyed. "Who was it?"

"A gentleman by the name of Yi Jichun."

"Yi?" Tan Yang said, shocked. "What's he doing in Sanya? He's supposed to be at this judicial training."

"Well, he's in Sanya," the mayor said, delighted that he had surprised his friend. "And staying at an expensive hotel, I might add, with a very attractive female friend—a judge who is going to be working in my court after she finishes training."

"She wouldn't happen to be Tibetan by chance, would she?" Tan Yang asked with a smirk.

"Tibetan? Yes, I believe so," the mayor responded. "She stopped by my office a few days ago and introduced herself. She told me she was here helping Yi investigate luxury resorts for a development in Shantou."

"What? That's a lie!" Tan Yang shouted into the phone. "He has nothing to do with the city of Shantou!" Tan Yang was silent for a moment as if trying to figure out what Yi could be doing in Sanya. He then continued. "He can't be trusted, Bao. I think he's lying about who he is and his background. He says he graduated from Tsinghua University and worked in the Haidian Court, but no one there remembers him. I've done a background check on him. Things don't add up."

"What about the girl who was with him?" the mayor asked.

"I wouldn't trust her, either. She's a fanatic about the American propaganda that the law must be supreme—totally disregarding our traditional ways. I tell you, Bao, you'd better watch both of them. They're up to something, and you better find out what it is."

"I'll keep an eye on him, but the girl checked out of the hotel yesterday," the mayor said.

"That's even better," Tan Yang replied.

A smile started to form on his face as an idea came to him. *If she's heading back to Beijing, I can make her tell me what they were doing in Sanya.*

CHAPTER 33

Yi printed out the five e-mails he received from Trenton Woodbury. The first three confirmed Yi's suspicions of the Hainan Net's operations. Woodbury wrote:

> The pictures validate the allegations in your report of planned attacks against American interests, most specifically targeting the Panama Canal and US seaports. Of great concern at this point, however, is the Hainan Net's operations center itself. According to your picture of the interior door, the Arabic characters indicate a biochemical laboratory on the premises. Without knowing exactly what chemicals are being developed there, we are limited in our options for how to deal with them. As for the web page with the unusual symbol, it appears to be a recruiting tool. From what we've compiled so far, and in combination with other intelligence reports we are now able to link to this group, the Hainan Net has major international connections and threat potential. Strategic planning and diplomatic arrangements are underway. I would advise you to leave the area as soon as possible.

The remaining e-mails dealt with Yi's list of corrupt officials. Woodbury wrote:

> I've personally delivered your list to the director of the CIA. He is scheduled to meet with his counterpart at the Chinese embassy. He will instigate thorough investigations. As you have requested, these will be deemed allegations only unless substantial evidence is obtained.

Because of the potential danger to you as the source of these reports, it is advised that you discontinue involvement in the judicial training program and return to the United States immediately.

Yi hurriedly keyed in his response:

I recognize the danger and appreciate your advice. However, if possible, sir, I believe it would be beneficial for me to stay and observe activities here in Sanya. If things heat up, I'll leave immediately, although I won't return to the States just yet. There's someone I hope to see in Beijing before I leave China.

CHAPTER 34

"This meeting has been called, gentlemen," US President Stephen Bradshaw began as he stood in the briefing room located behind the Oval Office, "to address a potentially serious national security threat to the United States and to international shipping through the Panama Canal—a threat which, according to this report, has been pinpointed as having its central operations on an island in the South China Sea." He held up a beige folder stamped with red letters: *HAINAN NET—CLASSIFIED*.

The president leaned his towering frame over the edge of the conference table, his hands pressed upon the polished mahogany surface. He peered around the table at the people he relied on most. They were expected to provide the answers he needed.

"You've all read the report," he said. "Now I want to know how we're going to handle this."

The resolute looks from each of his advisors assured him that they would deal swiftly and efficiently with the problem at hand.

"Let me start by saying that if this report is true, the uncovering of this Hainan Net is a major step in our antiterrorism efforts," Nathan Greenwald, antiterrorism task force director, spoke first. "We've received unsubstantiated telephone dialogue of suspected activity in that general area, but no concrete evidence existed until now. In fact, I had requested Colonel Stringer, our military attaché in Beijing, to look into this matter. Unfortunately, as you know, gentlemen, he was tragically killed in the airline crash off the northern coast of Hainan."

National Security Agency director Clark Mathews added, "A crash that this field agent who discovered the Hainan Net has indicated was a direct attack on Americans by one of the Net's pilots." He turned to the president then further stated, "And, it will be the first of many such planned attacks if we don't stop them."

"We don't have proof of that," Defense Secretary Warren Stricklan said, shaking his head. "China's investigation determined the crash was caused by a malfunction in the aircraft. It was a tragic accident in which the United States lost many of its high-level embassy staff and their families. We can't rely upon mere speculation by this field agent that the crash was linked to this Hainan group."

"We're dealing with more than mere speculation here," Mathews argued. "While the Chinese government may have ruled the airline crash an accident, they also verified that one of the pilots had been switched at the last minute for no apparent reason—and that he was Afghani, which fits with the Hainan Net's recruiting website, according to this report. That suggests a strong probability that the crash was terrorist related."

"I still don't see the connection," Stricklan replied. "If this crash was more than an accident, it could very well be repercussions for our botched NATO bombing in Belgrade. Hitting the Chinese embassy in error was a huge blunder. Although it's been two years and we've paid a ton of money in reparations, the Chinese people could still be harboring ill feelings toward the United States. Think about it: this crash resulted in a loss primarily of our own embassy people. We can't assume a link to this Hainan Net."

"I concur, Mr. President." Air Force General Mitchell Waldron, chairman of the Joint Chiefs of Staff, nodded. "And while the evidence seems to be irrefutable indicating a terrorist cell is operating in an island cave off Hainan, I'm still skeptical about the scope of this network's reach. We've flown routine reconnaissance flights over the South China Sea for some time now and have only detected sporadic communications signals—most of which are linked to fishing vessels in the area. This cell may be an isolated group."

"I would hardly call a Chinese sampan a fishing vessel, Mitch," Army General Frank Jankowski stated with a chuckle. "If the field agent's report is accurate—and for all intents and purposes it appears to be so—

then your high-tech reconnaissance aircraft have been outmaneuvered by a bunch of peasant fishermen. It's quite ingenious that this network thought to use them as short-range signaling devices."

President Bradshaw held up his hand as if to say "enough" then turned to the director of the Central Intelligence Agency and asked, "Mark, as convincing as this report is, what's the possibility that it's wrong?"

Mark Stanton removed his reading glasses and looked up from his notes. "Incredible as it may seem, Mr. President, all the intelligence we've gathered in this regard and the research we've done on the pictures as evidence support the claim that the Hainan Net is a valid terrorist threat, and it is growing."

"Then let's have a consensus on that point and move toward a strategic plan of attack," the president said as he sat down in the upholstered chair at the head of the table. "And remember, gentlemen, whatever you propose, I've got to convince China to play along."

Stanton nodded. "We need to take this group out quickly and do it while maintaining a high level of secrecy, or else we'll drive other terrorist cells further underground."

General Jankowski shook his head. "We need time to plan this. Our military focus up till now has simply been one-dimensional, and that's not going to provide us a good strategic position here. This whole thing has developed into a bigger, much more dangerous operation than we could have possibly anticipated, and we've got to get a handle on it before we go charging in. In case you've forgotten, besides the sensitive diplomatic element, we could be dealing with unknown biochemical weapons. I think we need a more thorough investigation before proceeding any further."

"No, I agree with Mark," Marine Corps General Edward Traynor interjected. "We've got to move as quickly as possible before this threat escalates. Terrorist cells have been recruiting throughout the Middle East, North Africa, and East Asia for years now. And those are just the areas we have confirmed. I suspect this network's reach goes worldwide."

"Come on. You know current extremists have no purpose except destroying the status quo," Secretary of State Tyler Jameson exclaimed. "How much of a threat can they be? They're fragmented and underfunded. Unlike the Islamic militancy of the 1930s and 1970s, these groups have nothing to back up their actions. They don't know or care about true Islamic history, morals, or even the history of their own countries. They simply want to create chaos and destruction."

Admiral Jeremiah Moser cleared his throat and spoke in his smooth, southern drawl. "I say we land a plane of Special Ops in there and . . ."

"Their radar tracking system would prevent us from landing with a planeload of soldiers," interrupted General Jankowski. "We would lose the element of surprise. And I doubt China would go along with it."

"Times have changed, Frank," Irving Maxwell, head of the CIA's directorate of operations and manager of their counterterrorism center and espionage/paramilitary operations, stated. "Beijing is sharing intelligence like never before. They've cooperated with us on providing information about terrorist training camps in Afghanistan. Granted, it's outdated information, but it's a show of good faith. I wouldn't jump the gun by assuming they won't go along."

"Well, we're still a long way from getting their approval and cooperation on an invasion," General Jankowski replied.

"I agree. Any strategy we come up with to take out this Hainan Net is going to require full cooperation from China, which over the past two years hasn't exactly been the best," the vice president interjected. "We're going to have to go in with kid gloves on for this one."

"I believe they would not only have to agree on whatever plan we suggest," Mathews stated, "but also participate in order for us to succeed in dissolving the Net. I mean, we're talking United States military forces flying into hostile airspace and landing in a Communist country, for heaven's sake! If it's not believable, we lose the element of surprise."

General Waldron shook his head. "Clark, we'd be opening up a can of worms if we involved China's military in this. It would be a logistical nightmare. We have the capability to do this on our own."

"I don't know, Mitchell," Admiral Moser replied. "We run a high risk of having our aircraft shot down if we enter China's airspace without their authorization. You know that. And the Chinese government would have inspectors and soldiers all over one of our planes the minute it set down. I don't see how we could do this without Chinese military cooperation."

President Bradshaw nodded then looked around the room. "What are you proposing, gentlemen?" he asked.

General Jankowski was the first to respond. "Mr. President, I think the only believable way for a US military plane to land on Hainan

Island, even with China's approval, would be if the aircraft were in distress—a forced landing after a mayday signal."

"Yes, that's an excellent point," General Traynor remarked. "We also need to consider the type of plane we would use. If, out of the clear blue, a US military transport showed up in China's airspace, anyone tracking it on radar would be suspicious. I think the only aircraft capable of slipping in over China and pulling off something like this would be a surveillance plane. They routinely show up in international airspace near there. It would have to appear that one of our surveillance planes somehow developed mechanical trouble or became distressed in some way and then entered China's airspace in order to land at the first possible airfield."

The room was silent for a moment as everyone mulled over the plausibility of what had been proposed.

General Traynor then continued. "And I too believe some Chinese military would have to be present when the plane landed in order for the situation to be believable."

General Waldron nodded in agreement. "You're right. Even with government permission to land, China would definitely require that they have military there—if for no other reason than observation. They're not going to let us set down sophisticated military equipment so close to their mainland without having soldiers and possibly inspectors present."

"That raises an important point," President Bradshaw interjected, leaning back in his chair and clasping his hands behind his neck. "Are we willing to risk China confiscating our aircraft if we were to land there? It could give them access to highly classified information and technology."

The room was silent again as the men contemplated the risks.

"General Waldron," Maxwell said, breaking the silence. "What types of surveillance aircraft have we flown in that area recently?"

"The navy's EP-3E Aries II surveillance aircraft routinely conduct electronic reconnaissance missions within the international airspace along the South China Sea," the general replied.

"Do we have any of those aircraft located near South China at this time?" Maxwell asked.

"Yes," the general answered. "They fly out of Kadena Air Base in Okinawa, Japan."

"And can the EP-3E Aries II surveillance aircraft hold more than its flight crew?" Maxwell continued his questioning.

General Waldron turned toward Admiral Moser who then answered the question. "Yes, in addition to the flight crew, the EP-3E can easily hold twenty soldiers in full gear."

"There ya go," Maxwell stated with a wave of his hand. "That's enough space for twenty Navy SEALs, who could easily take out the Hainan Net. The key question then is how can we stage a situation of distress in the air that would be recognizable by radar?"

General Waldron smiled confidently then explained, "Our surveillance flight crews in their missions over the South China Sea have spoken of a hotshot Chinese fighter pilot in an F-8 interceptor who regularly interferes with their flight path. He's clipped their wings on more than a few occasions."

Maxwell nodded enthusiastically. "So if we could get China to agree to have their pilot stage a wing clipping, it would look like a midair collision on radar and our EP-3E Aries II could issue a mayday, requesting permission to land. That's excellent, general."

"Are you serious?" Defense Secretary Stricklan clamored, looking skeptically at both Waldron and Maxwell. "You're suggesting that in order for this to be successful, the United States needs to negotiate a strategy with Communist China to fly into their airspace, have their air force launch some of their fully armed F-8 interceptor fighter jets, hopefully with clear instructions not to shoot, and maneuver a midair collision— not sufficient to damage the aircrafts, but enough to make it look good on radar—so our aircraft could then land at Hainan's military airfield?"

"Yes, I believe that is the general idea," Waldron replied matter-of-factly.

The vice president looked at General Waldron for clarification. "And after the staged midair collision, you're saying we need China's military to render what would appear to be a hostile takeover of our plane once it lands?" He, like Stricklan, wasn't sure if he had heard correctly.

"That's right," the general affirmed. "And the downed EP-3E Aries II would be fully equipped with the instruments necessary to extract critical Hainan Net operations information without detection. For example, in addition to the SIGINT system, the aircraft could be equipped with acoustic recording and analysis equipment, chemical analyzers, optical and electro-optical cameras, and multisensoring devices."

"Let's not forget that sending one of our highly advanced surveillance planes would be like handing China the blueprints. We risk them acquiring our latest and most advanced technology and intelligence information. I'll ask again, are we willing to take that risk?" President Bradshaw asked.

"We minimize the risk in that the aircraft won't really be in distress," General Jankowski remarked, fully supporting Waldron's plan. "The flight crew would remain onboard, and if Chinese soldiers start behaving like they have other plans, the flight crew would simply launch the aircraft."

"And leave the Navy SEALs?" General Traynor asked with concern in his voice.

"And what about hostages?" Admiral Moser asked.

"We can arrange diplomatic passage for our soldiers. I don't see a problem with the Chinese government holding the hostages until the rest of our operations can be carried out—it buys us some time," General Jankowski suggested.

"And after we dissolve the Hainan Net?" Jameson asked, wanting to clarify the rest of the plan.

General Waldron answered, "The Joint Chiefs of Staff will arrange for their respective military forces to implement the next phase of the operation—the activation of military units at other locations identified in the report—Thailand, the Philippines, Afghanistan, Colombia, and so forth."

"I hate to ask this, but someone has to . . . What if we fail?" Stricklan asked. "We've got to have some alternate plans in place before we go forward with this. Do you realize the potential for devastation if we fail in Hainan and these terrorists carry out their planned attacks? We are not prepared to handle attacks on our US seaports, let alone the Panama Canal."

"We wouldn't be able to get this under control if they were to move out to the open seas," Admiral Moser remarked. "The world's commercial shipping industry is so full of corruption, we couldn't begin to track the number of ships a terrorist network could have in operation—they illegally change their ships' names and repaint them on a regular basis, and nine out of ten crew members have fake identification papers."

"All the more reason why this operation has to succeed," the president stated in earnest.

Stanton nodded in agreement then said matter-of-factly, "For that reason, I believe the CIA's directorate of operations should handle this. It falls within our jurisdiction."

"It seems to me," Mathews retorted, "if the CIA had handled their intelligence properly to begin with, we would have known about this Hainan Net group before a hotshot attorney doubling as a field agent walked in and took pictures. According to his report, a good portion of his information came from a Chinese peasant woman who had tried to make contact with us on at least two occasions. What I want to know is, how come we didn't already know about this? Where were the CIA's guys on this in Beijing anyway, Mark?"

"Hey, come on, Clark. Given the loss of so many of our embassy staff in the plane crash, I think that's uncalled for," Stanton replied.

"He's got a point, though," Jameson added. "We all know the CIA's main model is still to have agents pose as diplomats and spot potential marks at cocktail parties. Well," he added with a chuckle, "these terrorist groups don't hang out at cocktail parties."

"Neither do Chinese peasant women," General Jankowski said with a snicker. "We're definitely out of touch on this one."

"What we need is a covert action," Maxwell interjected. "I suggest a secret attack, preferably on a day when there would be the least amount of activity . . . say, on a Sunday." He then turned to a calendar page in his notebook. "Looking at the calendar, realistically, I would suggest we plan to attack on . . . Sunday, April 1."

Several chuckles emanated around the room.

"April Fool's Day?" General Traynor chortled. "How appropriate would that be? Those fools won't know what hit 'em! I think it's a great idea—Operation April Fool's."

"That certainly gives us a little more time," Admiral Moser stated in a more serious tone. "I agree with Irv that hitting them a week from this Sunday is ideal."

"Well, whenever it's carried out," Jameson remarked, "the CIA's director of Central Intelligence is required to notify the Congressional Intelligence Oversight Committee. The finding documents that would outline the scope and justification of the action would have to be completed. You know it has to be submitted to Congress within forty-eight hours."

"Wait a minute," Stricklan said. "This requires military invasion. Therefore, it is not a covert action but a clandestine one. The public would need to know about it."

"I disagree," Jameson said. "Bringing the public in on this could further jeopardize US-Sino relations. No matter what the outcome, it wouldn't look good for either side. China's public is still angry with the US after the bombing on their embassy. They would view this as another example of Americans trying to be the world police. And the rest of the world would view China as weak and ineffective if the United States had to locate and clean up a terrorist cell that China should have known about and taken care of on its own. Under these circumstances, and according to Executive Order 12333, special foreign activities in which the role of the United States government is not apparent or acknowledged publicly must be classified as covert."

The tension level in the room eased as the meeting began to draw to a close. Everyone seemed pleased and confident about the decisions that had been made.

"Well, Mark," President Bradshaw said, exhaling deeply, "you'd better get the CIA moving on those finding documents. We're running out of time to get this through Congress. In the meantime, I'll contact China's president and start working on getting their agreement and cooperation." The president then stood to shake the hands of his trusted advisors.

"Do we wait for China's concurrence?" Mathews asked as he pushed back his chair. "What if we don't get it?"

"I say we go in anyway," General Jankowski said.

"Let's hope it doesn't come to that," President Bradshaw said, patting Mathews on the back.

"I and the directors of the joint staff will begin making the arrangements for the Navy SEALs Special Forces commandos and the EP-3E Aries II aircraft and flight crew out of Kadena," General Waldron stated as he shook the president's hand. "I also think we'd better involve the Defense Threat Reduction Agency at Yokota Air Base. We'll need their expertise in handling whatever biochemical weapons we find in Hainan."

The president nodded in agreement.

General Waldron turned to Jameson as they moved toward the conference room exit. "For what it's worth, Tyler, I agree we've got to keep this out of the public eye."

"That's impossible," Stricklan replied, overhearing General Waldron's comment. "The media's going to find out about this."

"Then we'll just have to spin it," President Bradshaw replied as they exited the room.

***

In a highly secured conference call to China's president and foreign minister, President Bradshaw carefully outlined the problem of a foreign terrorist cell targeting Americans and operating from an undisclosed location in China.

"As you are aware," came the response, "China is also a victim of terrorism and greatly sympathizes with America. We have long struggled with separatists in Xinjiang Province, the Uyghur people, and the East Turkestan Chinese, who are trying to split land away from our motherland of China."

"Then you understand our desire to quickly remove this threat," affirmed the US president.

"Of course. We can assure you that we will act swiftly to remove this cancer from among us, if you provide us the location and details of your facts. Surely you can understand our desire to verify this information. Additionally, if it is determined that our Chinese people, including any of our minorities, have been involved, we would wish to deal with them in our own way."

"In this case, however," President Bradshaw countered, "our sources have verified that this is a foreign faction operating with foreign funds. Because time is of the essence, the United States proposes a joint military cooperative to handle this situation in a discreet and judicious manner."

He then proceeded to outline the details of Operation April Fool's.

There was silence on the line for quite a while before the response. "This US-Sino strategic military cooperative you propose is acceptable to the People's Republic of China on three conditions: first, we must be assured the United States will not act in a hostile way toward China, its sovereignties, or embassies. The loss of our embassy workers in Belgrade is not so easily forgotten. Second, the United States must abide by our One-China policy and cease selling advanced weapons to Taiwan. And third, the United States must also agree to turn over to the government of the People's Republic of China any Chinese persons involved with this terrorist group, including officials who have given access to Chinese land, Chinese minorities who are connected with this foreign faction, or any who have fought or been trained in Afghanistan camps. Many of China's Uyghur minorities who fight to break away from China have gone to Afghanistan for terrorist training and have trained others upon their return. It is imperative that we stop this influx of trained terrorists."

President Bradshaw responded. "I assure you that during this joint military cooperation, the United States will not demonstrate any hostility toward China or its military, so long as China abides by the terms of this agreement. I cannot, however, assure you of the cessation of weapons sales to Taiwan, although I will agree that we will deny Taiwan their request for our most advanced systems—the Aegis and Patriot-3. As for your third stipulation, we will readily turn over any Chinese individuals involved in this terrorist network."

More silence.

"Then we agree," China replied.

"So it is agreed," President Bradshaw reiterated, "that at the designated time and place, China will authorize access to its airspace and specified land area and assist the United States military in staging a surprise attack to be carried out by US special forces under US military direction to eliminate this foreign terrorist group. Hostages, except those identified as Chinese, will be under the jurisdiction of the United States government. Any and all Chinese persons involved will be turned over to the People's Republic of China for appropriate action."

"That is correct."

"May I say," China's foreign minister interjected, "that I see this joint cooperative as a possible way to reestablish high-level military-to-military discussions with the United States. However, I must emphasize the importance of the United States adhering to our request of no hostility toward China, adhering to the One-China policy, and of returning to us any Chinese people affiliated with terrorist groups so they would face China's punishment. It is our desire to crush these separatists because our campaigns to reeducate those who openly advocate separatism have not been successful."

"In that regard you have my assurance," President Bradshaw replied.

The foreign minister continued. "Despite our past differences, it is our duty to assist in the world's fight against terrorism. By doing so, we may be able to move toward reestablishing closer ties with the West. A strong Sino-US relationship has been an important goal for China's president, who will soon step down. It is his personal desire to have his presidency end showing cooperation with the United States and a united force against world terrorism."

"I commend you for your efforts," President Bradshaw said. With one last item to discuss, he added, "There is one other area of concern to the United States, and that is how this incident will be reported in China's news. If the information becomes public too soon, we will be unable to execute surprise attacks on the other foreign locations affiliated with this terrorist network."

China's president chuckled. "Unlike the United States, we control our media. It is not a problem here. We will wait until we receive your prepared statement before we report the incident. And so long as your statement does not conflict with our own policies, we will report it as you wish."

"Thank you. I will have my secretary of state draft a statement."

CHAPTER 35

Yi logged on to his e-mail. Trenton Woodbury had finally responded to his request to stay in Sanya:

> *Continual surveillance and reporting is critical to the success of this operation. In particular, exact locations of all the cave's entrances are needed. Because of the unidentified biochemical weapons being housed there, an attack must be through existing entries. Blasting cannot occur until the chemicals are analyzed and properly secured. Your effort in identifying those locations is greatly appreciated. However, your safety is also our concern, and you should avoid any direct contact or suspicious action that could jeopardize your cover. I will advise you when to vacate the area.*

What action? Yi thought with disappointment. He had made a few trips downtown to investigate the business records of the Li-ren Culture Village, and he had uncovered several questionable and very large banking transactions with foreign banks, but other than that, his investigation had stalled.

He spent most of his time hiking on Wild Boar Island, looking for the above-ground entrance, and scuba diving—primarily to avoid Mayor Bao. And to take his mind off Sarah.

It had been a full week since she left. Optimistic that she had returned to Beijing, Yi sent a text message to her phone: "Welcome back! Please call me."

A call would mean she had returned to the judicial training program. Better yet, it would mean she had forgiven him.

But there had been no phone call from her, and his guilt and sadness only intensified. It would be his fault if she quit the program. Plus, he genuinely missed her.

Maybe she's back in Beijing and preoccupied with catching up on her studies. Knowing Sarah, that explanation made a lot of sense.

Yi decided to call her. At a few minutes past eight o'clock in the evening, he speed-dialed her cell phone. Much to his dismay, there was no answer.

CHAPTER 36

Tan Yang's anger had been building over the course of the week. Bao had said Sarah left Hainan on Tuesday, March 20, so Tan Yang had expected her back in Beijing a day or two later. When she still hadn't arrived by Saturday, he was furious. He knew Yi was up to something. And the only chance he had of finding out what that was, was through Sarah. His anger turned to rage as he stewed over the weekend, worrying that Yi was out to destroy him. He spent Sunday drinking liquor to dull the voices in his head. By Monday morning, he didn't trust his own eyes when Sarah suddenly appeared in class.

Later that evening he watched for her to leave her dormitory alone to study in the law library. He watched and waited from inside the dark alley behind the college cafeteria. As she passed, he grabbed her from behind, forced his hand over her mouth, and carried her into the back alley behind the cafeteria's kitchen. Open garbage bins were piled high with the smelly discards of the day's meals, and the ground was wet from buckets of waste water thrown out during cleanup.

Clutching her by one arm, Tan Yang backhanded Sarah across her face, splitting the corner of her lower lip with his gold ring.

"I want to know where you were last week," he seethed through clenched teeth, the reek of alcohol on his breath.

"I wasn't aware that you were my keeper," she replied with sarcasm, trying not to show the fear she suddenly felt as she wiped the blood from her lip.

He held up his hand, threatening to hit her a second time. "Try again," he smirked.

She put her hand to her jaw to regain her composure. "I was visiting my family in Tibet."

"I want to know what you and your friend, Yi, were doing in Sanya."

Sarah remained silent.

"What were you doing in Sanya?" he screamed, no longer caring if he could be heard by anyone passing the alley.

"Nothing, Tan Yang," she said softly, hoping to calm him down. "We just wanted a quiet weekend together . . . before the judicial training is over."

"Then why did you lie to the mayor?"

Sarah was confused. She didn't know what to say. How could Tan Yang know what she had told Mayor Bao?

"Who is Yi Jichun?" he yelled as he grabbed her by the throat, the increasing rage now spilling out uncontrolled.

"I don't know what you mean," Sarah pleaded, struggling to pry his hands off her neck. "He said he was . . . a judge . . . from Guangzhou. I don't know anymore—" she choked.

Tan Yang let go of his grip and struck her again. "He's not who he says he is, and you know it. Tell me!"

Sarah covered her face with her hands. She could feel the swelling around her cheeks and eyes. It would be difficult to see soon. She knew the only way to break free from Tan Yang in his drunken and enraged state would be to strike back. Reasoning, even lying, would be a waste of precious time. Bringing her knee up in a swift jerk, she struck him in the groin. He immediately let go of her, doubling over in pain.

She ran. If she could make it to the entrance of the alley, she was sure she could get someone's attention. Hopefully students would still be walking around campus.

"Help me!" she tried to shout out, but the pain in her throat stifled her voice.

The sound of shoes running behind her made her heart race even more. Then, a yank on her long hair snapped her head back and brought her to a halt.

"No!" she cried.

Tan Yang reached into his jacket pocket, took out a small handgun, and stuck the end of the barrel up under her chin. The defiant look on Sarah's swollen face told him that she was not going to say anything more.

"Tell me or you die!"

She knew he would kill her. Seeing no alternative, she broke down.

"He's an attorney," she began to sob.

"I don't believe you! Stop lying," Tan Yang screamed. He waved the gun in Sarah's face.

"From America," she turned her head and added in a whisper, hoping the words would go unheard.

Tan Yang staggered as the meaning penetrated his drunken mind.

"He's a spy?" Tan Yang sputtered. His rage grew even deeper. "I knew it!" he spewed out while shoving Sarah against the wall.

Sarah fell hard. The back of her head hit the brick ledge that extended out from the side of the building. Blood began to ooze through her hair, forming a puddle as she lay on the ground, unconscious.

Tan Yang stared down at the spreading darkness. He hadn't intended to kill her. The gun he brought to scare her wasn't even loaded. He only wanted information. Why had she been so stubborn? This was all her fault. Hers and Yi's. Tan Yang was not going to ruin his career or his life over their foolishness. Without even a second glance down at her prone body, he turned and ran.

At a few minutes past eight o'clock, the musical jingle of her cell phone sounded faintly from the pocket of Sarah's crumpled jacket.

***

Tan Yang ran until the burning in his throat and chest overshadowed the pain in his leg muscles. He had never run so hard or for so long in his life. Scared and gasping for breath, he needed to talk to someone. He telephoned Mayor Bao.

"Bao, the situation . . . is worse . . . than anticipated," he said, trying to catch his breath. "Yi's . . . an American spy."

"A spy? Are you sure?" Bao asked in disbelief.

"Yes, the Tibetan girl told me," Tan Yang breathed deeply.

"Well, that explains why they lied." Bao thought for a moment. "What are we going to do?"

"I don't know," Tan Yang muttered. "And what's worse . . . I think I may have killed her."

"What?" Bao shouted into the phone. "How could you be so stupid?"

"It was an accident, Bao. She fell and hit her head while I was questioning her."

"And you never touched her?" Bao asked accusatorily.

Tan Yang was silent for a moment as he began to fully realize what he had done. "She lied to me. I'm afraid I lost control." He began to whimper as his emotions overcame him.

"Then I suggest you leave Beijing immediately," Bao replied, hoping his name wouldn't be linked with Tan Yang's.

***

Afer disconnecting the call with Tan Yang, Bao keyed in another number on his cell phone. It rang one time.

"Yes," the voice replied.

"I'm sorry to bother you, my friend, but it seems we may have a bit of a problem here in Sanya."

"I'm listening."

"A man and woman have been snooping around the resort area and Wild Boar Island. He's been out diving several times near the island."

"It's a tourist area, Bao," the Foreigner replied with scorn. "That's what people do at beach resorts."

"They are lying about who they are and what they are doing here. They're supposed to be in Beijing at a training program. And, what's more, my friend, the man's an American spy."

"Are you absolutely sure?"

"Quite sure. I'm afraid the young woman may have sacrificed her life trying to keep his secret."

"You fool! You didn't kill her at the resort, I hope."

"Oh, no, no," the mayor laughed with relief. "I was not the one. It was Tan Yang. He killed her in Beijing."

"She's not American, is she? There would be a thorough investigation."

"No. Tibetan," the mayor replied.

The Foreigner chuckled. "That can easily be passed off." In a more serious tone, he then asked, "What about the American? How much do you think he knows about our operations?"

"Hard to say. But if he knows nothing, why would he lie about why he's here? And why would he stay after the girl left?"

"You tell me, Bao. Those are the kinds of things you're paid to know," the Foreigner said, his voice filled with disdain.

"I'm watching him," the mayor said in his defense.

"Just to be sure, Bao, I'll stop there on my way back from Bangkok. If he's still snooping around, I'll take care of him."

CHAPTER 37

What's the plan? Yi e-mailed Woodbury for the third time. Woodbury's reply was almost immediate:

> *The President has met with the Joint Chiefs of Staff. I'm guessing there may still be some diplomatic elements to iron out. I'll advise you when I know more. In the meantime, the CIA's directorate of operations is moving forward with attack plans. They have asked for clarification on the following details from your report: (1) Exactly how many entrances are there to the cave's center? (2) What are the markings identifying those entrance points? On their maps they are able to determine a close approximation to the underwater entrance, but from the picture you sent, there does not appear to be a distinct marker. (3) Please clarify the dimensions and characteristics of the tunnel into the cave. (4) What are your estimated time frames for locating these targets, particularly at night? Please respond ASAP. Then, Jason, I advise you to leave the area immediately.*

Yi quickly entered his response:

> *(1) According to my source, there are only two entrances—one from the surface of the island, and one underwater. (2) I have been unable, as yet, to pinpoint the above-ground entrance. It apparently has been moved and the original site destroyed. As for the underwater entrance, the tunnel opening is difficult to find. Locating it requires the use of shadows and finding my cut mark on the exterior rock. A foreign*

object or overly unique mark could draw the attention of other divers in this resort area. (3) The diameter of the tunnel at the smallest point is approx. 40 cm. There are 3 sharp turns. Total length approx. 18 m. Swim time approx. 2 min. 18 sec. (4) Based on trained divers with map and marker details, estimated time frame for locating the underwater tunnel without headlamp is approx. 15 minutes. At night with headlamp the time is reduced because shadows are more apparent. Estimated time is approx. 11 minutes.

Yi hit the send button on the computer then leaned back in his chair.

There's no way they'll find it.

***

Two hours later, Yi finished packing his bags. The extra clothing he'd had to purchase for his extended stay required a second suitcase.

As he stood at the hotel counter preparing to pay his bill, his cell phone rang.

Sarah!

Without taking the time to look at the number, he quickly answered, "Hello, Yi here," anticipating the sweet sound of Sarah's voice.

"Jason?" the male caller said.

"Yes," Yi replied, confused by the familiar American voice, since China's standard mobile phones were not allowed to receive international calls.

"Trent Woodbury here. Look, Jason, this call is not secured. I had a heck of a time even getting it authorized. But time is critical. There has been a change of plans."

"Okay, sir," Yi responded, a look of concern spreading over his face.

Woodbury continued. "Stay where you are. We can't afford lengthy search times. The directorate has requested that you be in scuba gear in a small boat above the underwater entrance point no later than 6:30 AM on Sunday, April 1. Do you understand?"

"Yes, sir."

"Be ready to dive as soon as you are approached. You will direct the divers to the tunnel entrance, Jason. Afterward you are to vacate the area immediately. You got that?"

"Not a problem, sir."

"Remember, Jason, once the chemicals in the cave are secured, the area will be destroyed. So get out of there!"

"Got it."

Yi smiled sheepishly at the hotel clerk then picked up his bags and returned to his room.

He speed-dialed Sarah's cell phone. Still no answer.

CHAPTER 38

YALONG BAY RESORT, HAINAN ISLAND
MARCH 30, 2001

The Foreigner arrived in Sanya tired and edgy. He was anxious to wrap up problems and return to Brussels. The organization's quarterly meeting was taking place in just two days, and he had to present a status update. His report was not going to be good news. The port of Laem Chabang was the Net's primary site for cruise ship navigation and crew training. Earlier that year he had stepped up operations there. Unfortunately, one of the explosives engineers had miscalculated his testing, and several of the cruise ships planned for use in the Panama Canal attack had been damaged. The Foreigner had flown to Bangkok to assess the impact and its effect on plans. Clearly, it would put them behind schedule. That information was not going to sit well with the organization directors.

On top of that, he now had to deal with what Mayor Bao believed was a potential threat to the Net's operations center in Hainan. If the mayor's judgment proved wrong, causing the Foreigner to waste time making a special trip to Hainan, someone was going to suffer the consequences.

He checked in at the registration desk of the Yalong Bay Resort, booking a suite for one night. He paid cash and collected the room key. The bellhop carried his only piece of luggage—a black leather hang-up bag.

"Bao," the Foreigner said into his cell phone. "I've just checked in at the resort . . . I'm on my way over to the island now to check on security . . . Yes, we'll see . . . Meet me at the resort restaurant . . . Five o'clock."

The Foreigner took a boat over to Wild Boar Island and hiked up the trail to the lighthouse. No matter how carefully he stepped, he couldn't avoid getting sand in his peccary leather dress shoes and in the cuffs of his expensive suit trousers, which only added to the anger already swelling inside him. He unlocked the security gate, then the lighthouse door, and descended the circular staircase to the operations center.

"Bao called me here to check on a security breach," he said to Abikar, the senior communications specialist sitting in front of the camera monitors.

"I'm not aware of any breach," Abikar remarked.

"No, I didn't think so. But I need to see the footage of two people, a man and a woman, nosing around on the hill about ten days ago," the Foreigner directed.

"Okay," Abikar replied and began scanning the dates.

After a few minutes, he said, "This is probably what you're looking for."

The Foreigner leaned in toward the security monitor for a closer look at the man and woman hiking on the hill. They appeared to be looking for something around the large cluster of rocks and in the scrub brush.

"Probably bird watchers," Abikar commented. "They often go looking for nests."

"Um . . ." the Foreigner mused then shook his head. "Not in a wet suit. He's obviously been diving."

"True," Abikar acknowledged. "The wet suit is unusual."

"They appear to be looking for something, and my guess is it's not bird eggs. Can you zoom in on their faces?" the Foreigner asked.

"Sure." Abikar zoomed in on Sarah.

Impressed by her beauty, the Foreigner remembered what the mayor had told him had been her fate. *Pity*, he thought.

Abikar then zoomed in on Yi. The Foreigner couldn't help but notice the startled look on Abikar's face.

"Is there a problem?" the Foreigner asked.

"About ten days ago this couple came upon our computer setup in the culture village. At the time I thought they were just tourists, but Wahid recognized him from an earlier visit. He thought the guy had taken pictures of his computer screen. He followed him back to his hotel room and confiscated his camera."

"Why didn't he kill him?" the Foreigner clamored.

"Apparently the man was scheduled to be on the flight we crashed."

"I told you that plan was a bad one."

Abikar thought it best not to argue the point.

"Obviously, this man took another flight," the Foreigner remarked sarcastically.

"That is a fact, sir," Abikar replied. "I had Wahid check the passenger lists for the flights that evening. He and a few other tourists were on the Shenzhen flight instead. But I had no idea he also came to this island. How much do you think he knows about our operation?"

"The mayor thinks he's an American spy," the Foreigner spouted, watching for Abikar's reaction. He laughed when he saw the look of sheer terror.

The Foreigner shook his head. "I don't think so. Clearly this man doesn't believe there is any danger here, or he wouldn't have brought his pretty lady friend with him—who, by the way, has already been dealt with."

Abikar's exhale of relief was almost audible. Thinking about the footage, however, he added, "I believe I've seen this man hiking the island alone since that time—several times, in fact."

"I'm not surprised."

The Foreigner focused in again on Yi. He wanted to make sure he recognized him when the time came. "Continue running the footage. I want to see where the two of them went on this island."

The screen showed Yi and Sarah stopping at the security fence at the lighthouse. They appeared to be discussing something as they both looked at the lighthouse and then back at the fence, scanning along its top that was strung with barbed wire. They talked some more, and Yi casually tugged on the padlock and chain. Seemingly satisfied they would not be able to get inside, they turned and left.

"So they never crossed the security fence?" the Foreigner asked as he stood and wiped the sweat from his brow with his handkerchief.

"No," Abikar replied. "If they had, the security alarms would have sounded. Tourists regularly wander up to the lighthouse, but they only go as far as the fence."

The Foreigner nodded in agreement. He had personally designed the cave's secured entrance. When the operations center was constructed, the entrance to the cave was moved to a circular staircase inside the lighthouse. The cave's original entrance, located at the cluster of large rocks, was destroyed. The barbed-wire, chain-link fence and the locked door on the lighthouse were to prevent tourists from accidentally stumbling upon the cave.

Despite the couple's seemingly harmless activities, however, the Foreigner wasn't convinced Yi was just a curious tourist.

***

Using binoculars, Yi watched the beach and Wild Boar Island every day at dusk from his hotel room window. After he and Sarah had seen the little man in black carry a package out to the island and come back empty-handed, Yi wanted to see if there was a repetition to the event. There was. Every third day or so, just after dark, the man took a package out to the island. Unfortunately, Yi was unable to see where on the island the little man went. Today, however, Yi noticed something different. At about 3:30 PM a foreign-looking man in a dark gray suit took a boat over to the island. Since it was still daylight, Yi was able to watch the man hike to the top of the hill, unlock the security fence, and enter the lighthouse.

Remembering where the circular staircase had been in the hallway to the right of the communications room, and the positioning of the room from the underwater entrance, Yi estimated the top of the staircase would be about where the lighthouse was located.

Well, well. I believe I've located the main entrance to the cave.

Yi quickly sent off an e-mail to Woodbury pinpointing the above-ground entrance.

I hope it's not too late!

***

"Hello, Mr. Yi," Bao said as he and the Foreigner approached Yi's table in the hotel restaurant. Yi had gone for an early dinner. Bao's wide grin looked as if he knew a secret and was dying to tell it.

"What do you want, Bao?" Yi asked, annoyed at his persistent monitoring.

"I thought we might join you for dinner. My friend here is interested in the research you're doing in Sanya." Bao's grin widened.

"Is that so?" Yi said. Glancing at the man standing next to Bao, Yi recognized the gray suit he had seen through his binoculars only an hour earlier. Suddenly, dinner with the annoying mayor took on a whole new appeal. Maybe he could extract some information from this gentleman.

Yi gestured for the men to sit down.

Yi started the conversation. "So, you're in the resort business?"

"I have a vested interest."

"My friend is a businessman with many investments in this area," Bao interjected proudly.

"And is this resort one of them?"

"One of many."

Yi raised his eyebrows in surprise. "I wasn't aware the Chinese government was now entering into foreign joint ventures in coastal areas—especially in areas bordering international waters."

The Foreigner paused then smiled before answering. "Many countries have found my expertise of great value, particularly in resort areas where national security is of primary concern."

"I see." Yi nodded, although he did not believe the Foreigner's answer. "You work in security, then. Is your company the one responsible for the fence around the lighthouse on Wild Boar Island?"

"Why do you ask?" the Foreigner postured.

"It would seem to me that an obvious tourist attraction such as a charming old lighthouse should not be kept behind a locked security gate," Yi said.

"It is old and condemned and would be a hazard to tourists," the Foreigner replied matter-of-factly.

"I would think that determination should be made by the local resort officials," Yi retorted, looking directly at Mayor Bao. "Any chance I could have a look inside? It doesn't appear to be structurally unsafe, and I can't imagine it would cost much to make it accessible to tourists."

Bao, flustered by the direct confrontation, stammered, "We rely entirely upon outside expertise for those decisions."

The Foreigner looked at Yi and smiled, as if conceding the point. "You may be right, Mr. Yi. I'll see what I can do."

He then leaned forward, his elbow resting on the table, a crease forming in his brow. "But you raise an interesting point, Mr. Yi. How did you know the lighthouse was in a secured area? The fence cannot be seen from the beach . . . where tourists usually stay," he added to see if Yi would lie about having been to the secured area.

"I have visited the island on several occasions to observe various species of wildlife," Yi replied innocently. "Recently, my friend and I visited there and became fascinated with the old lighthouse. We were, I must say, disappointed to not be allowed inside."

The Foreigner's eyes narrowed in scrutiny of Yi's every move. If he flinched or showed any trace of fear, the Foreigner would know it. Yet Yi held his gaze with ease, proving he was a worthy opponent.

"You seem out of character, Mr. Yi," the Foreigner frowned. "Chinese people are accustomed to being kept out of secured areas." Believing he had cornered his adversary, he added, "Might I ask where you are from?"

Without the slightest wincing or shifting of his eyes, Yi smiled. "I can understand your confusion. As an administrator specializing in international business ventures and especially luxury resorts, I travel extensively; therefore, I would not be a good representation of the average Chinese person."

"Of course," the Foreigner replied with a wave of his hand as if the question had been of no consequence.

Bao, having regained his composure, now went on the attack. "Yi, my friend Judge Tan Yang tells me you are supposed to be in Beijing at the present time attending the WTO judicial training program. Why are you here, and why have you taken such a strong interest in the culture village?"

Yi managed to refrain from showing his discomfort and surprise that Bao knew so much about his activities. "Yes, Bao, that is correct." He nodded as he cleared his throat before going on. "The Guangdong Administrative Council felt my background in international business ventures could be enhanced by the World Trade Organization's training program, which I had been attending. However, I assure you the portion of the training I was to participate in has now ended. As for my interest in the culture village here, our studies indicate an attraction such as the Li-ren site—like the famous Polynesian Culture Center in Hawaii—is an important tourist draw for an island resort area."

Bao frowned in disappointment at how believable Yi's answer sounded.

"And besides," Yi added casually, "local lore is a hobby of mine. For example, I'm fascinated with the Li tribe's matriarchal society and their strategic use of the island's caves for defense. It seems these islands have intricate cavern systems."

"I can assure you they do not," Bao hastily replied. "We have conducted extensive studies on that subject."

Right.

Yi couldn't resist provoking Bao further, so he added innocently, "You are native to here, correct?"

"For many generations," Bao responded proudly.

Yi smiled. "You wouldn't by chance have any family connection to the Li tribe then, would you?"

Bao turned as white as a sheet. Yi delighted in seeing him squirm. He guessed that Bao's thoughts, for the first time in probably a very long while, were now on his mother, Meijuan.

"No, no! No connection!" Bao muttered.

The Foreigner scowled at Bao then directed his attention back at Yi to change the subject. "I hear you enjoy diving, Mr. Yi. Any interesting sites in this area?"

"Several," Yi replied, fascinated by this foreigner to whom Bao seemed so reliant upon and who knew so much about the resort area and Yi's own activities. "I'm especially interested in the damaged coral out beyond Wild Boar Island." He looked from the Foreigner to Bao and then back again. "Any idea how it might have occurred?"

Yi waited for a reaction. The Foreigner leaned back, resting an elbow on the chair's padded armrest, his chin propped on his raised fist, his eyes fixed on Yi.

Yi broke the eye lock first. Seeing the Foreigner's watch unnerved him. It had the same gold tourbillon gear design that had been on the Macau gentleman's watch, on the computer logo, on Meijuan's letter, and on the plaque in the mayor's office.

"I see you wear a tourbillon," Yi said coolly. "The gear seems to be a popular design here in South China."

"My friend gives the watch as a gift to his closest business associates," Bao spoke up. Was he trying to bribe Yi?

Yi noticed Bao wasn't wearing one.

"Too expensive for my taste," Yi replied.

"Well, at least you have an eye for quality, Mr. Yi," the Foreigner said with a sly smile. "The tourbillon gear is unsurpassed in its accuracy."

Yi nodded, fully understanding the significance of the logo's meaning. Wild Boar Island was a self-contained nucleus of power carrying out its evil pursuits with focus and precision. *No wonder Meijuan was so determined to expose them.* If this organization succeeded in attacking America, there was no doubt they would hit hard, with exactness, and the results would be catastrophic. Suddenly Yi felt the weight of the world upon him.

"Well," the Foreigner said as he pushed his chair back from the table, "I believe we have taken up too much of your valuable time, Mr. Yi. Will you be staying here much longer?"

"A while," Yi replied as he stood to shake the man's hand.

"Then I wish you all the best in your research."

"Thank you, Mr. . . . I'm sorry, I didn't catch your name."

"Xabian," the Foreigner replied.

Yi nodded. "And you, Mr. Xabian, will you be staying here very long?" Yi asked, contemplating Sunday's attack.

"No. Sadly, I must leave for Brussels in the morning."

How unfortunate, Yi thought.

***

Back in his suite, the Foreigner analyzed the conversation he and Bao had had with Yi. Although not convinced the mayor was right about Yi being a spy, he was disturbed by the tenor of Yi's questions and answers and his reference to the tourbillon gear. *Should I kill him?* Yi had been so audacious in his approach. *Very uncommon here.* The Foreigner admired him. *I wonder what it would cost to have him on my payroll?* It would be worth following up after the Brussels meeting. *And if he can't be bought, then I'll kill him.* Taking on such a worthy opponent would require careful planning. *But now, I must prepare my report.* His plane was scheduled to depart first thing in the morning. *Well, Mr. Yi, you have managed to escape death twice now.* Xabian thought how tragic it would have been if Yi had been on that Guangzhou flight.

CHAPTER 39

KADENA AIR BASE, OKINAWA, JAPAN
0015 HRS, SUNDAY, APRIL 1, 2001 (D-DAY FOR OPERATION APRIL FOOL'S)

The crew of the *Dolly Mae* arrived at the briefing room of the Kadena Air Base in Okinawa, Japan. Although the muster hour was unusually early, the crew had flown other "special" missions requiring odd briefing times, so they suspected nothing out of the ordinary. That is, until they entered the room. There were at least two dozen people more than usual, and most of them didn't look like intelligence types.

"Some of these guys look like posters I've seen in the post office back home," Jake Newman, a radar navigator on the crew, whispered.

Major Frances Bachmann, who had walked into the room right behind Jake, acknowledged his comment with a broad grin. She obviously agreed with his characterization.

They located seats in the middle of the room.

"Attention!"

Everyone stood. The room grew quiet as General McMaster walked to the podium.

This is crazy, Colonel Brett Garfield, pilot of the *Dolly Mae*, thought. He could not remember the last time the general had briefed a mission, especially at that time of the day. He began to surmise the possibilities, given the general's presence. *I hope we're not going to drop a nuclear bomb somewhere.*

"Ladies and gentlemen," General McMaster began forcefully and with unmistakable clarity, "your mission this morning is one of the most delicate and dangerous missions you'll probably ever be called upon to perform."

The room grew even more silent.

The general continued. "We have been asked to conduct a surprise attack to eradicate an international terrorist training camp and control center located on a small island in the South China Sea."

Looks of confusion and murmuring passed around the room before silence again took over.

"Yes," the general said. "That means entering hostile airspace. And, yes, that means a change from your routine missions of surveillance and intelligence gathering. You will be transporting nineteen Navy SEAL special ops commandos and one bioweapons expert from the Defense Threat Reduction Agency, which I'll address in a minute. Your job is to get them there. Now, here's the tricky part. The success of the surprise element of this operation hinges upon your careful interaction and full cooperation with military forces of Communist China's People's Liberation Army. Specifically, people, you will need to stage a wing clipping with a certain Chinese fighter pilot."

Colonel Garfield had to stifle a laugh. *I know those guys well.*

"Here's how the action will break out," the general continued, a little more strongly to impress to his audience the fact that important details followed. "At 0100 this morning, Colonel Garfield will take off on what our observing friends and enemies will take to be a routine intelligence surveillance mission along the Chinese border. Your old friend, Lieutenant Wu Dawei of the People's Liberation Army Air Force, will approach you as you near China's airspace . . . about here." He pointed to a place on the wall map. "He will be his usual harassing self. However, this time he won't merely engage in his flight interference maneuvers; he will in fact attempt to clip the wing of the *Dolly Mae* sufficient to have the world think that the two planes have collided. The *Dolly Mae* will then issue a mayday distress signal requesting permission to land at the nearest airfield," he said, once again pointing to the map, "located here at Lingshui Military Air Base on Hainan Island."

The general paused, no doubt from the number of gaping jaws before him.

"Ladies and gentlemen, I cannot stress enough the importance of this maneuver. The ability to successfully carry out a surprise attack on this terrorist group's control center hinges on a convincing performance on both radar and radio by the *Dolly Mae*. Now, once the *Dolly Mae* has landed, Chinese military forces will surround the plane, and to the world, this will appear to be a takeover of the aircraft. However, I assure you this is being staged in full, friendly cooperation with the government and military of the People's Republic of China. This is not a hostile situation. Nevertheless, people, at no time—I repeat, at no time—are any Chinese military to gain access to the *Dolly Mae,* be it soldier, observer, inspector, or otherwise. In addition to the usual highly classified instrumentation installed on the *Dolly Mae,* there will be highly specialized, classified equipment on board specific to this mission. China is not to gain access to our aircraft or the equipment on board. Therefore, once the Navy SEALs have vacated the aircraft, the remaining crew will secure the aircraft until they return."

The general took a sip of water from the glass on the podium and cleared his throat. "Colonel Garfield, as I alluded to earlier, you will not be taking your usual crew on this mission. As you have probably noticed, we have members of the Navy SEALs special ops forces with us. In addition to their specialized combat training and bioweapons handling expertise, they are trained on the surveillance and cryptology equipment and specialized instruments carried on the *Dolly Mae.* In addition to yourself and Major Bachmann as pilots, Air Force Captain Jake Newman as navigator, and Marine Sergeant Vince Rotelli as flight engineer, these SEALs will substitute for the remaining members of your crew. They are the crux of this mission. Upon your safe landing on Hainan, they will carry out a surprise attack on the Wild Boar Island stronghold . . . located . . . here." The general pointed at the map to a small island off Hainan's southern coast. "Once the area has been secured, Mr. Siminski here," he gestured to a thin, awkward-looking man in white shirt and tie, "from the Defense Threat Reduction Agency will oversee the removal and handling of any and all bioweapons and explosives. This Department of Defense group, whose expertise is in handling weapons of mass destruction, has provided specialized equipment for this mission for the detecting, analyzing, storing, and handling of any chemicals, biochemical weapons, and explosives found in the biochemical laboratory believed to be located on the island. You will then return to Yokota Air Base near Tokyo, where Mr. Siminski has a trained crew standing by to take control of these weapons. I cannot overemphasize the need for caution and secrecy here, people.

The success of the overall mission depends on your ability to marshal a surprise attack and then carefully carry out your orders. Are there any questions?"

Questions? Brett thought. *Yeah, I have a few—like how do we know we can trust the Chinese? How do we know this isn't a trick to get the* Dolly Mae *on the ground so they can have access to our high-tech equipment? And what happens after the SEALs and Mr. Siminski here do what they're supposed to do?*

Suddenly, Brett became cognizant of the fact that his thoughts had been translated into sound and he was no longer sitting in his chair but was standing with all eyes upon him, including the general's.

"Your questions are noted, Colonel Garfield," the general said, somewhat impatiently because of the time. "This operation, designated as Operation April Fool's, was planned at the highest levels of both countries."

The general's strong emphasis on the word *highest* gave the audience an increased sense of the importance of this mission. "Answers to your other questions are contained in your written orders, which will be given to you by your commanding officer."

The general stepped from the podium, and he and his cadre left speedily through the crowd of stunned men and women, all now standing at attention.

"Brett, you sure like to put your foot in your mouth, don't you," Colonel Timpson said, moving quickly from the podium area to where Brett and his crew were sitting. "Didn't the significance of this mission get through to you? Anyway, we don't have much time. Here is a list of your specialists and the corresponding member of the SEALs team who will be taking their place. Get your men over to the *Dolly Mae* on the double so the SEALs can be briefed in the short time we have left."

Brett sensed the urgency in Colonel Timpson's instructions and immediately handed the list to Lieutenant Ben Jensen. Pausing long enough to realize his trusted crew members were in fact being replaced by unknowns, he said, "Ben, get on this now."

Ben had his people fall out one by one along with their designated SEAL replacements and Mr. Siminski. They loaded into the jeeps waiting to take them to the *Dolly Mae*. He returned to the group surrounding Colonel Timpson in time to hear, ". . . I'm not comfortable with this either, Brett, but it's all been worked out by men that I couldn't get near enough to spit shine their boots." The colonel continued impatiently, "All I know is the *Dolly Mae* is going to issue a mayday, enter Chinese airspace, and then land at a Chinese airfield where Navy SEALS will disembark to capture a terrorist control center and the plane with its remaining crew—yourself, Fran, Jake, and Vince here—will appear to be impounded by the Chinese government. That's what the world is supposed to think anyway. And, Brett, it's your job to make it happen."

Colonel Timpson then patted Brett on the back. "We're counting on you, Brett. Have a good flight."

Completely stunned by what was happening, Brett watched his C.O. walk out of the building. Looking down at the folder in his hands, he tried to ignore the array of sounds going off in his head. Pushing aside his concerns about what can happen in the air between two powerful hunks of metal, he walked out into the cold night air to join his new crew.

The *Dolly Mae*, specifically a Lockheed Martin EP-3E Aries II Signals Intelligence (SIGINT) aircraft belonging to the United States National Security Agency's Fleet Electronic Reconnaissance Squadron VQ-1 detachment out of Kadena Air Base in Okinawa, was chosen because its primary purpose was known to be surveillance—not strategic attack. For this mission, however, attack was exactly what was planned. Brett knew he would be ferrying a team of Navy SEALs specifically for the purpose of carrying out a subversive attack. The adrenaline flowing through his body created an altered state of mind that was both exhilarating and terrifying—a feeling he had never experienced before.

***

Wu Dawei knew they would be watching on radar. He knew it was dangerous, but the only way to make it appear convincing was to come in contact with the other aircraft. He had come close on several other occasions. The United States government frequently flew surveillance aircraft near China's airspace, and Wu Dawei and his fellow fighter pilots on several occasions had to fly interception to make the aircraft turn back. The United States had been warned many times. But this time was different. They were authorized to be there. And Dawei's ability to stage a collision was imperative to the success of this joint military operation.

Watching the US aircraft come into position, Wu Dawei slowed his jet and maneuvered alongside, his right wing just below the US aircraft's left wing. He then waved to the American pilots—something he had done many times before—not so much as a friendly gesture but more to say, "You're doing your job, and now I'm doing mine." This time, though, they were working together, and it was most important to him that it be done right. His success in accomplishing this critical military strategy would bring great honor to his family. The maneuver was risky, but he was good, really good—probably the best pilot China had. He was confident. He had done similar maneuvers before, and he knew he could do it now.

He tipped his wing up against the underside of the US aircraft's wing, brushing it ever so slightly but enough to look like a midair collision on radar. He then saluted the American pilots, smiled, and began to pull his F-8 fighter jet away from the US plane.

Just as Wu Dawei began to think of returning home to accept the government's bestowal of honor on himself and his family, the acceleration of the Chinese fighter jet drew the EP-3E to the left, catching the fighter jet's vertical stabilizer tail fin with its left propeller. As the tail section broke into pieces, a large chunk hit the nose radome of the EP-3E and sent both planes plummeting downward.

Colonel Garfield, Major Bachmann, and members of the crew worked frantically to stabilize the EP-3E but also watched in shock as the fighter jet spiraled out of control. With fire and black smoke spewing from the broken tail section of the fighter jet, they knew Wu Dawei was in serious trouble.

Suddenly, a parachute billowed out from the crippled fighter jet, and a collective sigh of relief spread through the EP-3E. The pilots and crew watched in sickening horror as the broken fighter jet plane crashed into the South China Sea.

CHAPTER 40

"Mayday! Mayday! Mayday!" Colonel Garfield issued the distress signal from the EP-3E at 6:02 AM. "Lingshui Air Base, this is United States Navy-1565. We have sustained structural damage from an in-flight collision and are requesting emergency authorization to enter Chinese airspace and land at your facility. Repeat, this is US Navy-1565 requesting authorization for emergency landing at Lingshui Airfield. Copy?"

There was no response.

Colonel Garfield repeated the distress signal several more times.

After a few minutes the response came. "United States Navy-1565, this is Lingshui Air Base. You are not authorized to land. Repeat, you are NOT authorized to land."

Colonel Garfield looked at Major Bachmann, who returned his puzzled look. Their briefing documents had stated China would give them authorization to land.

"Lingshui Air Base, this is US Navy-1565. Due to structural wing damage and engine failure we are not, I repeat NOT, able to sustain a change in course. We must land at your airfield—estimated arrival at 0625."

Minutes passed before a response. "US Navy-1565, you are NOT authorized to land. Change course immediately or prepare to be shot down."

Glancing to her right, Major Bachmann noticed a Chinese military F-8-II fighter jet maneuver into position and open cannon fire at them. She turned to Colonel Garfield. "They're firing on us, sir. What are we going to do? This turboprop can't outmaneuver their jets."

"Major," the colonel replied, "we follow our orders and hope they follow theirs. Let's slow this baby down and prepare to land. Maybe we can shake 'em off. The slower we go, the harder it'll be for them to stay with us without stalling out."

"Let's hope they don't shoot us full of holes before we can get this plane on the ground," the major replied.

The officers in charge of each of the four Navy SEALs attack groups reviewed their orders as they readied themselves for combat. Of the nineteen SEALs, six were outfitted as frogmen, dressed in black wet suits with blackout face masks and Draeger LAR V breathing units. The total weight of their gear exceeded seventy pounds—twenty-five of which were C4 explosives. They would be the first group to engage the Hainan Net's operations center by entering through the underwater tunnel leading to the cave. They would secure the communications console, disarm the security systems, and radio the other teams.

Four SEALs, dressed in camouflage combat gear and equipped with M4 rifles, would attack the Net's operations center from above ground on Wild Boar Island. The last-minute intelligence information that the center's main entrance was located inside the lighthouse was a major coup in strategic planning. They would be able to attack from above ground as well as underwater. Once the Net's soldiers, computer systems, chemicals, bioweapons, and explosives were removed, the underwater demolition team would blow the infrastructure of the operations center and both entrances to the cave.

Two SEALs, one male and one female, were dressed in civilian clothes carrying hidden weapons. Along with a few plainclothes Chinese soldiers, they would proceed to the culture village and remove the terrorist presence located there. Their orders were to capture Net soldiers and couriers and confiscate the computer system, electronic files, and any hard disks.

The remaining seven SEALs, also dressed in camouflage combat gear and carrying M4 rifles, would join with Chinese military forces to capture the combat training facility next to the beach resort area.

All hostages would be detained in China until transport arrangements could be made. The confiscated computers and communications equipment, along with any bioweapons, would be transported back to Yokota Air Base on the EP-3E.

Except for the loud noise from the two still-functioning turboprop engines, the nineteen Navy SEALs sat in silence as they mentally prepared for their courses of action.

"That's an interesting breathing apparatus," Mr. Siminski shouted to one of the frogmen as he clumsily put on his own camouflage flack jacket and helmet. "I've never seen scuba gear like that."

"The Draeger's pure oxygen breathing loop is much more complicated than a standard regulator but also much smaller than scuba gear with air tanks. It's ideal for maneuvering in narrow spaces," the frogman replied.

"That'll come in handy," Mr. Siminski added with a nervous chuckle as he contemplated the events about to unfold before them.

The US Navy EP-3E Aries II surveillance aircraft landed at Lingshui Military Airbase at 6:33 AM Sunday morning, April 1. No sooner had the aircraft come to a halt than it was quickly surrounded by hostile-looking Chinese military forces with rifles raised and ready to fire.

Minutes passed. The crew on the *Dolly Mae* looked at each other, wondering what would happen next.

The pilot scanned the crowded airfield. Out of the corner of his eye, he noticed four Chinese military transport vehicles coming toward the *Dolly Mae*. As they pulled alongside, one soldier jumped out and saluted the pilot.

"Here we go!" he shouted to his crew.

CHAPTER 41

Yi looked at his watch for the tenth time. It read 6:50 AM. Although it was still dark, Yi knew the sun would start rising soon. Still no sign of Navy SEALs.

What could have happened? Yi decided to give it a few more minutes.

He offered a silent prayer. *Father, please watch over this operation . . .*

Suddenly, a single beam of light swept across the water. Yi's adrenaline starting pumping. *Inhale. Exhale.*

A black, motorized raft pulled up to Yi's rowboat. One of the six frogmen saluted Yi then gave a thumbs-up. Without a word, Yi positioned his face mask and regulator. He slid into the water, and the six frogmen followed.

Dropping to twenty feet, Yi switched on his headlamp. As they reached the ocean floor, the beam of light cast a bell-shaped shadow on the rocky base of the island. Yi was relieved to have found the mark so quickly. He positioned himself at the back of the outcropping and pointed to the opening. The head diver gave Yi another thumbs-up and entered the tunnel. One by one, the other frogmen entered behind their leader.

Caught up in the moment, Yi had a very strong urge to follow them. But he resisted. Instead, a sense of pride and homesickness for America overcame him. He wanted to go home. But he knew he had to finish his mission first. And, more than anything, he wanted to see Sarah.

He slowly maneuvered back to the surface and climbed into the rowboat. He removed his gear then started up the little engine and steered toward shore.

The first hints of light were beginning to appear on the horizon. Yi could just barely make out the tent area of the Net's training camp near the Yalong Bay Resort. Shouts and gunshots rang out followed by machine-gun fire. Tiny flashes of light interrupted the last of the night's darkness.

Yi could see both Chinese and American forces rounding up soldiers in the uniforms he had been unable to identify. *What a historic event,* he thought as he watched the successful outcome of this Sino-US military operation. He hoped the judicial training cooperative would have the same result.

Thinking of the training program brought back the pangs of guilt and sadness he still harbored for Sarah. Now, at least he could return to Beijing, or fly to Tibet if necessary, to talk to her.

As he walked up the sandy beach toward the hotel, he planned to call her yet another time once he got back to his room and had a chance to clean up. He felt drained. *A hot shower will feel great.*

"Aiya!" came a maniacal scream from behind Yi. As he turned, he saw Bao, red faced, running at him with his hand raised in the air, a knife blade glinting in the early morning sun.

Yi stopped immediately and dropped his gear. His defense training took over. He spun around and caught Bao in the jaw with his foot. The blow stunned Bao, and he fell to the ground. The knife disappeared in the sand.

As Yi bent over to grab hold of Bao, Bao threw a handful of sand in Yi's face.

"You've ruined everything!" Bao shrieked.

Blinded, Yi scrambled to clear his vision of the stinging sand. Before he could do so, Bao located the knife and lunged again at Yi. Still unable to see clearly, Yi didn't fully block Bao's thrust. The tip of the blade grazed his forearm.

Instinctively, Yi moved in the direction of the knife and caught Bao's wrist, twisting it around behind his back. Bao's knees buckled as he squealed in pain. This time when the knife dropped, Yi kicked it out of reach. Bao slumped over, whimpering like a small child.

"It's over, Bao," Yi said and released his grip.

In one swift motion, Bao swung both arms up, hitting Yi under the chin and knocking him back. Stunned and enraged, Yi pounced on Bao, grabbing him by the throat and forcing him to the ground. As Yi thought about this annoying creature and the despicable way he had treated his mother, Meijuan, and all the suffering he had caused, Yi's hands began to tighten. Bao gasped for air.

"Do you realize how many people you've hurt?" Yi growled. He could feel his self-control slipping away. His grip tightened even more.

Yi thought about the Book of Mormon story of Laban, who was delivered by the Lord into the hands of Nephi to slay him for his wickedness.

Had this wicked man been delivered into Yi's hands for the same purpose?

Bao grew weaker from lack of air. Yi knew at that moment that he could end Bao's life. It was tempting. But a voice came into Yi's mind, saying, *No, it is not the same. There are proper courses to follow.*

Yi loosened his grip around Bao's neck.

As he pulled Bao to his feet, Yi said out loud, "And that's the rule of law."

"What?" Bao muttered, still gasping for air.

"Nobody's above the law, Bao. Not you, not me."

Yi called out to where the Chinese military soldiers were assembling the Hainan Net hostages. "Can I get some help over here?"

Several soldiers ran to where Yi was holding Bao. In Chinese, Yi instructed them to take Bao into custody for corruption.

"But I am the mayor of Sanya." Bao struggled to regain his voice. When his title didn't influence the soldiers, he added, "I can pay you a lot of money."

"He may be the mayor here," Yi stated, "but he's the one responsible for all of this. Don't let him fool you." He then turned to Bao and patted him on the shoulder. "Your mother will be relieved to know this has finally ended."

Yi picked up the knife and his diving gear and headed back to the hotel.

***

"Please return my calls, Sarah," Yi mumbled after leaving yet another message on her cell phone. He was beginning to be more than a little concerned. This really wasn't like her. If she had decided to drop out of the training program and never see Yi again, she would at least have the courtesy to return his messages.

Yi decided to call Lincoln and get a feel for the situation back at the Judges College. He would be able to tell right away from Lincoln's reaction to his call if anything was amiss. He dialed Lincoln's cell phone.

"Lincoln, this is Yi. How are things?" Yi asked casually.

"Yi," Lincoln exclaimed, seemingly pleased to hear Yi's voice. "Where are you? We thought you were only going to be gone a few days."

"I know," Yi replied, delighted to hear his friend's voice and relieved that Lincoln sounded as if nothing were wrong.

"When are you coming back? You are greatly missed, my friend. This judicial training is grueling," Lincoln remarked.

"I'm on my way back. I should arrive late this evening."

"Things must really be terrible there in Guangzhou," Lincoln said.

"Why do you say that?"

"Because Tan Yang left as well. Except he didn't tell anyone he was leaving—he simply disappeared."

"That's odd," Yi responded, trying to sound casual while alarms were starting to go off in his head. "No one knows where he went?"

"Everyone assumed he returned to Guangzhou."

"Did the college administrator check with his office?" Yi asked. "She should know if he's left the training program or not."

"I'll ask her," Lincoln offered.

"Thanks, Lincoln. By the way, I've been trying to contact Sarah. Did she return to the college by chance? She's not answering her phone."

"Yi, don't you know?" Lincoln was surprised Yi hadn't heard the news. "She was attacked last Monday evening here on campus. Come to think of it, it was right before Tan Yang left. Anyway, she's hospitalized and in pretty serious condition. Yi, I'm sorry. I thought you knew."

Shock hit Yi like a tidal wave. He could feel the color drain from his face as the thought of Sarah being seriously hurt fully culminated in his mind.

This is my fault.

Yi quickly ended the phone call and collected his already-packed suitcases. He checked out of the hotel and left for the airport in the first available taxi. No matter what it took, he would be on the next flight to Beijing.

CHAPTER 42

Yi had been in Beijing since the evening of April 1, staying by Sarah's hospital bedside while she recovered from the vicious attack. She was in a coma. Seeing her lying there—her head bandaged, her face bruised and swollen, with numerous tubes and medical apparatuses connected to her—brought stinging tears to Yi's eyes. With complete disregard for his cover, he gently laid his hands on her head and gave her a blessing. But even that brought him little solace. After all, it was his carelessness that had exposed her to such harm. There was no doubt in Yi's mind who had done this to her and why.

He stayed by her bedside around the clock, leaving only to e-mail Trenton Woodbury that he had completed his responsibilities in the Hainan Net attack. He was hoping to hear back from Woodbury with complete details of the entire operation. So far, Woodbury had not responded. Now all Yi could do was wait for Sarah to heal. But patience was not one of Yi's strengths.

Late in the evening on April 3, with the hospital room quiet and Yi resting in a metal chair next to Sarah's bed, she finally opened her eyes.

It took her several moments to clear them and adjust to the darkened room. She slowly glanced around at her surroundings. She stared at Yi as if she were dreaming. But as the pain throughout her body began to take hold, she remembered what had happened to her. Although it had been a nightmare, it was all too real.

"Yi?" she said, trying to make some sound but only getting a whisper.

"Yi?" she tried again, this time with a little more sound. It was enough because Yi shot up in the chair.

"You're . . . here?" she asked him.

Realizing Sarah was awake, he joyfully and impulsively reached to embrace her. "Oh, Sarah!"

She flinched from the pain of his touch, and he realized how fragile her condition still was. He gently kissed her on the corner of her swollen mouth.

"Why?" she mumbled.

The hurt look in his eyes told her that he had misunderstood her meaning.

Forcing herself to stay conscious and using all her strength, Sarah tried to form the words she needed Yi to hear. "I'm . . . glad," she said and tried to smile.

"Sarah, I'm here with you now. Everything's going to be fine. But you should rest." Yi struggled to hold in his emotions. "I need to go let the doctor know you're awake now."

"How long . . . have I . . . slept?" she asked, confused that he would make such a fuss over her waking up in the middle of the night.

"About eight days," he replied and lightly kissed her again.

***

Woodbury had not responded to any of Yi's e-mails. *That's strange.* Yi began watching the news for some mention of the attack. He could find none.

Then, on April 8, an item pertaining to Hainan Island and the United States appeared in the *Beijing Times* newspaper. It stated:

A People's Liberation Army Air Force F-8 fighter jet was rammed by a United States spy plane at approximately 6:00 am local time on Sunday, April 1. The fighter jet was one of two Chinese F-8 aircrafts sent to shadow the spy plane and force it back into international airspace after it crossed into Chinese airspace only sixty-two miles southeast of Hainan Island. The American plane maneuvered abruptly into the Chinese fighter jet, causing it to crash into the South China Sea. Wu Dawei, the heroic pilot, is presumed dead. The spy plane's unauthorized landing at China's Lingshui Air Base in southern Hainan violated Chinese sovereignty and international law. China's

Office of Foreign Ministry declared in a statement that it made a "serious" protest and that "the US plane abruptly turned toward the Chinese plane, its nose and wing colliding with the Chinese plane. The United States should take total responsibility for this incident."

The United States, however, has not offered any apologies. Reports indicate the United States blames the Chinese pilot for recklessly flying into what they say is a slower, less maneuverable plane. They also say their emergency landing on Chinese land followed standard international practices. Liu Linhua, a Chinese fighter pilot who has experienced similar occurrences with American spy planes, said, "This is not the first time American spy planes have had to be forced out of Chinese airspace, and the Chinese government officials should take a tough position against the United States." According to Chinese military experts, the United States' electronic intelligence flights off the Chinese coast are part of a deliberate plan by the American government to draw a harsh response from China, further diminishing Sino-US relations.

Shocked by the newspaper's false account, Yi turned on the television and flipped through channels until he found the story. The news station reported:

News coverage confirmed an American spy plane illegally entered Chinese airspace and Chinese air force fighter jets tried to intercept its path. After a midair collision at the fault of the United States, one of the Chinese jets crashed, and the pilot was unaccounted for. The American plane managed to land at Lingshui Air Base near the southern coast of Hainan Island but was taken captive by Chinese military forces.

Yi bought a copy of each of the Chinese newspapers to read the different accounts of the incident. They all reported basically the same information. There was no mention of an attack on a terrorist group or of a joint military cooperation between the United States and China. In fact, from what the newspapers and television media were reporting, this was an unfriendly hostage situation that was fast becoming a potentially volatile political predicament.

What?

Why withhold key facts? Why not tell the world that China and the United States had formed a joint military alliance to capture the Hainan

Net? It didn't make sense. And why would the Chinese government wait so long to report anything? Since they control their media, what purpose would it serve to withhold information, let alone report only part of the facts—especially when those facts would antagonize rather than enhance foreign relations?

***

"It must have been a dream, Yi. But it was so real," Sarah explained, "like angels encouraging me to stay, but I wanted to go with them. Then I felt these gentle hands on my head, and I heard a voice—like your voice, Yi—and I knew I had to come back. I wanted to come back."

Yi sat next to Sarah's hospital bed, silently caressing her hand as she told him of her dream. He smiled, grateful that his prayers had been answered.

"But it's too late," she continued, disappointment obvious in her voice. "The judicial training program is over."

"I'm afraid so, Sarah," he replied consolingly.

"Then I have let many people down," she said, trying to control her emotions.

"You haven't let anyone down."

"Yes, I have, Yi," she said, forcing back tears. "My family convinced me that I should continue the program and pursue a scholarship. Now that's not going to happen."

She paused as if her next thought had been more painful than the previous one. "Most of all, I've let myself down. I worked hard to further my legal studies, and it was always my dream to study at an American law school. I realized that even more while I was in Tibet."

Yi squeezed her hand. "Because of your hard work, Sarah, I have no doubt that if it's meant to be, there will be other opportunities for you to study at an American law school." He leaned in and kissed her tenderly. "And for us to be together."

She responded in kind, but Yi could see she still felt sad about the program. Not wanting her to dwell on negative thoughts, he inquired, "So how was your trip to Tibet and the visit with your family?"

The smile beginning to form on her face told Yi he had made the right choice in changing the subject.

"Tibet was just as I remembered. Seeing my family again and my hometown after such a long time made me happy and very much at peace."

"I'm glad to hear that," Yi replied warmly. "And did you say hello to your family for me?" he asked jokingly.

"As a matter of fact I did," Sarah said. "I spoke quite a bit about you to my family."

"All good things, I hope." Yi suddenly felt a little insecure.

"Actually, I talked to them about how confused I was regarding my feelings toward you—especially since I believed you had misled me."

"Hmm . . . they must think I'm awful," Yi said, feeling even worse.

"To tell you the truth, they were very supportive. Even when I told them you were American and would return to the United States and I would probably never see you again." She thought for a moment. "In fact, my mother told me basically the same thing you just did."

Yi paused, a look of confusion on his face. "What was that?"

"My wise mother said, 'Deckey, you must take happiness where you find it. If it is meant to be, where he is from won't matter; there will be other opportunities for you to be with the man you love, either here or in America.'"

Yi smiled at Sarah then kissed her again. He couldn't agree more.

CHAPTER 43

The Foreigner arrived at the boardroom on schedule as always. The thick, wooden-paneled doors were closed as usual. He reached for the doorknob. It was locked. Looking at his watch, which read 5:00 AM, he wondered if he was the first to arrive. *Not possible.* This meeting had been specially called by the chairman himself.

He hesitated as a feeling of uneasiness came over him. Tiny beads of perspiration started to form on his brow. Out of habit, he removed his folded monogrammed handkerchief and wiped his forehead.

He rapped lightly on the door.

A moment later the white-haired man opened the boardroom door and gestured for him to enter. He did not greet the Foreigner with his usual hug and kiss on each cheek.

The Foreigner glanced around the room. The meeting was already in progress. By the looks of the used coffee cups on the sideboard, it had been going on for some time.

The Foreigner's uneasiness began to intensify as he walked to the cabinet and poured himself a cup of Grand Earl Grey tea. He could feel all eyes upon him. The silence was deafening. The only sound was the tinkling of the spoon against the fine porcelain cup as he stirred in lemon and sugar. He took his time. He dreaded this meeting because no doubt they would hold him accountable for what had happened on Hainan Island.

But they cannot blame me, he thought. *I could not possibly have known about an underwater entrance to the cave on Wild Boar Island or that the mayor's mother was still alive.* He allowed his mind a fleeting glimpse of the torture he would inflict upon the mayor of Sanya when he returned there.

Finally, he turned and walked to the conference table. He took his usual seat to the left of the white-haired man. He shifted in the leather upholstery and glanced again at his watch. It was now 5:06 AM.

The chairman nodded to one of the directors who then placed a telephone call. The white-haired man cleared his throat and began to speak. He did not stand but spoke from his position at the head of the table.

"You will please give us your report on the recent events at Hainan Island," he said to the Foreigner, his hands clasped in front of him on the table.

The Foreigner looked at each of the eight directors, all of whom avoided eye contact. He took a sip of his tea, wiped the corner of his mouth with his handkerchief, then stood and gave his accounting of the incident. When finished, he sat down.

The white-haired man leaned forward in his seat, pursed his lips, and touched them to the tips of the index fingers of both hands. He stared at the center of the table.

"Although this incident has resulted in a setback," he began, "the organization's objectives are still intact. One minor item of concern, however, is the media's explanation of what has happened. Gentlemen, we must ensure that what is published is merely an unfortunate incident between a Chinese fighter plane and an off-course US surveillance aircraft that thought it was in international air space. There will be no mention of Wild Boar Island or military activity there."

The white-haired man stood and walked to the side credenza. He poured himself a cup of coffee. As he was stirring in some cream and sugar he added, "The board will now take a ten-minute break."

He nodded at one of the directors who proceeded to make another telephone call.

Turning to the Foreigner but avoiding eye contact, the white-haired man said, "You may leave."

Without saying a word, the Foreigner stood and walked toward the boardroom doors. He didn't hesitate or turn around to the directors as he opened the door.

A strange crackle sound caught his attention as he stepped outside the room and closed the door behind him. He realized that instead of standing on the antique Persian rug lying in the vestibule, he was standing on plastic sheeting. An opaque tarp had been placed wall-to-wall over the polished wood floor and rug outside the boardroom.

He hesitated only a moment before slight bursts of noise reverberated in the air. The sounds, although barely perceptible, were familiar to him. Yet, before his mind could grasp the full reality, the bullets penetrated his forehead and heart. The folded handkerchief he still held in his hand fell to the floor, blood splattered across the finely stitched letter *X*.

Two of the guards lowered their guns, silencers attached. As ordered, they quietly gathered up the plastic tarp and its contents, clearing away any trace of its unpleasantness.

In the boardroom the directors finished their coffee break and resumed their meeting. There was much to do to proceed with operations.

"Our purpose is still clear," the white-haired man stated. "We will continue to manipulate governments, even have them overthrown if necessary, in order to dominate the earth's resources and the financial markets they influence. These resources of food, water, oil, and gas control the world—life does not exist without them—and are, therefore, the ultimate source of power. Gentlemen, we will use whatever means necessary to gain this power. With the exception of my son's most unfortunate handling of events in Hainan, the Net has served us well. I propose that a new director of Net operations be selected and that temporary facilities be set up on our island in the Philippines. Much of our stockpile of explosives and weapons is already located there, and many of our trained pilots and sea captains frequent Manila in their travels."

"What about existing plans of attack?" a director asked.

"Unfortunately, attacks on seaports and the canal must be postponed until new virus strains can be cultivated. However, other attacks will be carried out as scheduled. Are there any further questions?"

The room was silent.

"I second the proposal," one of the directors said.

"All in favor say aye."

The vote was unanimous.

"Very well. This meeting is adjourned until July," the white-haired man said, breathing a deep sigh. Relieved that this slight setback to his plans had now been dealt with, he dabbed at his forehead with his linen handkerchief, a monogrammed cursive letter X finely stitched in the corner.

CHAPTER 44

SENATE EXECUTIVE OFFICES, WASHINGTON DC
APRIL 30, 2001

"Welcome back, Jason. It's good to see you," Trenton Woodbury said, shaking Yi's hand as he entered the room for his final debriefing. Yi had spent the few days since his return from China engulfed in intensive meetings and debriefings with the Central Intelligence Agency and the Department of State. He had been required to give a detailed report of his activities and answer a myriad of questions. Now in the final debriefing, he and other members of the legislature who had been involved in Yi's assignment and the judicial training program—Trenton Woodbury and Senator Boyle among them—would be briefed on the overall effectiveness and success of the program.

"It's good to be back," Yi replied.

"How's Sarah?" Woodbury asked with sincere concern.

"She's doing fine, sir. The doctors say she is making remarkable progress and should recover fully."

"That's good news, Jason," Senator Boyle interjected as he sat down beside them. "We understand the man who attacked her was finally caught."

"Tan Yang," Yi responded, thinking about the senior judge from Guangzhou who had caused so much grief. "Yes, the Chinese government located him hiding in a massage parlor in Shenzhen."

"If I'm not mistaken, I believe he faces execution if he doesn't win his trial," Boyle commented.

"More so for his involvement in corrupt dealings than for his attack on Sarah," Yi replied. "Personally, I think he deserves whatever the courts decide. But Sarah has asked the government to spare his life." He sighed as he added, "She's an incredible woman."

"It looks to me," Boyle said with a sly smile, "like there might be something developing between you two. Am I right?"

"Possibly." Yi nodded as if he were thinking about it for the first time, wanting to keep his personal life somewhat private. In actuality, he had thought about it a lot and hoped to find a way to pursue the long-distance relationship.

"She is remarkable." Woodbury nodded in affirmation. "And how about you, Jason? You've been back only a few days, yet you've been locked away with the CIA and Department of State darn near round the clock. How are you holding up?"

"Still adjusting to the jet lag, sir. But I'm eager to hear the final briefing on the outcome of this assignment. I have a lot of questions at this point." Yi was most interested in why the Chinese newspapers had completely misrepresented the facts.

"I can imagine you have questions." Woodbury nodded in understanding. "Well, it's good to have you home," he said and patted Yi on the back. "I think we'll all rest a little easier now that your assignment has been such a success. I have to say, Jason, it was truly an amazing discovery on your part—to expose the Hainan Net in such a short time and put together such an extensive list of corrupt officials from so many provinces around China."

"Believe me, sir, I had a lot of help."

"Well, it was ingenious on your part to consolidate everyone's lists into one anonymous list. That way, no one risked personal repercussions," Woodbury stated. "You've done an incredible job, Jason."

"I couldn't have done it without Sarah and the other judges, sir, or Meijuan," Yi replied. "They are incredible people. With the exception of a few of the judges, I don't think I've met more honorable and hard-working individuals. They want to do so much for their country and fellowmen. That list was the result of their personal willingness to take a stand against corruption. I can't say this about too many people, but I would trust most of those judges with my life."

"I believe, Jason, that's exactly what you did," Boyle said warmly. "And through that trust, you accomplished more than any one person could have done on his own."

"What's also amazing is the domino effect your list has had on the corrupt officials," Woodbury added. "They are turning in other officials because they don't want to be the only ones being prosecuted for the corruption in their provinces. China couldn't have hoped for a better outcome."

"Thank you, sir. I'm glad to hear there's been such a positive ending to this program."

Woodbury hesitated before broaching what he anticipated would be a sensitive subject for Yi. "Jason, I'm sure you must be disappointed in the results for the two scholarships. I'm terribly sorry."

"Don't be, sir," Yi replied, trying to sound positive. The sting still penetrated deeply, knowing Sarah had lost her dream because of him. He forced a smile. "My dear friend, Jerry, and the other judge—I believe he went by the name Thomas—are exceptional judges and very deserving of the opportunity to attend Temple's law school."

"But Sarah must be disheartened," Boyle said. "She had the highest score prior to her attack."

"Yes, she's very disappointed, Senator. But she understands." Yi looked off in the distance as the full impact of the pain he had caused her washed over him again. Sarah had forgiven him, but he could not forgive himself.

Yi thought about seeing Jerry and the other judge. He was happy for them. And he looked forward to their meeting.

"I imagine you have established some valuable friendships through this judicial training experience," Woodbury commented to cover Yi's silence.

Yi turned his focus back to the conversation. "Yes, sir. It's hard to describe, but I feel a strong familial bond with those people. While I was there, I learned a lot about who I am as a Chinese person and as a human being. I guess it takes more than a large ocean to sever ties with one's heritage."

"I can understand you feeling that way," Boyle said warmly.

"In fact," Yi added, "I'm going to continue using my real name . . . my Chinese name. So, if you wouldn't mind, I'd be honored if you would call me Yi instead of Jason."

"Very well, Yi," Boyle said and patted him on the shoulder.

Woodbury cleared his throat. "You know, Yi, speaking of Meijuan, it's a shame her son, the mayor, managed to escape after his trial. I understand from a reliable source that he was to be executed."

Yi shook his head. "I was afraid he would get away—the slippery weasel. I guess I should have finished him off when I had the chance."

Boyle responded. "No, you did the right thing, son. It's a shame they couldn't hang on to him. I'm just amazed, though, at how quickly the Chinese government can send someone through their judicial system."

"As I said before, Senator," Yi replied, "there's a lot the United States could learn from China. Not that I agree with execution as an outcome, but China's policy of only one appeal certainly speeds up the judicial process."

They all nodded in agreement.

Yi thought for a moment longer then in a reflective tone added, "One thing I find interesting is how the Stillmans unknowingly led me to Meijuan. I wouldn't have uncovered the Hainan Net without the letter she left with them. It's amazing to me to see how things seem to work out." *Divine intervention,* he thought. He then chuckled sheepishly. "I certainly hope the Stillmans understand why I had to be deceptive. How are they, by the way?"

"They're fine," Woodbury responded. "I understand they returned to the States two weeks ago, after BYU wrapped up the final testing. I hear they've indicated an interest to teach in the next training program."

Yi nodded and smiled. "I'm not surprised. The judges loved them." He paused. "Getting back to your mention of Hainan, sir. I'm a little confused by the news reports. I haven't had a chance to review the newspapers here in the States, but in China they only mentioned a midair collision between a US surveillance plane and a Chinese fighter jet."

Boyle interrupted. "That hotshot cowboy of a pilot they had flying their fighter jet almost cost us our aircraft!"

Woodbury held up his hand to calm Boyle down. "Rand, the man sacrificed his life for this cause."

"Well, we don't know for sure. No one ever found his body," Boyle replied, somewhat appeased.

At that moment, Mark Stanton, the director of the Central Intelligence Agency, entered the room with a gust of bravado and headed straight to the podium without a glance around the room. All eyes turned toward him. "Ladies and gentlemen, let's begin this final debriefing session." Putting on his reading glasses he read, "We have completed our first successful mission in assisting China in the elimination of corruption preventing the implementation and adherence to World Trade Organization laws. China's foreign ministry has extended their gratitude to the United States for assisting in this breakthrough in their work. This is the first of what will be many more Sino-US judicial training programs. Many of the corrupt officials named have been arrested, and substantial evidence has been accumulated in proving their involvement. In addition, the United States has eliminated a significant leak of highly classified information through the American embassy in Beijing. A Chinese minority by the name of Zou Kai, who was on staff at the American embassy, has been arrested for espionage and terrorism connections. The United States has requested extradition for him to be held here until the international trial. However, China has informed us they intend to try him there. Others on the list are still being verified and will be arrested when and if sufficient evidence can be determined.

"During Mr. Yi's assignment as an undercover judge in the WTO judicial training program," the director continued, "he was able to gain access to important information that has proven vital to our country's national security. Because of the classification level of the resulting operation, the facts will not be discussed in this briefing. I will tell you, however, that the Hainan portion of the operation was a major success thanks to Mr. Yi and the endeavors of two Chinese women. One of them, Miss Sarah Decker, a judge from Tibet, unfortunately suffered a severe assault as a result of her efforts. I can assure you she is recovering well and will be recognized for her valuable assistance to Mr. Yi. As for the other woman, I'm afraid we do not know her current location. All we know at this point is her name is Meijuan, and she is, or at least was, an editor of a news magazine in Beijing. Both the United States and China would like to commend her for her bravery in uncovering the threat to America's national security."

Yi began to raise his hand to correct their information. He knew Meijuan's whereabouts. His thoughts turned to the e-mail he had received from her only a few days earlier.

Mr. Yi, thank you for restoring peace to the precious island of my heritage. I will be forever grateful to you. I have returned to Hainan and have assumed a leadership position. This is where I belong. Zaijian, Meijuan

P.S. If you ever return to the land of your heritage (and it is my belief that you will), I pray you visit Hainan again.

Yi lowered his hand.

"Did you have a comment, Mr. Yi?" the director asked.

Yi shook his head. "No, sir, sorry." He decided it was best to keep Meijuan's location a secret. *She would want it that way.*

The director continued. "As for Miss Sarah Decker . . ."

Thinking about Meijuan and wondering how she was doing, Yi wasn't paying attention to what the director was saying. Hearing Sarah's name mentioned, however, brought him back into full focus.

". . . although she was unable to finish the judicial training due to her injuries suffered at the hands of Tan Yang, the United States and China have agreed to fund a third scholarship on her behalf. She will arrive in the United States the end of May."

The director looked out over his reading glasses directly at Yi and, with warmth in his voice for the first time, said, "Mr. Yi, she has asked if you would please meet her at the Philadelphia International Airport. My assistant will fill you in on the details of her arrival."

Yi was shocked but thrilled, to say the least, and grateful to the United States and China for recognizing Sarah's valiant efforts in this way.

They couldn't have chosen a better reward.

The CIA director continued. "You are all to be commended for this highly successful mission in helping eliminate corruption as China moves forward under permanent normal trade status in the World Trade Organization. Thank you." The director then stepped away from the podium and exited the room.

***

The week of debriefing had been intense for Yi. He now looked forward to catching up on news and e-mails. The first thing he planned to do when he returned home was send an e-mail to Sarah congratulating her on the surprise scholarship and letting her know how much he looked forward to seeing her.

Yi was also eager to read the full account of the Hainan incident in the US papers. Because of the debriefing, his newspapers had accumulated in unopened bundles on the entryway floor of his apartment. After scanning them, he was even more confused by the conflicting news reports presented by the media in both China and the United States. Neither country included reports on the identification of a terrorist cell operating in Hainan or on the successful US-Sino military attack to capture it.

Yi pondered both sets of reports. The events of April 1, as reported in the news in both the United States and China, were drastically different from what Yi knew had happened.

Why would there be such a misrepresentation of the facts? Was the distortion deliberate? For what purpose? Before stepping down, China's leader had wanted to establish solid relations with the West, particularly the United States. Strong relations were essential for success in the World Trade Organization and would certainly enhance preparations for the 2008 Olympics if Beijing received the bid. The coordinated military efforts and resulting success of Operation April Fool's certainly proved that a solid relationship had been formed.

Why would this important fact not be reported? Powerful individuals within the political structure of the People's Republic of China might seek to thwart their leader's goals, to hurt his legacy of being the one to launch China into a growing economy through entrance into the World Trade Organization and strong Sino-US relations. *But China's media is controlled by its own political power.* In the United States, however, where freedom of the press is an inalienable right, the facts should not have been distorted. Yi chuckled at his naïveté. *Freedom of the press doesn't guarantee the truth.* Even in the United States, the media is not above following their own agenda or being influenced by powerful outside forces. Yi thought about the individuals and organizations who would not want strong Sino-US relations established. Could they persuade the media to color the facts or even change them? *Definitely.* But as to the reason for the misrepresentation? Yi could only speculate.

CHAPTER 45

Yi parked his Honda Prelude then rushed into the Philadelphia airport. The announcement was just coming over the Delta concourse loudspeaker: "Delta flight 5244 from Beijing is now arriving at gate thirty-four."

Wearing his finest black suit and carefully cradling twenty long-stemmed red roses wrapped in clear cellophane, Yi passed through the airport's metal detectors and hurried toward the arrival gate. It was 6:12 AM. He had been on the road for more than three hours.

As he passed gate thirty-two, he could see people coming out of gate thirty-four. Her plane had arrived. Anxiously, he looked for her through the crowd, afraid he might have missed her. It appeared she had not yet disembarked from the plane. Yi took a deep breath as he stopped at the waiting area to watch for her. He ran his hand through his hair, trying to smooth it out and wishing the long ride hadn't taken such a toll on it.

As he stood there watching for her, he became aware that he was lightly tapping his foot. *Impatience?* He took inventory of his emotions. No, he was nervous. Chuckling to himself, he realized he felt like a schoolboy on his first big date.

Get a grip, Yi! He took another deep breath to calm his nerves. What was there to be nervous about? *Lots of things.* A flood of questions poured into his mind: *Have her feelings for me changed? Will she be excited to see me or just elated to finally be in America? How should I act toward her? What do I do? Do I shake her hand? Kiss her? Will she want to kiss me?*

And then he saw her.

The telltale hint of yellow bruising on her face was the only remaining trace of her injuries. Even that could not mar her beauty. Her glossy black hair was tucked behind one ear, and her wide-set eyes twinkled with the excitement of beginning a new experience. She was dressed in black slacks and a pale blue blouse. The cuffs were neatly folded back almost to her elbows. The black leather strap from her briefcase hung over her right shoulder. In two months' time, Yi had almost forgotten the profound effect she had on him. She totally mesmerized him.

Sarah scanned the crowd for Yi's familiar face. She had not yet seen him. As Yi watched, he detected a hint of nervousness in her. She was biting her lower lip. He couldn't help but smile.

"Sarah," he called to her, holding up the roses.

As her eyes found his, a broad smile lit up her face and tears began streaming down her cheeks. There was no doubt about her feelings for him. All his nervousness and anxiety vanished. At that point, his sole objective was to hold her in his arms. And this time he wasn't going to let her go.

She rushed into his embrace and hugged him, not caring at all about propriety. At that moment, for both of them, it was as if no one else existed. He held her tight and breathed in the faint smell of jasmine in her hair.

"How was your flight?" he asked her.

"Long," she replied. "I couldn't wait to get here." Looking around the spacious airport, she added, "I still can't believe it!"

Taking her briefcase, Yi handed her the flowers, which she smelled and then beamed her beautiful smile at him. There was the dimple. Oh, how he had missed it!

"Thank you, Yi," she said. "And thank you for meeting me." She squeezed his arm. "I hope it wasn't too much of an inconvenience."

"Sarah, you know I would meet you anywhere," he replied tenderly.

Putting his arm around her shoulders, they walked to the baggage claim area. The silence between them was not as comfortable as when they had walked along the beach on Hainan. Yi realized it would take some time for their relationship to heal. But he was confident it would be even stronger for having survived the Hainan incident.

As he loaded Sarah's luggage into the trunk of his car, he said, "For the next fifteen months, I intend to occupy as much of your time as you'll let me."

"That's what makes you so different from other men, Yi. You are strong willed and determined, yet you never fail to consider the feelings of others. I love that about you."

To her surprise, he opened the car door for her. She shook her head and added, "I just can't figure you out."

A smile came to his face as he walked around to the driver's side of the car and got in. Starting up the engine, he said, "I believe I have something here that might help you with that."

He reached behind the passenger seat and brought out a gift-wrapped box.

She studied him for a moment then took the gift from his hands. Setting it in her lap, she began to carefully lift the taped ends of the red and gold wrapping.

Yi wanted to rip the package open for her but restrained himself, smiling as he watched her enjoy the anticipation of the unknown gift inside.

After removing the wrapping paper and carefully folding it, she lifted the lid on the box. Inside was a leather-bound Book of Mormon with her name etched in gold in the lower right corner.

She looked at Yi, and he could see tears welling in her eyes.

"You are Mormon?" she asked.

Yi nodded.

"Now I understand," she whispered with a smile.

ABOUT THE AUTHOR

DM Coffman lived in the People's Republic of China from 2000–2004. She and her husband taught with the Brigham Young University China Teachers Program and the US-sponsored WTO China Judicial Training Program. She is the author of *A Peking University Coursebook on English Exposition Writing*, published by Peking University Press, and has served as an editor and foreign consultant for English educational texts. Prior to China, the Coffmans lived in Northern Virginia and worked in the legal profession in Washington DC. She has a M.Ed. from Brigham Young University and a BBA from National University. She is the winner of awards for short writings, and *The Hainan Incident* is her first novel.